Love & Money

Collaboration between Justan Autor & Katerina Dunne

A screen play written by Katerina Dunne, adapted by Justan Autor

Staten House

Love & Money

First Edition 2026
Justan Autor Copyright © 2026

Published by Staten House

Cover illustration by Justan Autor
Cover and interior design by Justan Autor

Copyediting and Proofreading by Justan Autor & Katerina Dunne
The right of Justan Autor & Katerina Dunne to be identified as the authors of
this work has been asserted in accordance with the Copyright, Designs and
Patents Act, 1988.

A CIP catalogue record for this book is available from the British Library

ISBN: 979-8-89965-993-5

Contents

About The Authors

Justan Autor

Katerina Dunne

Preface

Kind Reader,

Permit your Author, before you embark upon the ensuing pages, to offer not an apology, but a brief bill of fare, outlining the territories through which you are invited to travel.

While the present narrative may not concern itself with kings or battles, it lays claim, nonetheless, to a certain veracity — not perhaps in every minute particular of time and place, but in its earnest endeavour to portray the intricate workings of the human heart.

Herein, you shall find a gentleman whose charms are more readily apparent than his prudence, and a heroine whose spirit is as considerable as her fortune. You shall also find those whose motives are governed more by avarice than affection, and whose machinations serve to drive our narrative through sundry trials and misunderstandings.

For Love and Money, those twin pillars upon which so much of mortal existence is precariously balanced, shall be our constant companions—sometimes as allies, but more often as antagonists in the intricate dance of our characters' fates.

If, along the way, some gentle satire upon the foibles of the age should inadvertently slip from the Author's Pen, he trusts it will be received with Indulgence. And so, having detained you sufficiently upon the threshold, we invite you now to step within.

Your Humble and Obedient Servant,

THE AUTHOR

PS: Do forgive this author, who has performed all his own copyediting & proofreading, should any **wily typo** have escaped his scrutiny.

Act the First

Chapter the First – A Libertine, A Lady, A Thorny Rose

Wellington Hill area, Somerset – July 18, 1865

'Tis a truth universally acknowledged — though whether first proclaimed by the wise, the love-stricken, the poet, or the pawnbroker is a matter of some debate — that every bouncing Tom and buxom Bess in possession of a beating heart is doomed to be in love at least once in their lives! But whether this affliction should prove a gentle roll down Parnassus or a headlong plunge into Bedlam is a proposition to which I should be loath to stake my reputation, let alone my purse.

For you see, often this divine affliction first manifests as a youthful fever — a giddy delirium of stolen glances and hastily dropped kerchiefs, where prudence is sacrificed with alarming alacrity upon the pyre of passion. Later, it too frequently settles into a more mercenary malady of maturity — where a suitor's ardour is assayed against his annuities; affection is measured in acres; appraisal is governed by pedigree. At any rate, for those somewhere in between, 'tis seldom a sublime romance and more a high-stakes farce. Here in this grand amphitheatre of attachment, vows are bandied about like promissory notes, and the only unbreakable bonds are those secured by solicitors. 'Tis a game played with marked cards, where Cupid appears less a cherubic archer but as a shrewd bookkeeper, tallying the dowry. 'Tis a confusion particularly prevalent, one might observe, in certain genteel shires.

And so, with a clear eye on this curious duality, let us then, gentle Reader, turn our coach towards that most amiable of counties, Somerset; for nowhere else, 'tis said, does Eros and Economics, Venus and Avarice, dance with such indefatigable vigour. Indeed, were you possessed of a spyglass this very night, and your gaze directed to Thornfield Hall — that imposing pile standing sentinel against the dim summer sky and slumbering fields — you might witness the curtain rising upon the first act of our comedy.

Scarcely had the sighs of satisfaction ceased to echo against the damask bed-hangings, nor the warmth entirely fled the limbs so lately intertwined in that most ardent of congresses, when Lady Grant — whose ripe charms have lured many a fop into her silken snare — cast a compliment upon her companion. "Oh,

Francis!" breathed she, her voice still bearing the husky timbre of exertion. "You are... *beyond* compare! As is your wont."

Said Francis, the very beau whose fortunes (and misfortunes) these pages shall chronicle, adjusted a stray lock of his fair hair and returned the compliment with the easy grace of one for whom such post-coital flattery is both expected and routine. "The pleasure, madam, was, as ever, entirely my own."

Yet, the Fates — or, what is often the same thing, an ill-timed nocturnal ramble by the master of the house — decreed this tender (*ahem!* — I do not condone such amorous activities) tête-à-tête be most abruptly aborted. For sudden as Doom, there fell upon the chamber door such a battery as might have roused the Seven Sleepers of Ephesus.

Verily, our two sinners — ripe for the rod — who but moments before had been models of languid satisfaction now froze into a tableau of pure alarm. Their cheeks blazed not with shame, but with detection's vulgar flame.

From without, a voice thick with choler and patriarchal authority bellowed, "Virginia!" (For this, Reader, was the jade's Christian name, though her recent exertions might undermine its sanctity) "Open this instant!"

Lady Grant's orbs did widen to the size of shillings. "My husband!"

"Blast!" muttered Francis, along with other such words that spoke to a vocabulary as rich in profanity as it was in seduction. His wits galloped at a clip that rivalled his recent palpitations. "Must the old cuckold choose his moment with such *damnable* precision?"

Galvanised by a terror that lent her a surprising agility, Her Ladyship scrambled from the tumbled sheets and snatched at a silk wrapper that lay discarded upon a nearby chaise longue. "Fly, Francis, ere that choleric Cyclops claps eyes upon us!"

The battery renewed. Louder now and accompanied by the ominous rattle of the door handle. "Virginia! Do you hear me? Open this door, thou filthy strumpet, or I shall have it from its hinges!"

Mr Sheringham — for such was the libertine's patronymic — meanwhile, thus found himself embroiled in that most ignoble of battles: a man versus his own breeches. Hopping gracelessly on one booted foot, he sought to ensheathe his other limb whilst snatching up from the floor his second boot, his shirt, and coat.

"Open this door, madam!" came the furious ultimatum from beyond the quaking oak. "Or, by heavens, I shall splinter it!"

His attire now hastily reassembled in a manner more befitting a scarecrow than a rake, Francis made for the tall casement overlooking the bedarkened gardens.

As he fumbled with the obstinate latch, Lady Grant, in a flurry of desperate passion, pressed a frantic, fleeting kiss upon his cheek, followed by a last, clinging embrace. Then, steeling herself, she administered a nudge meant merely to expedite his egress — yet terror lent such vehemence to her thrust that it served less as a gentle encouragement and more a direct propulsion into the treacherous void beyond.

Earthwards plummeted Francis with a most unheroic yelp. His descent, alas, terminated not upon the soft turf, but squarely amidst the barbed embrace of what proved to be Her Ladyship's pride and joy — her much-trumpeted champion roses.

From the prickly darkness below arose a sermon of profanity, wholly unfit for repetition in polite society. His once-fine coat got comprehensively snagged, his hide perforated in more places than a colander, whilst his self-respect sustained the direst casualties of all.

Still and all, he finally extricated himself from the fiercely defensive, thorny blooms and, after casting a final malediction windowwards (with perhaps a soupçon of pique at his paramour), melted into the shadows.

Back within the boudoir of sin, Her Ladyship, showing a remarkable presence of mind for one so recently compromised, lit a nightlight, smoothed her hair, adjusted her wrapper to a semblance of modesty, and arranged her physiognomy into such an aspect of drowsy innocence as would've earnt bravos at Drury Lane.

With a deep breath, she turned the key.

Like Boreas unbound — all thunderous choler and darkly charged air — Lord Grant erupted into the room. A gentleman of some threescore winters, beef to the heels and florid as a side of bacon, with martial whiskers bracketing a visage now purple as a bishop's nose, he cut a somewhat comical figure clad only in his nightshirt and cap. His orbs, however, blazed with anything but mirth as they reconnoitred the disordered bedchamber.

"*Where* is he?!" His voice vibrated with enough rage to shake the rafters and rattle the windowpanes. "Where *is* that scoundrel?!"

Lady Grant batted her eyelashes with studied bewilderment. "Where is *who*, my lord? Good heavens, what *is* amiss? Have the night-terrors plagued your sleep again with their fancies? Pray, return to your bed ere you do yourself a mischief in this state."

But His Lordship's eyes did fall upon the gaping casement, the curtains yet astir from our hero's precipitate exodus. With a beastly harrumph, he charged the portal, thrust his head into the night, and ocularly assaulted the darkness below. Espying naught but the molested shrubbery and the silent, untenanted lawns, he drew back with a snarl. "Admit it!" He wheeled his basilisk glare upon his suspect spouse. "*Admit it*, madam! It was that young pup Sheringham here again, cupping your disloyal doe between his fornicating palms, was it not?"

"*Sheringham*?" Her Ladyship attempted a tinkling peal of dismissive laughter that, alas, sounded more than a trifle strained to even the most amateur of ears. "La, you conjure bogeys from moonbeams, my lord! There was *no one* here but *me*, I *assure* you. Those base phantasms have bedevilled your slumbers again!"

"Nay, I am *not* deceived!" Lord Grant jabbed an accusing finger at the compromised dame and then at the equally compromised window. "His visitations have grown altogether too bold these past weeks! The insolence of the worm! His filthy calligraphy is writ large upon these chambers! But he shall answer for this night's depredations! Upon my honour! That satyr shall pay dearly for his transgressions!"

A sigh escaped Lady Grant's lips — whether of capitulation to her husband's suspicions or vexation at his predictability, 'tis not for me to say. She wagged her head in a well-rehearsed charade of martyred connubial forbearance.

"The Sheringhams!" His Lordship expelled the name from his mouth as if it were poison. "Ever a blight upon the good name of this county! The father always dicing away a fortune at the tables. The mother's virtue was a matter of public debate long before her demise! And the son...!" Here, he broke off, nostrils a-flaring, jowls a-quivering as he groped for epithets adequate to the younger Sheringham's infamy. "A libertine! A profligate and a scoundrel, treading dutifully in his begetter's disgraceful footsteps!"

Chapter the Second — An Unexpected Invitation

Blackdown Hills area, Somerset – July 19, 1865

Let us now, Reader, quit the imposing grandeur and nocturnal dramas of Thornfield Hall, and direct our coach some miles distant to alight before Brookside House the following day. This dwelling, though fashioned of good stone and possessed of a venerable air of the previous century, presented a marked contrast to Lord Grant's palatial residence. Where Thornfield sprawled with arrogant magnificence, Brookside sat in a state of honourable decay, hinting — in its want of fresh paint and the slightly undisciplined nature of its shrubbery — at fortunes somewhat diminished from their former glory.

Within, we find the master of this house, Sir Andrew Sheringham, seated in his study — a chamber lined with bookshelves whose dust-jacketed contents spoke more of past than present scholasticism. He occupied a great leather chair that bore the honourable scars of long service to a thousand ponderings. Though but midway through his fifties, the baronet wore the countenance of a man considerably his senior. For life, or perhaps the particular way he had seen fit to live it, had etched crevices deep as the wan Westcountry valleys upon his brow and pulled down the corners of a mouth that had long forgotten the habit of smiling. His shoulders stooped, burdened by cares far exceeding the management of his modest estate. With an air of profound contemplation, he held in one hand a stiff, cream-coloured card — evidently an invitation.

Before him stood his son and heir, Mr Francis Sheringham. Despite the previous night's... *athletic*... exertions, he maintained an attitude of studied composure; though if a faint crimson scratch upon one cheek escaped a casual eye, it did not escape ours.

At length, he broke the gravid silence: "Well, Sir? Your verdict?"

Sir Andrew sighed, expelling breath like a bellows gone flat. He tapped the invitation against the worn blotter; a soft percussion, doubtless accompanying his cogitations. But finally: "His Lordship has not deigned to favour me with his society these five-and-twenty years past," stated he. "What reason, pray tell, could he have for doing so now?"

Francis permitted a slight vulpine smirk to warm his lips. Through his mind there cavorted — nay, jigged with unrepentant élan — sundry reasons Lord

Grant might begrudge his presence at the Manor. But such impious exploits our libertine naturally concealed in that equally impious strongbox within his bosom. "Perchance age has softened him, Father."

Sir Andrew looked at him.

"Perchance the old curmudgeon," continued Francis, "that puffed-up old badger, that dyspeptic, blustering goat..."

His father's orbs contracted to incandescent slits.

"... I mean, that worthy *gentleman*," amended Francis, indeed marking his father's scolding stare, "has resolved upon a policy of amnesty and amnesia regarding ancient broils."

"You govern that viperous tongue of yours, Francis! Lord Grant remains our neighbour, whatever grievances subsist between us, private or public. Remember your station and show some deference, even when glossing over the infirmities of others — especially your superiors!"

"My apologies, Father." Francis executed a bow nicely calculated between open contrition and secret irony.

Sir Andrew grunted, a sound partaking of both anger and resignation. He looked down at the card again before raising his eyes to his son with a searching look. "And you believe, then, that we should accept this... *olive* branch?"

"Most assuredly, Sir!" declared Francis with studied insouciance, knowing precisely which string to pull on the melancholy instrument of his father's soul. "Is it not high time you vouchsafed yourself some trifling divertissement beyond these musty walls? An occasion to cut a figure once more? To mingle again? Surely," appended he, with as persuasive a tilt of his head as he could muster, "a morsel of genteel jollification amongst the *beau monde* would prove a most welcome tonic for your whimsical humours of late."

The notion seemed at first to curdle on Sir Andrew's features, mingling with his habitual bitterness that had fixed upon his countenance of late a most severe frown. Yet, a flicker of something — perhaps sheer weariness with his own solitary existence, perhaps a reluctant acknowledgement that his son's point held the ring of reason — flitted across his phiz. "Hmph. I suppose you may have the right of it for once. My existence has grown morose enough to chill the marrow in a younger man's bones. Very well. We shall attend this... soirée."

To be sure, this was exactly what Francis desired. In playing the solicitous scion — feigning concern for his sire's welfare where, in earnest, he rather pursued his own ends — he had prevailed by indirection where frontal assault would've foundered utterly. His purpose achieved, he made to pivot on his heel and depart the study's somewhat sepulchral ambience. But then, arrested by a sudden, vital afterthought, he paused and turned back to the baronet.

"Only pledge me one article, Father," began he. "You must vow not to…"

He got no further. Sir Andrew cut him short with an abrupt, reflexive wave of his hand. His features tightened anew with a look in which annoyance visibly fought a losing skirmish with shame. "Yes, yes, Francis, spare me the confounded homily!" His gaze skittered away. "I apprehend your meaning entirely. You have my solemn vow — my word as a gentleman. This occasion shall not be marred by… *former* indiscretions."

Chapter the Third — A Trap and A Bewitching Stranger

July 22, 1865

The Great Hall of Thornfield blazed with the light of a thousand candles; their flames glinted off the polished floors, gilded mirrors, and the dazzling chandeliers that served as costly testimonies to their owner's fortune. Here gathered the cream, or at least the richest curds, of South-West Somerset society. The air hummed with a symphony of polite conversation (and rather less polite gossip), punctuated by bursts of laughter, the clinking of glasses, and the strains of a string quartet valiantly attempting to impose order upon the cheerful chaos.

A stark contrast, as always, prevailed in attire: the gentlemen, sombre pillars in black and white, formed dark islands amidst a swirling sea of ladies arrayed in gowns of every hue. Silks, satins, and velvets vied for attention; décolletages sparkled with diamonds, rubies, sapphires and pearls, each gem a silent boast of a father's land or a husband's bank ledger.

Amidst this throng, one might spy Sir Andrew Sheringham, looking somewhat adrift. Surrounding him was a knot of country squires whose talk ran chiefly to crop yields and foxhounds — subjects upon which Sir Andrew offered little contribution. He clutched his wine glass rather tightly; his gaze occasionally wandered as if seeking an anchor in this unfamiliar sea.

But let us turn our roving eye elsewhere, to where that arrant rake and all-too-willing votary of Venus' court, Francis himself, presented a veritable study in contrasts. Encircled by a twittering bevy of admiring females — from blushing, wide-eyed debutantes through to the more seasoned, full-blown matrons in desperate want of pollination — our young coxcomb held court with the practised ease of a Lord Chesterfield upon the stage. Witticisms, airy persiflage, and scandalous anecdotes flowed freely from his lips, honeyed enough to put the Royal Beekeeper to shame. His charming, Puck-like smile elicited flutters and giggles both. He was, in short, performing that role for which nature and inclination had so perfectly equipped him: the captivating, irredeemable rogue.

I say *performing*, Reader, for despite his masterful display of engagement, his gaze was a privateer, constantly scanning the crowded room for a prize of more compelling interest.

And there, amongst a cluster of gaudy satins and silks, a singular figure stood in arresting contrast. A young woman dressed entirely in unrelieved black; mourning attire, clearly — strange, considering if that was so, why then was she *here*? At any rate, the gown's starkness did nothing to diminish the quiet intensity of her presence. A grave serenity radiated from her like heat from a banked ember. Lustrous dark hair, simply coiffed; classical lines, like those of a Grecian statue, formed her profile; skin, luminous as marble, shimmered against the ebony fabric. She was, in short, an islet of quiet composure in a sea of ostentatious artifice; as serene and compelling as the eye of a storm.

Francis had never seen her before; of that he was certain. Who *was* this sable-clad creature, this startling note of sobriety in Lord Grant's opulent chorus? Here was a fortress he had not yet laid siege to; a mystery he felt a sudden, undeniable compulsion to solve. For the first time that evening, our hero's easy smile became a thing less practised. In that moment — and whether we are to blame Cupid for the wily shaft, or merely a rake's vanity for the target, is a matter for debate — Francis Sheringham found his heart aflame, his every faculty enraptured by the stranger's grave and remote allure.

She was, he noted with a private scowl, engaged in low-toned conversation not only with that insatiable Sheba, Lady Grant, but her dastardly son, Vincent, who hovered near them not unlike a terrier guarding a prize bitch.

Valiantly, Francis attempted to maintain a semblance of focus upon the twittering ladies who surrounded him, nodding and assaying smiles where required. But his eyes kept stealing back to that solitary figure in uncompromising black. She had turned slightly, speaking now with an older woman — quite possibly her chaperone (also dressed in economic black, save for the rather ill-complemented accessory in the form of an opulent, hand-painted silk fan, which she waved with the fury of a sultan between her meaty paws).

An impulse, most unusual for its directness, seized our hero. As Lady Grant turned aside, Francis shifted his stance, angling himself to catch the dark-clad beauty's eye; a silent overture, an invitation from a man unused to issuing them.

Her reaction, or rather, the pointed lack thereof, was a masterclass in social annihilation.

Without so much as affording him a flicker of acknowledgment, the raven-tressed vision seemed to sense his attention upon her person as assuredly as if he had coughed loudly in her ear. Moments later, she placed a gloved hand on the middle-aged woman's arm and guided her away, putting a wider distance between herself and Sheringham's orbit, without so much as a backwards glance.

A flush crept up Francis' neck, hot and mortifying. He, Francis Sheringham, a veritable dauphin amongst the doxies of the *beau monde*, accustomed to commanding female attention with a mere tilt of his head, had just been pointedly dismissed — waved off like some buzzing, importunate fly, and without even the common courtesy of a direct snub!

Stung by so unaccustomed a taste of rejection, an irrational surge of vexation so profound it masqueraded as hatred flared in his breast. Fine! If the remote, dusky waxwork wished to be so coldly untouchable, so be it. Let her cloister herself in her faux-funereal airs. Let her simper and plot with that chaperone. He would banish her striking image and unforgivable slight from his thoughts.

With a renewed and almost aggressive charm, he turned back to his harem of hopefuls. "You were saying, Miss Russell?" enquired he with a brilliant, albeit hollow smile, bestowing the full sun of his regard upon the silly, blushing chit beside him.

And so, the performance resumed. Francis laughed, rallied, and once more reigned as sovereign in his glittering court of sycophants. But despite the thespian's mask, a slender thorn of vexation would not be banished. His pride, more than his heart, had suffered a grievous wound. And for that reason, above all others, the mysterious woman in black remained, in vexing defiance of his will, unforgotten.

Meantime, in a slightly recessed alcove, partially screened by a large potted fern, stood the evening's host, Lord Grant, conferring in hushed tones with his son and heir apparent, Mr Vincent Grant.

A callow youth of two-and-twenty, yet already afflicted with a case of self-regard so advanced it might be deemed terminal, Vincent embodied the very acme of the fashionable dandy. His coat was of so amplified a cut as to lend him the silhouette not of a man, but of a small-masted sloop under full sail. His cravat was a monument of starched linen that threatened to decapitate a lesser man. He employed a lace-trimmed handkerchief not for necessity, but as a weapon in the arsenal of ennui, fluttering it to accent his studied, languid airs. As he attended his father's murmurings, his expression was incontrovertibly one of profound, almost somnambulant boredom.

Like a duellist sighting his mark, Lord Grant fixed his eyes on the oblivious Sir Andrew. "When I give the signal," murmured he to his son, "I shall convey the gentlemen upstairs under some pretext for cards and further refreshments. Your task, Vincent, is to ensure that young jackanapes Sheringham remains firmly entangled with the ladies. He must be kept apart from his father. Do you comprehend?"

Vincent undulated his handkerchief idly before his face. "Scarcely a challenge, Father," drawled he, casting a contemptuous glance at Francis' laughing circle. "The capering popinjay is glued to their petticoats by his own vanity. He shan't stray unless borne off at bayonet-point, you may wager your soul on it."

Satisfied, His Lordship nodded. Moments later, Vincent detached himself from the shadows and glided towards his mother, who was observing her paramour's performance with a "knowing" sparkle of amusement.

Leaning close, Vincent whispered a brief directive. Her Ladyship's face brightened. She clapped her hands, commanding the room's attention with that universal semaphore of genteel entitlement. "My dears!" trilled she to the lasses orbiting her gallant. "The hour grows chill and uncivilised, and I fear the gentlemen threaten to bore us with politics! Shall we, ladies, decamp to the drawing room for a game more befitting our spirits?"

A chorus of eager assent arose:

"Yes! Oh, yes, Lady Grant! A delightful notion!"

"A game! How perfectly ripping!"

"Lead on, I beg you, and away from these droning stovepipes!"

"Excellent!" Her Ladyship clapped again to corral her flock. "Let us repair to more congenial precincts and play Blind Man's Buff! And *you*, Mr Sheringham" — she transfixed him with a sportive, provocative regard that might have discomforted a more prudent young blood — "you, sir, shall be our first blind man!"

What fitter diversion, Reader, for a society so determined to grope blindly for what it desires?

Before Francis could frame either assent or protest, he found himself borne along by a freshet of rustling taffeta and feminine laughter, swept drawing-room-wards.

Yet, even as he was thus shanghaied, he cast one last glance for the vision in black. She hovered near the vestibule, a footman draping her mourning coat about her shoulders. And then, the enigmatic creature who had called forth in his breast such contrary impulses to worship and to crush, vanished entirely, with scarce a backwards glance over her exquisitely insolent shoulder.

And so, in the drawing room, a transformation was already afoot. Chairs were thrust wall-wards, and Lady Grant, wielding a silk scarf, advanced upon Francis. "Now, sir, stand fast and submit to your fate!" She deftly tied the blindfold over his eyes, plunging him into Stygian murk, whereupon the ladies scattered about the room, suppressing giggles, their slippered feet whispering on the polished floorboards.

With the fox thus occupied in the henhouse, the coast was — as they say — clear for a more serious hunt to begin. Lord Grant, having marked Francis' capture with indubitable satisfaction, accosted Sir Andrew and the other gentlemen. "My friends," said he, oozing a spurious bonhomie, "shall we withdraw upstairs?"

Nods of agreement followed; the male contingent drifted towards the grand staircase.

Anon, in a chamber designated for masculine pursuits, they settled around a gaming table. Brandy circulated; cigars were lit. And then Lord Grant — or Lord G, as we shall style him henceforth, for brevity is the soul of a good conspiracy — produced a fresh pack of playing cards.

Oh, Reader, mark the effect upon the hapless Sir Andrew! At the sight of those two-and-fifty painted devils, a palpable tension seized him. His complexion turned to chalk. His hand, bound for his snifter, petrified mid-voyage.

"Gentlemen" — Lord G shuffled the pack with a cardsharp's fluency — "I propose we try our luck at a novel amusement lately arrived from America. They call it... 'Poker'. A test of mettle and nerve, I'm told." His gaze fastened upon Sir Andrew, a mute, barbed gauntlet as he deposited the deck upon the green baize.

Sir Andrew gulped audibly. "My lord... I..." tried he in a somewhat throttled croak, "I fear I must abstain. I gave my word... no more gaming."

Lord G placed a comradely arm around his shoulder. "Oh, come, come now, Sir Andrew! A trifling hand amongst intimates, to commemorate our renewed rapprochement!" He kneaded the shoulder gently. "Let bygones be bygones."

"But I..." Sir Andrew's utterance trailed off into a wretched murmur. "I have forfeited so much..." He threw back his brandy as if it were poison and antidote in one.

At a paternal signal, Vincent discreetly replenished the vessel.

"Entirely understandable," purred Lord G. "Pray, feel no compulsion. Merely spectate, then. Savour the brandy, the fellowship. No harm in looking on."

Meanwhile, downstairs, in the lower circles of this social inferno, the game was in full swing. Blindfolded, arms outstretched, Francis navigated by the sound of squeals and whispers. His fingers closed on a shoulder. He commenced, as protocol dictated, to explore with his digits the captive's lineaments — tracing the jaw, the nose, the elegant slope of the neck... and onwards to the — *ahem*! This modest chronicler colours and forbears to venture further into such treacherous terrain.

Thus, hands and fingers a-hoisted back towards more becoming regions!

"Hmm," murmured Francis, concentrating. "The rather charming, if slightly pronounced, earlobe... Dare I hazard... Miss Russell?"

A jubilant shriek ratified his inference.

"Yes! Oh, bravo, Mr Sheringham!" chorused the ladies.

Amidst the merriment, the apparently roseate Miss Russell was released, and Francis was returned to the room's epicentre to renew his prowl.

Back upstairs, the first hands were dealt. Chips clinked. *Sotto voce* observations circulated. Sir Andrew merely watched, his knuckles blanched to bone. Yet his eyes — oh, those dilating orbs — followed the fall of the cards, the wagers' placement, with an intensity that belied his status as a mere spectator. He was a drunkard locked in a distillery; a lotus-eater compelled to witness another's euphoric inhalations.

While appearing engrossed in his hand, Lord G missed none of it; a faint, yet undeniably sardonic smirk played on his lips.

At length, the tension became unbearable. Sir Andrew thrust back his chair and started up, capsizing his snifter. "I... I wish to stake," declared he with a squeal.

Lord G elevated his gaze and cupped a hand to his ear with studied politeness. "I beg your pardon, sir? The din from below proves rather penetrating. Did you say something?"

Sir Andrew sucked in a quavering breath. "Deal me in the next round," reiterated he with that ghastly resolution so common of the foredoomed. "I wish to play."

Lord G's brow ascended fractionally. He traded a swift glance with Vincent — a look that passed between them like the closing of a steel trap.

Again below, Francis had bagged fresh quarry. This time, his eager paws — alas, Reader, the rascal outpaces your humble author's sense of decorum! — encountered a figure altogether more generously proportioned. His fingers, emboldened by the blindfold, lingered with scandalous appreciation upon the dame's abundant frontispiece. Said Dame, far from bridling, inclined into his ministrations with an audible exhalation of delectation.

Francis could scarcely suppress the wicked grin tugging at his mouth-corners. "Ah," declared he with mock-solemnity, "judging by this... *munificent* testimony... surely this can be none other than... Lady... *Plenty!*"

The captive gasped, then dissolved into throaty laughter, while the other ladies erupted into near-apoplectic giggles at his audacious, if apt, appellation. The sport, it seemed, waxed rather more piquant than simple Blind Man's Bluff.

Within the game room, the air, now a veritable Tartarus of smoke and spirits, bore witness to Sir Andrew Sheringham's wholesale capitulation to the game. His phiz, erstwhile pallid, glowed with an unhealthy flush, and a marked palsy afflicted the fists clutching his cards — tokens not merely of chance, but of his evaporating fortune.

Across the baize sat His Lordship, a picture of calm, save for the devilish glint in his eye. For Lord G, you see, was not merely a player but a sharper — deploying a stratagem as old as deceit itself. He'd positioned a brass lamp on a corner console adjacent to the gaming table. How exactly he wielded this device to his opponent's demise shall, for the time being, be known only to himself. Thus armed, His Lordship played with the placid assurance of one who commands not only his own hand but his adversary's. The other gentlemen, possibly sensing the current's perilous undertow, had long since withdrawn, abandoning the lamb to the wolf.

Swiftly, the contest reached its crisis. A hillock of markers, promissory notes, and hastily scribbled IOUs on the table had grown to a formidable Himalaya, representing a sum to stagger a nabob.

Sir Andrew squinted at his dealt cards. A flicker of desperate hope illuminated his haggard features. "I... I see your wager, my lord," croaked he as he pushed forward the last of his ready cash. "And I raise!"

Lord G reclined, steepling his fingers. "A bold move, Sir Andrew." His smile broadened. "But may I remind you, sir, that your coffers appear somewhat depleted? To match my own considerable advance, you must pledge something more substantial. Your remaining acres at Brookside, perhaps? Or... the *house...* itself?"

Below, having quite spent themselves, the ladies now lolled upon settees and ottomans, plying fans and chattering like starlings at dusk. Observing that the hour advanced and her duties as hostess required attention elsewhere, Lady Grant deftly disengaged Francis from his circle of admirers and spirited him from the room.

And so we turn, dear Reader, from a tableau of fiscal catastrophe to one of carnal decay. In the dimly lit corridor, decorum had been summarily abandoned. Francis and Lady Grant were locked in ardent congress, regaling themselves — or rather each other — in time-honoured degenerate fashion, mingling stolen kisses with vows of passion.

"Oh, Francis," sighed Her Ladyship, clinging to him, "I fear I shall pine for these trysts most abominably! We must be exceedingly discreet henceforth. Lie low, as they say."

Puzzled, Francis drew back slightly. "Lie low? But wherefore, my dearest Virginia? Has something occurred?"

Lady G — let us agree to call her — averted her gaze while worrying a ribbon on her gown. "My husband," breathed she, "he... he harbours suspicions. Indeed, he *knows.*"

"*Knows?*" echoed Francis, aghast. "Impossible! How could he ascertain...?"

"Alas," confessed she, "I was constrained to intimate... *something.* He threatened else to confine me to my chambers for three days entire! Three days without society, Francis! Conceive the ennui!"

Not long did it take for the pieces to click into place with horrifying finality. Did Lord Grant separate him from his father on purpose? Was his sire perhaps ensnared to gamble his life away by a man who knew his son was horning him? The invitation wasn't about forgetting the past; 'twas about vengeance.

"Good God!" Francis pushed her away with unkind force. The lover vanished, supplanted instantly by the panic-stricken heir. With horror dawning upon his brain like a hailstorm, he wheeled and bolted towards the Great Hall.

Bewildered and slightly offended by his precipitate dash, Lady G gathered her skirts and hurried after him. "Francis! What is it? What discomposes you so?"

Chapter the Fourth — A Crushing Debt

Into the cavernous Great Hall, Francis burst like a summer tempest, only to find it nearly deserted, dimmed and drained of its recent festivities. Two weary footmen were extinguishing the candelabra while two other liveried fellows, not less weary-looking, stooped to collect the evening's discarded glasses, soiled napkins, and other stray ephemera littering the aftermath of society's convivial storm.

"My father?!" demanded Francis of the nearest servant. "*Where* is Sir Andrew?"

Startled by so brusque an enquiry, the footman gestured towards the curving staircase. "Still upstairs, sir. In the game room, with his lordship."

"The *game* —?" Without another word, Francis flung himself towards the upper floor, taking the polished oak steps two, even three at a time.

Behind him, like a frigate of fashion foundering in a squall of silk, Lady G came in breathless pursuit, her elegant gown snagging and tearing in a most undignified chase.

By the time she'd attained the stairs' upper reaches, 'twas too late. Francis had already reached the game room's arched portal and flung it open with such pent-up violence that the thick oak panel rebounded from its frame with a resounding BANG, causing the room's remaining occupants to start in their chairs.

Framed in the doorway, Francis stood trembling, chest heaving from his headlong flight. All raging inferno within, he scanned the room. His gaze at length fell upon the card table, its once green baize obscured beneath scattered playing cards and various other gaming effects — tokens, burnt matches, an overturned tumbler shining wetly in the candlelight, and there...

There sat his father, slumped in a carved chair. His face ashen as a limestone statue, he stared blankly down at the ruinous cards carpeting the table before him. Truly, the baronet appeared in that moment the very picture of a soul devoured; a man whose substance had been gambled away, leaving behind a mere husk of bloodless despair.

"Father!" Francis crossed the chamber in three strides.

Alas, Sir Andrew did not respond, did not even seem to hear him. He remained as motionless as the graven effigy atop his own future tomb; as though some malign spectre had reached into his breast and plucked forth his soul, leaving but a vacant, scarcely breathing shell.

A piteous sight, in truth, and one Francis found himself ill-prepared to grapple with despite his reputedly tumultuous history with the elder Sheringham.

His hands hovered over his father's trembling shoulders, utterly impotent. All his life, he had wielded words like a rapier, deflecting consequences with a well-timed jest. But looking at the hollowed, broken exterior of the man who had raised him, he realised with terrifying clarity that no amount of cleverness could hoist them out of this abyss.

While coolly observing the scene, Lord G made a curt gesture to the few remaining gentlemen who had lingered, perhaps out of morbid curiosity. "Leave us," commanded he. "Lady Grant, perhaps you too should retire."

Silently, they filed out, casting pitying glances at the tableau. Only Vincent remained, lounging near the fireplace, casually fanning himself with his absurdly delicate handkerchief.

Francis bent over his sire. "Father? Are you quite well? Speak to me."

Sir Andrew finally stirred, his hollow eyes blinking as if rousing from a nightmare. "Lost," breathed he in a hoarse whisper. "All is lost... Everything..."

"*Everything*?" A chilling dread coiled itself in the pit of Francis' belly. "What can you mean, Father? For the love of God, what is this... 'everything'?"

But the broken baronet could not, it seemed, articulate the catastrophe. He merely shook his head; his sunken eyes augured a bitter, unceasing deluge.

Frustrated and aghast, Francis straightened and whirled about, his blazing gaze seeking a target. He found him — Lord G, seated by the hearth, swirling a glass of brandy with a smile of such unalloyed malice.

"You..." Francis levelled an accusing finger. "What fresh devilry have you visited upon my family this night? What possessed you to drag him down into such utter ruin and —"

"Your patrimony, young man," interrupted Lord G. "Brookside House, its lands, its contents... they now belong to me. A fair exchange for the debts your father has incurred." He continued to idly swish the contents of his glass, causing the liquor to shiver against the crystal in a maddening display of nonchalance.

The sheer audacity struck Francis like a physical blow, causing him to rock back on his heels. He tore his gaze from the gloating victor to the slumped form of his father, who now turned his face to the wall, indubitably in an agony of shame.

"You fiend!" Francis glared again at Lord G and spat with all the violence he was master of. "It was *I* you sought to punish from the very start, was it not? For... for *imagined* slights!" He could not, of course, name his dalliance with the man's wife, but the implication hung in the air. "Why must you ruin my father?"

His Lordship chuckled. He took a sip of his drink, almost performatively, before replying. "Why not punish both the sinner and his vainglorious spawn? Revenge, Mr Sheringham..." he all but purred, "... is indeed sweet. Even after these five-and-twenty years, it retains a most *delightfully* saccharine bouquet I find impossible to resist."

"All this... chaos and heartbreak," scoffed Francis, his brain pounding with despair and disgust, "merely because the woman you both desired chose my father over you in the end? Can your pride not stomach defeat, even after all this time?"

Lord G's smile vanished, replaced by a contemptuous, feral-like baring of teeth. "*Chose*?" His chest swelled with some inscrutable emotion. "Do you even have the faintest conception of how your sainted father 'won' your mother's hand? The vile methods he employed?"

Francis could only stare at his father's accuser in mute disbelief, an expression Grant no doubt took as an invitation to continue prodding at this festering, decades-old wound.

"He compromised her!" Lord G leant forwards in a grotesque parody of paternal condescension. "He lured your mother into a situation... ensured she spent a night under his roof, unattended... unchaperoned... ruined her reputation so thoroughly that she had no choice *but* to accept his hand! That is how the noble Sir Andrew *won* his bride!" He sneered the final accusation directly into Francis' stunned face.

"Ridiculous!" Francis' own chest dilated with vengeful reproach. But alas, as he glanced at his father, noting a look somewhat culpably hued, a seed of doubt, cold and unwelcome, began to sprout within him. "That... that is a vile and monstrous lie," resumed he nonetheless, transfixing the arrogant lord, "and I'll thank you to hold your venomous tongue, ere I find myself provoked to —"

"Believe what you will." Grant shrugged so very dismissively. "Indulge in what little comforting delusions and lies yet remain; I care not. The fact remains: Brookside and all its holdings now belong solely to me. I shall derive considerable satisfaction watching you and your disgraced parent remove yourselves from *my* property with all due haste."

Trembling now with a rage he dared not fully give vent to, Francis clenched his fists until they verily ached. "May you roast in the deepest pit of Hell, you black-hearted villain! May you —"

"Francis!" Sir Andrew's voice, though weak, held a note of command, cutting off the vulgarity.

At this juncture, as if sensing the dramatic spotlight had strayed from him for too long, Vincent stepped forwards. With a flourish betokening rather more thespian pretension than true martial aplomb, the callow youth tossed his lace-trimmed handkerchief onto the disarrayed card table. "Sir!" He struck a posture he doubtless fancied heroic. "Your unforgivable insults and calumnies against my own father's most upright character demand immediate redress! I demand satisfaction from you, sirrah — forthwith!"

Lord G, having until this point been thoroughly engaged in the far more engrossing sport of watching his ancient foe bleed out his dignity, rolled his eyes heavenwards as if entreating the very furthest realms of patience from an indifferent cosmos. "Hush, Vincent, you fool! You barely comprehend which end of a duelling pistol will produce the decidedly unintended effect of removing that massively inflated head from its shoulders. You spend more time playing dress-up with your mother than learning some honourable, manly art. Do not make yourself even more ridiculous than Nature already has, boy!"

His Lordship turned back to Francis. "We are all grown overwrought," said he, his tone regaining its cold composure. "Tempers are frayed. Why not take your leisure to depart, Mr Sheringham, and return to us on the morrow? In the sober light of day, we may discuss the... *practicalities* of your removal with all due decorum."

The calculated insult, delivered with the blandness of a business arrangement, was a masterpiece of cruelty. Francis, however, betrayed no reaction save a grinding of his jaw. He gently took his father by the elbow. "Come, Father. Let us leave *this* place."

Sir Andrew rose, appearing for all the world like some venerable piece of architecture from antiquity. He leant heavily on his son; an act which seemed an indignity too far, aging the once-proud man a decade in a single, gasping breath.

As they departed, Lord G watched them go with incontrovertible satisfaction — a most gratifying conquest of vengeance realised at long, long last.

Vincent, meanwhile, chastened into irrelevance, scooped his fallen handkerchief from the litter of gaming debris with a petulant sniff.

The heavy doors groaned shut upon the utterly crushed and impotently furious Sheringhams, who departed into the damning silence of their disgrace.

Vincent turned to his sire. "Practicalities of their removal, Father?" A distinct crease furrowed the space between the young fop's carefully cultured brows. "What manner of arrangements remain to be discussed?" He adjusted the starched and billowing folds of his cravat in that habitual, self-consoling gesture so endemic to the loftier rungs of etiquette when discomfited. "Have you not fairly won the entirety of their pitiful estate?"

His Lordship permitted himself another thin, dry chuckle. "Indeed, Vincent," answered he. "And yet... a swift and unceremonious eviction, whilst eminently satisfying in its own way, somehow lacks a certain degree of... *finesse*, shall we say?" He began pacing the chamber's length with hands clasped behind his back.

Verily, had one the ability to read his mind, one would have known how he savoured that long-awaited blaze of absolute victory with every measured tread, tasting its dark succulence upon his palate with something very like rapture.

He paused before the marble mantelpiece with its yawning mouth of darkened brick just visible beyond the andiron's latticework. He cocked his head slightly; his gaze fell upon the insensate pile of pale ash and glowing embers smouldering in sullen silence. "Yes," murmured he, almost to himself. "I shall grant them a period — let us say, six weeks — wherein they may attempt to *repurchase* their lost inheritance."

Vincent stared at him in stunned incomprehension. 'Twas manifest how he utterly failed to penetrate the depths of such baroque reasoning and unexpected leniency towards those who had spurned them so egregiously. "Repurchase it? But... wherefore, Sir? And whence could they possibly procure such a sum?"

"Precisely, my boy! Whence, I ask you in turn, could those bankrupt rapscallions ever hope to procure such an astronomical sum? Whence indeed?" He surveyed his son over one shoulder; his eyes glinted with the first sparks of a more sadistic fire fuelling his entire stratagem. "Sir Andrew's pockets have long been as notoriously empty as his pretensions to honour and decency."

He resumed his pacing. "The sum I shall require to even consider entertaining their futile protestations must, by necessity, be quite impossibly exorbitant! Let us fix it at a pleasingly round five thousand pounds, shall we? A figure so ludicrously beyond their narrowed means!" He turned to face his son directly. "Think, Vincent! Perceive the exquisite dimensions of their torment! For six perfect, agonising weeks, they shall frantically scrabble — begging favours, currying obligations, mortgaging what little remains of their sullied reputations!"

He chuckled again, rubbing his hands together. "They shall endure, hour upon day upon night, the exquisite, slowly twisting torments of degradation and utter humiliation! Oh, such metered devastation shall prove infinitely more gratifying than a single, brutish stroke of dispossession or beggary ever could have hoped to provide! After so many years, watching that pompous fool Sheringham enjoy the fortune and the wife that should, by rights, have been mine, I find my appetite for revenge is sharp indeed. I wish to draw it out, to savour every moment of their despair."

Here, a profound silence blossomed and filled the room like a sudden fog rolling in off the moors.

"Unless, of course," resumed he, "the esteemed Sir Andrew fancies he might win back the entirety of his squandered holdings, birthright and all, through the virtuous tossing of chance upon... oh, let us say another intimate evening of cards and wagering?"

This final, blasphemous and utterly gratuitous cruelty took a moment's labour to truly penetrate the decorative ironwork of Vincent's wits — labyrinthine and beset by so many preening mirrors on all sides as they were. A lascivious smile of dawning comprehension spread itself across the young fop's face. "I... comprehend you fully now, Father." With something very like reverence, his head bobbed in time to some added, unheard but profound realisation. "Such... exquisite cruelties you have prepared for them. A true connoisseur's bouquet of tantalising mortifications and degradations most... poetical, I must confess!"

"Poetical indeed, my son. Furthermore," continued Lord G, turning away to resume his pacing, hands now steepled before his lips, "I shall permit them to remain *in situ* during this period. Let them act as caretakers of *my* property. It serves a dual purpose: it feeds their futile hopes, making the final dispossession even more bitter, and it ensures the house and grounds are kept in good order until such time as *you* might take possession."

Vincent's eyebrows rose. "Until *I* take possession, Father?"

"But naturally," affirmed His Lordship. "Whether they somehow contrive to find the five thousand pounds — which I sincerely doubt — or, as is infinitely more probable, they fail, and the estate becomes irrevocably mine, the outcome benefits you directly. Consider it, my boy: either a handsome sum of ready money or the entirety of the Brookside estate. Either," concluded he, clapping Vincent lightly on the shoulder, "will make a most suitable wedding present for you and your intended, would it not?"

Vincent's smile broadened into one of incandescent avarice. The prospect of acquiring either a fortune or a neighbouring estate, particularly one obtained through the ruin of the irritatingly handsome Francis Sheringham, appealed greatly to his sensibilities. The subtle cruelty of his father's plan now seemed not merely clever, but positively inspired.

***

While the embers of conspiracy still glowed at Thornfield Hall, the morning light that fell upon Springfield Castle — in the village of Staplegrove near Taunton — was of an altogether different quality. 'Twas a chilly, architectural light, streaming through tall, arched windows to illuminate a scene of vast and sombre grandeur. This was the inheritance of Miss Vanessa Lockwood, and today, more than ever, it felt less like a sanctuary and more like a beautifully appointed prison.

Vanessa herself stood near a mahogany desk piled high with ledgers and correspondence — the tangible tonnage of her new responsibilities since her father's passing. Dressed as she was, still in deep mourning black, the severity of her attire only emphasised the restless energy simmering beneath her composed surface.

Her brow was furrowed, not merely from scrutinising estate accounts, but from the weight of her guardian's expectations. Lord G made his intentions regarding her future — a future shackled to his son, Vincent — suffocatingly clear. Were it not for this obligation thrust upon her, she would gladly have evaded all society at present — nay, forever! If only His Lordship had not prematurely dragged her out of mourning's shadows! Though indeed the end of this period was a mere handful of days away, Lord G's lack of propriety on this score horrified her.

Ms Brown, her loyal chaperone and accomplice in all things ladylike, entered with the quiet tread of one accustomed to sorrowful houses, carrying a silver tray. "More papers, Miss Vanessa?" She placed the tray on top of the desk, observing her mistress' tense posture with concern. "You mustn't tire yourself so. Your father — God rest his soul — would have wished you to take some ease. Oh, to think we had to quit the joys of Paris to return to... well, gone are those days of freedom."

Vanessa gave one of those sighs so accustomed to the weary and turned from the desk. "*Ease*, Ms Brown? There seems little chance of that. It seems my duty now is merely to exchange one set of chains for another. And all his lordship cares about is parading me before his guests! The audacity of his demands! To force upon me an obligation to attend his silly little gathering when I have not yet reached the end of my mourning period."

Her gaze fell upon the velvet-lined box resting on the side-table, an unwelcome emissary of her guardian's intentions. Inside, there lay the heavy, ornate gold bracelet set with pearls. 'Twas a harbinger, a gift procured in anticipation of an engagement she abhorred.

"Lord Grant seems to believe my future is as easily settled as signing a deed!"

She snatched it up, seeing not the pearls' lustre, but the symbol of her entrapment; the expectation that she, and her fortune, would soon belong to Vincent Grant.

"He speaks of suitability, of alliances," murmured she, her fingers tightening around the cold metal. "He speaks of everything but choice." Her voice dropped to a near-whisper, a quiet declaration of war against the silent, opulent room. "*My* choice."

Chapter the Fifth — The Bracelet

July 24, 1865

Two days later we find Sir Andrew Sheringham slumped within the embrace of the large, wing-backed armchair in his study — that same sanctum where, as we earlier witnessed, he reluctantly agreed to attend Lord G's ill-omened gathering. The very air was thick and oppressive with the melancholic pall of ruin. Dust motes performed their indifferent dance in the afternoon sun's pale shafts; several beams illumed the faded Turkish carpet; others, the leather-bound, colour-starved spines of volumes lining the shelves like silent witnesses to a dynasty's fall.

On the small table before him, a cup of tea grew cold, untouched. He essayed to lift it, but his hand trembled so violently that the porcelain rattled against its saucer. After a second, equally feeble attempt, he relinquished the modest effort with a sigh so devastatingly deep it seemed to dredge the very nadir of his soul. He let his hand fall limply onto his lap. The architecture of the man within had collapsed; his clothes, once the very acme of sartorial precision, now hung in slackened folds from his forlorn frame.

His eyes, red-rimmed in abject desolation, stared at the polished surface of his desk, where an incongruous collection of once-cherished objects lay gleaming dully: a heavy gold pocket watch, its cover shut as if it had ceased to mark the hours of a life now measured only in loss. Two signet rings, widowed of the fingers that gave them meaning. A Dresden porcelain figure of Terpsichore caught mid-pirouette and a Staffordshire shepherdess clutching a basket of posies to her bodice. And coiled amidst the clutter, a delicate gold and diamond bracelet, its intricate scrollwork casting miniature spectres on the lacquered wood. With this sad congregation of heirlooms lay a few pieces of silver, all awaiting immolation upon the pawnbroker's counter.

Into this scene of quiet devastation, Francis entered. He paused on the threshold, taking in his father's dejected posture with pained assessment. His own face — as shown to him in the mirror opposite — was no less pale and etched with worry; he adjusted his expression to hold a firm, albeit fragile, composure. "Father?" softly enquired he, advancing into the room. "How... how do you find yourself this afternoon?"

Roused from his stupor, Sir Andrew slowly raised his head. The raw glint of unshed tears lent his eyes a profoundly vulnerable aspect, more befitting an injured child than a baronet of long lineage. "How do I find myself?" echoed he. "I find myself *contemptible*, Francis. Contemptible beyond absolution." His chest heaved as a fresh wave of anguish broke across his waning features. "I... I gave you my solemn vow. My sworn promise those thrice-damned tables would know me no more. And yet" — he gestured weakly towards the desk — "at that black-hearted fiend's very first temptation, I succumbed like the weakest of fools."

For his part, Francis' gaze followed the trajectory, alighting on the pitiful collection. "These items, Father... Why have you brought them here?"

Sir Andrew seemed to shrink further into the chair. "To raise what meagre coin we might!" His voice cracked with shame or self-defensive instinct — 'twas difficult to discern which. "In preparation... for the road. For I fear that is our dismal destination once Lord Grant's intolerable demands resume their inevitable course."

His rheumy gaze panned across the scattered valuables with a look of profound resignation and disgust. "It shall not even begin to approach the outrageous sum that serpent demands of us!" He sighed only the louder. "But the mercer knows my coffers are as barren as the pit. Any pittance raised might stave off the poor-crib a day or two longer when... when we are turned out to make our way as beggars on the king's road."

To be sure, at this maudlin pronouncement, Francis' jaw tightened. He turned towards the gleaming bric-a-brac and, reaching out, plucked up the coiled golden bracelet; his long fingers traced its diamonds. "This was Mother's," murmured he. "Her favourite, if I'm not greatly mistaken, gifted from her father when he served as an officer in India." Glancing up, he met his father's watering gaze. "Whatever else must go to feed the fires of Grant's Tartarean machinations, Father, you must swear to me you'll not part with *this*. It is..." — Francis swallowed back down the poignant sensation — "it is all we have left of her, save for fleeting memories and aching dreams."

Indeed, the mere mention of his late wife seemed to open further the older man's already profoundly raw wounds. A fresh wave of dark-hued sorrow washed over his face. "Ah, your dear mother..." Something like pained regret pulled at the hollows beneath his cheekbones, tightening the skin. "Eleanor... Sometimes, in my deepest fits of black despair and weakness, I find myself... blaming her, you see.

Railing at her cruel abandonment of us." He again sighed, a ragged, mournful sound, and shook his greying head heavily, eyes downcast in apparent contemplation of the unseen. "If only her constitution had not failed at that final, most crucial hurdle! If only she had persevered against those last agonising confinements and sweats, she might yet walk amongst us today, bolstering my own waning spirits with her radiant hope and... and..."

"Such thoughts are fruitless, Father," gently interrupted Francis. "What is past is past. We cannot alter it. Darker paths yet loom before us." He paused, then, steeling himself for a subject that had indeed plagued his thoughts of late, continued, "yet, speaking of the past... that night... the vile and frankly untenable accusations Lord Grant saw fit to level against you and your manner of winning my mother. Tell me they hold not a solitary grain of truth?"

For a moment, a spark seemed to stoke the guttering flames of the older man's spirit. Sir Andrew straightened in his chair and threw back upon his patrician hauteur. "*Truth*?" retorted he in a tone utterly incredulous. "Of course not! Grant's slander holds not one whit of truth, Francis; this I aver most absolutely! That poisonous, spite-bloated viper forever twists and perverts all to suit his warped narrative! Insult the virtue of the woman I adored above all others?" He shook his head most vehemently.

"Never, oh *never* would I so besmirch her maiden modesty with vile whispers of illicit revels!" resumed he. "It was a stratagem, Francis — a ruse Eleanor and I conceived in *joint* desperation to thwart the mercenary, cold-blooded schemes of her own obdurate parents to sell her off as chattel to that... that..." he faltered, possibly searching for epithets sufficiently damning, "... to Lord Grant, for his ill-begotten wealth and lineage over her every tear and protestation!"

Visibly worked up at these recollections, he broke off, chest heaving as his outburst ebbed. "We merely facilitated circumstances that made our own union appear the only respectable course. A subterfuge, yes, but one born of love and desperation — not dishonour! To pledge our troths in the sight of God and all society, title and fortune be forever damned!"

Francis dipped his chin in an economical nod, accepting his father's words at face value — for now. "Forgive me for dwelling upon such painful histories." With a measure of relief softening his temper, he carefully replaced the bracelet back amidst the sad clutter. "But again, promise me, Father, whatever difficulties yet lie before us, this piece at least shall remain with us."

Sir Andrew seemed scarcely to register his son's plaintive request. He shook his head slowly from side to side; his gaze had taken on a distantly haunted character. "Oh, Francis..." groaned he, giving voice to whatever fresh mordant visions swam behind that hollowed stare. "Would that I had possessed the simple resolution... the courage to put a pistol to my head last night when the full, monstrous measure of my ruin became horrifyingly clear!"

A sudden, menacing chill clamped onto Francis' chest. He involuntarily recoiled a pace or two, feeling as though his father's hushed confession had taken on a fleshy, serpentine form. His father could not have been serious? To take his own life? Immediately, Francis closed the distance between them and firmly clasped his shoulder.

"No, Father, no! This... this shall not be borne! I cannot allow you to surrender so utterly to these black fantasies of self-violence! Do not speak, do not even think in such malignant, unrectifiable terms, I beg of you!"

He tightened his grip on the older man's shoulder until his knuckles shone pale. "This... catastrophe upon our family is not solely of your making, sir." An inrush of eloquent emotions beset him. "Indeed, I fear the greater portion must inevitably lie with me and certain... decisions of a most regrettable nature to which I have been incumbent these recent weeks."

At this solemn pronouncement, Sir Andrew raised his head. "With you, Francis? Whatever nonsense is this you speak?" He reached up, his grasp surprisingly firm on his son's hand. "In what possible manner could any portion of this... wretched misery have emanated from *your* actions?"

Aye, in this moment did Francis fully realise his err. In his bid to succour his father's sufferings, he had inadvertently let slip a most inauspicious allusion to his nocturnal activities. Drawing his errant emotions back under some semblance of mastery, and desperate to disguise the burning rush of colour which stole across his cheeks, he turned away and crossed the room.

Soon standing by the window, he feigned an interest in the vista of gardens. Though try he did, his mind had already succumbed to the painful reality. How was he ever to give voice to such profound mortification interred deep within his soul? But at length, braving the inevitable, sacrificing his meagre honour to his father's, he took a bracing breath and: "It... it concerns Lady Grant, Father," began he at last to confess the awful truth. "Her Ladyship and I... we... we..."

Alas, for all Francis' courage, his words faltered; those yet unspoken, their implication traversed the silence which, suffocating and suddenly airless, descended upon the study. Though he kept his back to his father, he felt — as all such libertines, rakes, and general delinquents are wont to do when they let slip inconvenient truths — Sir Andrew's stare boring into his shoulder blades. Then, a choked sound, a gasp, as if from a physical blow, broke upon the terrible silence.

When Francis braved to turn, he beheld a sight almost terrifying:

In the span of several heavy heartbeats, a green pall seemed to leach what colour remained from the baronet's face, leaving him waxen and trembling. "Oh, merciful God," breathed he. "Tell me this is some cruel jest at my expense, Francis! Tell me this... this implication you have drawn is not... *cannot* possibly be true!"

Despite his own shame — if shame it may be called — Francis refused to offer up any such convenient fictions as a salve against the searing wound of truth's harsh disrobing. "I fear it is the unvarnished truth, Sir," replied he, somewhat shakily. "For these past two months, I have been... paying Her Ladyship visits. There were near discoveries of our... congress. Moments of peril beyond even my arrogance to cavalierly dismiss." Having already confessed so much, he found sudden confidence to utter the whole more steadily. "But I, fool that I am, blinded by vanity, by indolent self-absorption... I never truly suspected for an instant that her husband, Lord Grant, had, in point of bitter fact, uncovered our... liaisons."

Sir Andrew had shaken his head in stunned negation from almost the first admission; but as his son's sordid accountings multiplied in compound condemnation, so too did his countenance grow ever sicklier and more haunted. Now, as the full, unmitigated implications exploded in chorus all about him, he cast a look of such pained disbelief upon his heir as might have felled a lesser man at twenty paces.

"Flirtations with impressionable debutantes and eligible misses," rasped he at last. "Foolish... boyish jests... and vapid compliments ill-befitting your station — those I have seen, Francis, and despaired at. But *this*...!" He broke off, visibly struggling to contain the storm of outrage and hopelessness. "But this!" The word re-erupted, raw with palpable disgust. "To utterly debauch a married woman? To so flagrantly and callously cuckold the very man whose ill-fated hospitality we have so assiduously cultivated and accepted within his own household? Were you entirely bereft of sense, boy? Of honour? To so wantonly disport yourself in such a lurid, unthinkable fashion?"

Even Francis, notwithstanding his own arrogance, wilted beneath the onslaught of his father's opprobrium. As the air, long pent-up, rushed from his lungs, deflating his posture, the scalding enormity of his selfish indiscretions rained down in righteous fury all about him.

For the first time in his careless existence, the true price of his amusements stood before him like a castigating spectre. He had not merely offended society; he had handed his father's dignity to a monster on a silver platter. The realisation of this consequence crushed him.

Steeling himself, he crossed the chamber and sank to one knee.

"Forgive me, Father. My folly alone has crippled us and brought us to this unthinkable pass." He seized his sire's trembling hand in his own. "But I swear to you, upon my very soul in this life and any hypothetical next, I shall undo the damage and thwart the Devil's bargain he so eagerly embraces."

He squeezed the older man's papery hands with a gentle urgency. "You must rest here, sir. Cease tormenting yourself. Leave everything now to me!"

A fresh surge of horror and despair, this one utterly impotent and soul-shaking, seemed to sweep across Sir Andrew's ravaged features at this final oath. He gripped Francis' hands with a sudden, startling intensity. "My boy... my poor, foolish boy... I fear nothing short of divine intercession could deliver us from the utter annihilation Lord Grant so plainly intends for us both!"

At so dire a prognostication, Francis attempted a wan smile, a mere flicker of filial bravado amidst the settling gloom. "Perhaps, Father. And yet, as the saying goes... miracles have indeed been known to transpire upon occasion..."

However, even as he spoke such hollow words of consolation and stared into his father's devastated eyes, the weight of his own indiscretions bearing down redoubled with the seeming impossibility of their situation, found the word "miracle" leaving behind naught but a charring residue of bitter ashes upon his tongue.

****

Four days later, many miles from the shadowed study at Brookside, a different kind of weight pressed down under an overcast sky. The air of Springfield Castle's private graveyard was thick with the scent of damp earth and old stone. It was exactly one year since Sir Lockwood had been laid to rest.

Vanessa stood before the substantial marble tombstone, a solitary figure of grief. The formal mourning she wore was a uniform now, a second skin that had become a cage. Beside her, Ms Brown stood as a silent, supportive shadow. The vicar had just offered his final prayer, his words swallowed by the stillness, before he retreated with a respectful bow.

Vanessa remained behind, her gaze fixed on the chiselled letters of her father's name. With a gloved hand reaching out, she traced the inscription. The cold marble offered no comfort, only the stark finality of loss. A single year. An eternity since she had felt guided; since his laughter had echoed in the halls of Springfield Castle. Now, only silence and the menacing weight of Lord Grant's guardianship remained, and his relentless plans for her future.

Her eyes drifted to the stone's base; a sheaf of white lilies lay in stark contrast to the turmoil in her heart. She drew her mourning cloak tighter against the chill, a cold which rather emanated entirely from within.

Finally, with a steadying breath that hitched in her throat, she turned away. The walk back through the weathered graves of Lockwood ancestors felt impossibly long, each step heavier than the last, burdened not just by grief but by the gnawing anxiety of her present.

Back within the imposing stone walls of Springfield Castle, the composure Vanessa had maintained before the vicar and her father's grave instantly fractured. With a long, soul-dredging sigh, she entered her spacious bedchamber; again, its familiar luxury felt hollow, almost mocking. With weary indifference, she removed her bonnet and gloves, dropping them onto the chaise longue.

Following behind, Ms Brown was all "aahs" and "oohs", her round face a canvas upon which concern had been painted in broad, anxious strokes. "Will you take some tea now, Miss Vanessa?" said she, craning her neck. Her dark eyes, which ordinarily possessed all the penetration of raisins in a pudding, manifestly studied her mistress' countenance. "Or perhaps lie down for a while?"

Though indeed fatigued by grief's outpouring, Vanessa, restless from other feelings, shook her head and glided towards the tall window, which overlooked the sprawling parkland. "Rest," murmured she, "is a luxury I cannot afford, Ms Brown."

The day's solemnity had stirred not just sorrow, but a potent commingling of anger and helplessness. Anger at the fate that had taken her father; exasperation at the position she was now forced into; aggravation at the expectations closing in around her. Her gaze swept the room and snagged anew on the velvet jeweller's box still resting on her dressing table; still untouched. The bracelet, that symbol of Lord Grant's intentions, of the marriage she dreaded, of the future being dictated *to* her, not chosen *by* her.

The memory of her father's kindness, his trust in her judgment, collided violently with His Lordship's manipulative control. Grief for the past warred with fury at the present. She happened to glance at the stack of cheap, thrilling novels hidden beneath her vanity. *How pathetic that the only place a woman of her means could experience freedom, danger, or a choice of her own was within the dog-eared pages of a penny dreadful.*

Caught up in the tempest of a year's suppressed injustice and swelling rage, she snatched up the box, wrenched the heavy gold bracelet from its velvet bed, and flung it across the chamber.

It struck the cold fireplace with a sickening crack. Gold links scattered; pearls rolled across the polished floorboards like fallen tears.

"Oh, Miss Vanessa!" Ms Brown rushed forwards. "That beautiful bracelet! Such craftsmanship!"

"Mere craftsmanship for a cage!" Vehement heat burnt her cheeks, tears pricking at the corners of her eyes. "Let it lie broken. It is more honest that way."

Having hovered in that peculiar attitude of distress which servants adopt when witnessing the destruction of their betters' property, Ms Brown at length descended to her knees. Her expression being a mixture of shock and sympathy, so common to her station, she began gathering the ruined pieces. "A costly piece like that..." muttered she.

Then, as if the sight of such abused finery awakened some dormant faculty of commerce within her breast, she added, "it reminds me... when I was in Taunton yesterday, fetching the wreaths you required, I saw the most dazzling things in the window of that little pawnbroker near the market square. Rings, brooches... sundry bracelets, not unlike this one, though not so fine, to be sure."

Having finally gathered up the last melancholy fragments, she cast a glance of no small apprehension towards her mistress. "I shall take this there, too, Miss. When I next go to town. We wouldn't want Lord Grant to be cross.

Chapter the Sixth — A Black Eye and A Desperate Vow

August 7, 1865

Oh, let us turn our roving gaze awhile and cast it unabashed upon the jolting, careening interior of a certain carriage, labouring through the midnight ruts of some forgotten country lane! For within this compact theatre of dalliance, lurching and swaying upon the roads that had evidently known better days, do we espy our young, still untamed rake, Mr Francis Sheringham. Having ostensibly abandoned all thoughts of familial and financial discomfiture, he appears to have sought solace therefrom in that oldest and most time-hallowed of consolations afforded the bereft and despairing sons of Adam's accursed seed.

Beside our hero sat that full-figured paragon of feminine plenitude whom his irreverent wit had christened Lady "Plenty". Both passengers, it must be confessed, had partaken of the grape and were considerably elevated by it. Their laughter echoed perhaps a trifle too loudly within the carriage's quarter-sphere confines. The lady in particular — her amber curls elaborately dressed and liberally perfumed, escaping their pins — punctuated her amorous sighs with bursts of incoherent nonsense, while Francis (ever the vaulting opportunist when borne aloft by Bacchus' blushing favours) employed one bold hand in languid ministrations along the plump alabaster column of his inamorata's swan-like throat. The path his lips traced I shall, for fear of impropriety, chronicle not here. As for his other digits, they were quite shamelessly engaged in the dexterous unfastening of a rather magnificent cabochon emerald that bedecked her ladyship's heaving corsage.

Yet, just as this louche transference of feminine *spolia opima* was about to conclude, the careening coach shuddered to a bone-juddering halt.

The immutable laws of nature and physics, being no respecters of persons, passions, or genteel pretensions, thereupon asserted their ineluctable prerogatives. Our two entangled lovers found themselves pitched headlong from their seats into a most undignified heap upon the floor of their rolling boudoir.

"Ooof!" gasped the lady.

"What in the very Devil's unholy name...?" spluttered Francis, still struggling — as men of his kind ever have and ever shall — to disentangle himself from the siren's generous, if momentarily inconvenient, curvatures.

At any rate, some brief and unseemly tussling, punctuated by mutual bony elbows and unparliamentary plaints, preceded the pair at last scrambling atop their dislodged cushions in passable array.

'Twas at this precise juncture that the carriage door flew open.

And lo, silhouetted against the full moon's unforgiving cast, there stood a most alarming apparition. This unsavoury customer, 'pon whose disreputable person and lineaments we shall shortly become more intimately apprised under the coach light, possessed a visage and general mien scarcely calculated to inspire confidence in even the most charitable of Christian souls. He stood at some thirty-odd perplexities in seasons past the gateway to maturity, and his countenance, rugged and as ill-shorn as the coastal moors, bore the hallmarks of a life lived in defiance of soap and societal niceties. A great nimbus of unruly hair, dark as a starling's wing, crowned his uncivil pate and merged seamlessly with a feral beard that bespoke more of wild hedgerows than barbers' ministrations. As for his clothes — what tattered remnants persisted in their dubious office upon his person — they spoke of an intimate acquaintance with wharf-side ditches and cross-roads hostelries leagues removed from the callow refinements of the *beau monde*.

And most unambiguously, this unprepossessing individual brandished in one grimy, untutored fist a rather menacing pistol.

Lady "Plenty", whose eyesight penetrated the alcoholic haze more quickly than her companion's, was the first to register the unwelcome intrusion. "Good heavens, Francis!" She clutched his arm. "What... what in the name of God's mercy is... is *that*? Do the restless dead truly wander at their own pleasure amongst the all-too-living?"

With her talons digging into his flesh, a somewhat squinting Francis peered at the figure in the doorway. "Pay it no mind, my dear," slurred he. "'Tis merely some species of monkey-faced booby who has mistaken our private vessel for a common public house, no doubt."

"But, Francis!" Her cries only took on a keening desperation. "The monkey-faced booby appears to be positively armed! It clasps a firearm about its person!"

Thus accoutred and duly acknowledged, the trespasser drew himself up, his chest puffing beneath its ragged vestments. "Stand and deliver, ye scufflers!" growled he in accents distinctly redolent of the Borough Shambles. "Abide ye now the dread visage o' Black Harry hisself!"

At this rather rough-on-the-ears proclamation, our Sheringham, menaced not by the rascal or his weaponry, calmly raised an ironic eyebrow. "Black you are, beyond dispute, varlet! Though such sable hues owe less to lineage, methinks, and more to a manifest aversion to bathing. A right vigorous curry-combing and a good scrubbing might render you a more palatable turnspit designation. How about 'Grubby Harry' instead?"

Ignoring this sally with the dignity of one whose intellect was unequal to appreciating its wit, the highwayman shook his weapon with renewed emphasis. "Yer money or yer lives! Quick about it, or Oi'll be decoratin' this 'ere road with yer pretty brains!"

"Oh, wretched me, oh thrice undone and accursed!" wailed her ladyship. "He intends to deprive us of our very lives, Francis! Oh, sir, you verily must intervene and safeguard us against this felon's ravishments!"

Whether it was the damsel's *cri de coeur* pricking what dormant martial enthusiasms yet slumbered within our hero's wine-soaked breast, or perhaps merely the intrinsic obligation any gentleman of quality (however compromised) to be overtly discommoded or shorn of his chattels (or those he intended to relieve others of), Francis reassumed his prerogative. He cast off the role of Dionysiac satyr and took up instead that of doughty defender of feminine virtue

"See here, you most egregious and unwelcome wastrel!" He strove to sit up properly on the dislodged cushions. "Such conduct is entirely unacceptable! One does not address a lady in this peremptory fashion! Have you no manners?"

Incidentally, as the lout leant into the coach's stuffy confines to press home his vulgarian demands, his gaze betrayed a certain wavering. Those rheumy fen-pits masquerading as vision-slits widened with a different cast of interest altogether. They strayed southwards, magnetically affixed upon the remarkable — nay, the absolutely *staggering* — expanse of Lady "Plenty's" décolletage, which, in consequence of that earlier tumble, had unexpectedly unfurled for a roving inspection considerably more generous than strict decorum might allow.

"Cor blimey! Me old mushrooms an' truffles!" exclaimed the robber in a tone not unlike a toad ribbiting amidst the rushes. Forgetting entirely his foul purpose in open-mouthed rapture, he continued. "B-b-beggin' yer pardon, missus" — he shifted his grip upon the trailing artillery-piece to better serve as a pointer's wand — "but Oi ain't never been blessed to clap me blinkers upon the like o' *them* afore in all me wanderings... no offense-like meant, o'course!"

That this unwashed rapscallion should dare to so brazenly leer upon his ladybird's considerable Venusian assets proved too final, too great an emasculating insult for Francis' taxed dignity. The wine that had moments before rendered him languorous now fired his blood with righteous indignation.

"How dare you, sirrah!" roared he, struggling to attain his feet within the coach's rocking confines. "Your impertinence demands satisfaction!"

With these immortal words, he lunged forwards.

While his choreographed intent was indeed that of a seasoned prizefighter delivering the *coup de grâce*, his execution rather lent him the pitching momentum of a landsman newly shipped.

One might charitably surmise that our hero intended to plant as punishing a blow upon the impudent fellow's undefended munnings. Yet, the brigand — his apian reverie having been so rudely disrupted — reacted with the brutal economy of one whose entire existence had been a protracted education in brawls. The unshaven raptor, devoid of all gentlemanly artistry but pregnant with all the force of a sledgehammer's wallop, released a single swing of his meaty fist.

To be sure, the impact detonated with a crunch that echoed through the carriage. Bereft of vigour in a single, devastating instant, Francis was launched like a cannonball payload across the interior — his back re-acquainting itself with the cushions' disarranged upholstery. A faint grunt escaped him as pinpricks of stabbing brilliance exploded in little stellar nebulae of agonising vertigo behind his eyelids, whilst his consciousness took temporary leave of its customary residence.

Harry, for his part, sneered, revealing a landscape of decidedly rotten and absent teeth. "Satisfied now, y'poxy guv'nor?" mocked he with a derisive snort billowing from his putrescent caverns. "If not, I'll be right chuffed to reinforce the lesson with me other fambles!" His gaze now fell upon the emerald necklace lying glinting on the floor. He snatched it up greedily.

"Right-o then!" He turned his attention and that infernal pruning-hook upon the now thoroughly terrified and inert Lady "Plenty" herself. "Let's be 'avin the rest o' yon fripperies while we're at it, eh ducky? Rings, bracelets, shiny pretties — the lot on 'em, an' be a good 'un fer Black Harry now!"

Seeing her erstwhile cavalier sprawled before her in an insensate, groaning heap, the prudent Lady commenced surrendering up her remaining bijoux. Rings slipped from trembling fingers, pearl ear-bobs were hastily unclasped, and a diamond cluster that had graced her stomacher was surrendered with sobs.

Having perceptibly satisfied his magpie's appetites for the nonce and stuffed his plunder into a capacious pocket, Harry favoured the lady with one final, gap-toothed grin, displaying the full pestilential splendour of that ogreish deathtrap purporting to be his mouth. Whereupon, with unexpected brusqueness, he slammed the carriage door shut.

Thus left alone with the battered, semi-conscious, and now quite thoroughly maltreated escort: "Francis...! Francis...!" cried her ladyship. "Wake yourself now! I beg you most earnestly!"

But, receiving no response save a series of incoherent mumbles, she employed that most traditional and robust of revivification rituals known to womankind: a series of stinging, percussive slaps across his noble cheeks.

"Wake yourself, Francis!" again cried she, her palm connecting with his countenance in a rhythm that would have done credit to a military drummer. "Rouse and declare whether any lasting injuries have been dealt to your precious person!"

Natch, such blows, however well-intentioned, served only to further mortify his masculinity. "Unhand me, madam, this instant!" He pushed her away before gingerly prodding the angry rise of a painful contusion already forming beneath one eye. "Your attentions are as unwelcome as they are, I must say, excessive! Confound you, I am perfectly able to recover the use of my faculties without such energetic intervention!"

***

We find ourselves now transported to the intimate confines of Francis' bedchamber — a room reflecting, perhaps, more of the young master's somewhat disordered situation than any conscious application of refined or elegant décor. Garments lay strewn with studied carelessness over the back of a Chippendale armchair, their rich silks and velvets cascading in flagrant defiance of proper valetry — for alas, much like their dwindling fortunes, their household staff were daily depleting too, driven away by the twin spectres of unpaid wages and uncertain prospects. An upended volume of Pope's translations, its gilt-edged leaves splayed in mute testimony to interrupted reading, gaped from its abandonment upon the carpet.

By the sputtering bougie of a single tallow candle — beeswax being among those luxuries recently deemed beyond their reduced circumstances — Francis reclined in dishevelled posture amid the worn but still accommodating depths of a padded *bergère* chair. The evening's vinous festivities had long since evaporated, leaving in their wake only the throbbing malaise of both contusion and disgrace. Ah yes, that bruise — a most unwanted floral of ecchymotic hue — had well and truly blossomed like some monstrous tropical orchid upon his aristocratic cheek and brow.

Attending upon this wincing invalid was a most unlikely and unlooked-for ministrant: his own father. Clad in the homely austerities of a nightshirt and brocaded dressing gown, the baronet exhibited all the tender solicitude of a hospital sister as he hovered over his prodigal offspring. With hands that trembled slightly, he dipped a linen cloth into a basin of cool water, and with painstaking care pressed the damp compress to his heir's injured noggin.

At length, with a countenance that bore testament to decades of worry over his scion's manifold follies, Sir Andrew mused aloud:

"Highwaymen..." His voice held a note of mild astonishment. "Truly, I had thought their era long past, consigned to the dusty annals of history. I recall tales from my own childhood, certainly — formidable figures they were said to be, haunting the lonely crossroads like spectres of the night. But the dragoons were despatched, the roads systematically patrolled... the county was declared quite clear of such ruffians these thirty-forty years past." He shook his head. "To think such primitive villainy yet persists in our enlightened age..."

From the depths of Francis' tormented soul, there escaped a dismissive snort, though he winced anew as the cold cloth touched his tender flesh. "Highwayman!" scoffed he. "Pray, elevate not that uncouth wretch to such romanticised heights, Father! He possessed not a whiff of the noble rogue's mythic gallantry about his grubby person, I assure you!"

Francis shifted irritably in the chair, unable to appease his aching musculature and outraged dignity both. "Any craven bully can procure a rusty firearm and terrorise honest travellers under cover of darkness! It requires no particular valour, merely opportunity and a comprehensive absence of moral scruples. He was naught but a common footpad, a gutter-spawned cur, nothing more!"

Having vented his immediate spleen, Francis paused; a flicker of his usual arrogance returned to defend his shamefaced ignominy. "Why, even I could doubtless manage such a feat with tolerable ease, were I so inclined to embrace the criminal arts!"

At this bold statement, Sir Andrew froze as though struck by a lightning bolt; his hand hovered over the basin. Slowly, he lowered the cloth and fixed his son with a stare so sharp, so laden with disappointment, it proved more afflicting than any physical blow.

The ensuing silence stretched like a bottomless chasm, heavy and suffocating with unspoken rebuke.

Francis shifted beneath so judicial a gaze; indeed, he even shrank from him, for his father's disapprobation verily possessed the power to compress his very being. The weight of that stare proved, to his considerable discomfort, more excruciating than his still-swelling contusion.

Our hero was accustomed to his father's anger, but this quiet comingling of shame and grief was unbearable. It held up a mirror to his soul, and the reflection staring back struck deep.

At length, he raised his hands in a gesture of mock surrender that fooled precisely no one but himself. "Forgive me, Father," mumbled he. "An ill-considered jest, uttered without proper reflection or discretion. Pay it no mind, I beg you. Fatigue and... and the lingering effects of the evening's encounter make me speak foolishly."

Act the Second

Chapter the Seventh — A Highwayman's Gambit

August 8, 1865

The next night had fallen, thick and starless, casting the world in blackness, save where the gibbous moon cast a fleeting silver upon the seldom-travelled byway. 'Tis here we find Francis Sheringham engaged in an enterprise far removed from the salons of polite society; an enterprise, on this occasion, that might have raised considerably more than just a few eyebrows.

Mounted upon a steed of commendable stoutness — a bay gelding purloined, we must assume, from his father's now-imperilled stables for so ungentlemanly a purpose — our hero, or perhaps anti-hero, depending upon your moral compass, lurked within the embrace of an overgrown thicket that bordered the lonely stretch of country road. His attire bespoke a dramatic, if somewhat anachronistic, transformation: a flowing black cloak enveloped his form; a hat of such generous brim it might have sheltered a small family from a downpour cast his noble features into mysterious shadow; completing the ensemble of a traditional highwayman, a silken mask veiled his aspect.

Presently, the nocturnal symphony of crickets and sighing branches was disturbed by a crescendo of sound most welcome to Francis' expectant ears: the grinding of iron-shod wheels against the earth, the musical jingle of harness, and the steady percussive clatter of hooves that heralded the approach of potential... benefactors, as it were.

Francis, whose heart, it must be confessed, performed a rather lively contradance against his ribs, peered through the concealing foliage. His fingers, with a volition of their own, found their way to the cold butt of the pistol nestled in his belt — an instrument whose provenance, one presumes, was as shadowy and suspect as the purpose to which it was about to be dedicated.

Part patience, part suspense, part terror, part... well, part many things not easily catalogued by moral philosophy, he waited for the lumbering conveyance to draw almost abreast of his leafy sanctuary. Then, with a suddenness calculated to inspire alarm, and a cry of "Stand and deliver!" he spurred his mount from its verdant lurking-place, presenting himself squarely in the oncoming carriage's path.

The coachman — a stout fellow, whose belly strained valiantly against the buttons of his many-caped greatcoat — reacted with a celerity that did him credit. He yanked on the reins with such vehemence and loosed such a volley of curses as might have shocked a Billingsgate fishwife, whilst the horses reared tall in equine protestation, and the coach skidded to a halt.

"Oi!" roared he, his whip poised in the full heat of his indignation. "You rotten reprobate! You cursed son of a diseased doxy! Remove your carcass from the road, ye damned fool, lest my beasts make a proper pancake of ye!"

To this rather coarse invitation, Francis responded not with words, but with the far more persuasive argument of his pistol; he produced and levelled it with a calmness that, given the riot in his breast, quite belied his novice status in this particular field of endeavour. Even the moon, as if eager to play her part in the nocturnal melodrama, cast a sinister gleam upon the weapon's barrel, transforming it from mere metal into an arbiter of mortal fate.

"Saints and martyrs defend us!" gasped the coachman in what can only be described as a squeak.

At this unaccustomed commotion, natural curiosity from within the carriage prompted investigation. A window in the lacquered door screeched downwards upon its brass runners, and a head, crowned with a periwig of formal, if slightly askew, magnificence, protruded into the uncertain light like some turtle emerging from its shell.

Reader, you may well recall this very same cranium, and the portly gentleman to whom it was securely affixed — none other than Mr Russell, that prosperous merchant whose acquaintance we previously made amidst the glittering gaiety and subsequent spectacular ruin of Lord G's fateful gaming party.

"What in thunder is amiss, Smith?" cried he to the coachman. "Why this unseemly delay? Proceed, man, proceed with all haste! Time, as they say, is money, and you are squandering mine with unconscionable profligacy!"

"Begging your pardon, Sir," interposed Francis, pitching his voice lower than its natural register, yet losing none of the genteel accents (a curious juxtaposition, one might observe, in a knight of the road), "but to proceed would be, I fear, most injudicious at this juncture. For this, I must with sincere regret apprise you, is a hold-up. Might I prevail upon you, and any companions within, to do me the single honour of stepping forth from your conveyance?"

Smith, whose enthusiasm for arguing with a loaded firearm was understandably minimal, required no second bidding. He scrambled from his perch with an agility surprising in one of his girth and, with hands that danced a nervous jig upon the latch, flung open the coach door as though it were aflame.

Thus, from the shadowed interior there reluctantly emerged, first, Mr Russell himself, holding aloft a hand-lantern, whose glow revealed a countenance bearing indignation and apprehension in equal measure. Mrs Russell followed — a lady whose figure, it might be said without undue exaggeration, presented a formidable challenge to the structural integrity of any carriage doorway; and whose expression, as again illumed by the lantern's uncertain radiance, conveyed the sort of profound moral affront typically reserved for stray dogs and itinerant peddlers. Lastly, like some timid woodland creature startled from its bower, came Miss Jenny Russell, their daughter — that maiden of some eighteen summers, whose delicate beauty possessed that ethereal quality which, whilst Francis had continually ignored, poets are wont to celebrate in their more inspired moments. Her large, wide eyes, indeed flashing with the righteous anger one might expect from Russell blood, betrayed in the lantern's amber haze a dawning confusion as to why Papa was not immediately vanquishing this impertinent fellow.

This unhappy trio arranged themselves uncertainly by the roadside.

"Ladies, and you, sir" — Francis swept a bow from the saddle that was a masterpiece of courteous brigandry, though it nearly cost him his balance and his hat — "I pray you accept my profoundest apologies for this... *unscheduled* pause in your peregrinations. Certain pressing circumstances compel me to relieve you of your ready money and such portable trinkets of value as you might currently have about your person."

Mr Russell, whose barrel chest visibly inflated with every syllable of this outrageous preamble, turned a shade of purple hitherto unseen outside of a dyer's vat. "Oh, monstrously sorry, I've no doubt!" spluttered he. "A thousand pardons for the inconvenience! How terribly civil of you to express such regret whilst robbing us blind! Tell me, you audacious rogue, has society no more *honourable* profession for earning one's bread than terrifying ladies and plundering the possessions of law-abiding citizens?"

Francis inclined his head slightly. "Indeed, sir, the avenues for honest employment are manifold, as you rightly observe. Yet, efficiency, sir, must sometimes take precedence over convention. And now, if you would be so obliging as to divest yourself of your purse?"

"Your civility, sirrah, is positively overwhelming!" retorted Mr Russell with tones that left precious little doubt as to his sarcasm; "it quite makes up for the loss of one's property!" With a sigh that might have powered a small windmill, he nonetheless produced a plump wallet that spoke of commercial success and a gold watch that gleamed with insolent luxury. "You are practically murdering me with your charm, you villain!" He handed them over with ill grace. "Next, you'll be asking for my teeth, I suppose!"

As Francis accepted the plunder, he maintained all the theatricality he was master of. Yet, beneath this bravado, something like bile rose into his throat. He, a Sheringham of Brookside, was reduced to terrorising merchants in the dark like a common footpad.

Mr Russel's wife and daughter, meanwhile, divested themselves of their glittering burdens — necklaces that whispered of Bond Street, rings that winked with costly fire in the moonlight, and brooches that pinned their indignation as much as their finery. Mrs Russell, particularly, upon unclasping a diamond necklace of such ostentatious sparkle, lamented in a tone that suggested the loss of a beloved child rather than mere carbon. "Oh, my dearest, dearest stones! How they did set off my complexion! I shall be quite undone without them! I shall look positively sallow!"

"Madam," responded Francis, receiving the cascade of jewels with another bow, "allow me to venture that a lady of your manifest charms and — if I may be so bold — your striking natural complexion, stands in no need whatsoever of such vitreous trinkets to advertise her inherent radiance to the world."

'Tis a testament, dear reader, to the peculiar workings of the female heart (or perhaps merely to Mrs Russell's particular constitutional susceptibility to flattery) that, notwithstanding her present despoilment, a distinct ray of sunshine pierced the gloom of her countenance. That said, she immediately cast a withering look at her husband. "Did you hear that, Russell?" demanded she. "A veritable desperado possesses the discernment to appreciate my finer qualities! When, I ask you, was the last occasion *you* troubled yourself to utter a sentiment half so gallant?"

Before Mr Russell could even reply to this matrimonial ambush (and, judging by the tightening of his jowls, it was likely to be a spirited one), Francis pocketed the loot. "It has been, despite the somewhat unorthodox nature of our introduction, an undeniable pleasure." He touched the brim of his hat with a flourish, both deferential and dashing. "I bid you good evening and trust the remainder of your travels will be entirely devoid of... further unscheduled diversions."

With those parting words, our gallant rogue wheeled his mount around and was gone from the violated coach, swallowed by the same accommodating darkness from which he had so dramatically emerged, leaving the Russell family standing by the roadside in a state of bewildered indignation.

At length, as the still trembling Smith clambered back onto his box, Mrs Russell rounded upon her spouse, her now barren bosom heaving like a storm-tossed sea:

"Well, I *never*!" She quite drowned out the droning of the crickets. "To think that a man of the road, a common highwayman with holes in his boots, for all I know, should exhibit more genteel consideration than my own lawfully wedded husband! Mr Russell, this — *this* — is the absolute, unmitigated, final indignity! I shall consult my proctor! I demand a divorce, sir, a *divorce*! And I shall tell everyone it was your snoring that drove me to it!"

***

And so, good reader, began Francis Sheringham's improbable career as the most paradoxically polite purloiner of purses ever to grace, or rather, disgrace, the king's highways. His name, his *nom de guerre* whispered in hushed tones (for none knew his identity, save perhaps his tailor, who might have wondered at the sudden demand for black broadcloth), began to acquire a local notoriety — a curious blend of trepidation and, dare we say it, distinctly flustered admiration.

Now, to chronicle each of these nocturnal adventures would, I fear, unduly tax your patience, and my own reserves of ink. Let us therefore avail ourselves of that most convenient literary artifice: the swift and illuminating montage.

Picture, if you will, our hero, a recurring shadow against the countryside's moonlit tapestry. Night after night, ever masked and dramatically cloaked like some protagonist from a gothic novel, he would halt coaches with a most deferential of authority that was all the more effective for its underlying urbanity — a velvet glove, as it were, encasing a hand that gestured with a pistol. We observe him addressing his victims with so unfailing a civility amidst so felonious an enterprise, offering such elaborate lexicons of apology. To the gentlemen, he paid a respectful inclination of the head and a calm explanation of the unavoidable transaction. But for the ladies — *ah*, for the ladies — there was a particular brand of gallantry reserved, a chivalry so out of place in the circumstances as to prove utterly disarming.

Imagine the scene, repeated with charming variations across the length and breadth of the county: Francis dismounts with a flourish, thereafter assisting a matron of formidable wealth, or a blushing maiden of tender years, to alight from her violated carriage. Hands, which moments before had clutched reticules and jewellery with desperate tenacity, were now offered to his grasp. Upon these hands, whether wrinkled with age or smooth with youth, he would press a most reverent kiss before delivering his heartfelt regrets for the encounter's "most unfortunate necessity" — and all with so respectful a low sweep of his hat that one might think he was performing a distasteful but essential public service.

The effect on the female portion of his unfortunate clientele was, it must be recorded, nothing short of astonishing. Far from succumbing to the vapours, or shrieking in a manner one might reasonably expect given their circumstances, a remarkable number of these fair victims appeared, if truth be told, rather... *captivated.*

We witness through our narrative spyglass sighs escaping from corseted bosoms — sighs that spoke less of terror and more of a delicious, thrilling flutter. Dainty lace-edged mouchoirs, instead of staunching tears of distress, waved wistfully after his departing silhouette. Indeed, on more than one occasion, as he spurred his horse into the night's welcoming anonymity, kisses wafted upon the breeze in his direction — a fragrant tribute to this perplexing paragon of politeness and pillage, a most bewildering triumph of exemplary manners over manifest malfeasance.

Yet, for our gentleman-turned-thief, such success went not, as he fondly imagined, entirely unobserved. For villains, much like mushrooms, often spring up in company; the shadowed byways of England were home to more than one rapscallion.

One evening, while Francis executed his latest masterpiece of courteous confiscation, there lurked behind a gnarled and ancient clump of oaks none other than Black Harry. This worthy — whose appellation was, as we learnt, derived from the general blackness of his character, his clothing, his teeth, and the grime beneath his fingernails — watched the proceedings with an intensity that transcended mere professional curiosity. 'Twas not, however, the glittering plundered pearls that gnawed at his vitals with the sharp teeth of resentment; no, 'twas a far more infuriating phenomenon: Master Sheringham's inexplicable, almost supernatural success with the fairer sex.

How, in the name of all that was unjust and contrary to the natural order of criminal enterprise, did this perfumed popinjay contrive to systematically divest women of their valuables and yet leave them sighing as if he had just presented them with a posy of roses, or whispered a particularly fetching sonnet in their formerly bauble-adorned ears?

Harry, whose own methods of persuasion tended more towards the guttural threat and the brandishing of a cudgel, scratched his thoroughly lice-infested pate in patent bamboozlement. "Blast-n-damn 'is pretty manners!" growled he into the oak's rough bark. "What devil's trick does the toff possess?"

***

About a fortnight had now transpired, during which the image of that paragon of polite plunder did continue to haunt Black Harry's every waking thought. Thus, inspired perhaps by such perplexing and galling observations, our less-favoured ruffian came to a momentous, if ill-conceived, resolution: if fine manners were the key to unlocking not only strongboxes but also the female heart, then fine manners he, too, would attempt!

Consequently, Fortune — that mischievous goddess who delights in arranging the most improbable and mortifying of circumstances — soon provided him with an opportunity to test this newfound philosophy.

Having, with his customary lack of finesse, brought to a halt a rather modest chaise, he discovered its sole occupant to be a lady of middle years and of a most stern countenance. After divesting this formidable dame of a purse, whose contents proved as meagre as her smile, and a tarnished silver brooch, whose chief value was... well, very little, Harry paused.

Rather than vanishing into the night with the speed of a startled stoat, as was his wont, leaving behind an odour of unwashed linen and resentment, tonight — *ah tonight* — was to be altogether different! He, Black Harry, would not be outdone in the niceties! He would demonstrate that he, too, could play the gallant, even if his audience proved a singularly unpromising specimen of womanhood.

Therefore, venturing upon his novice repertoire, he thrust his decidedly uncomely visage into the carriage's dim interior. "Righty-o-then, me duchess," declared he in tones that possessed all the mellifluous quality of a rusty hinge. "A little kiss for yer trouble, eh?"

And with these words, he lunged forwards, his lips puckered into a shape that bore less resemblance to a Cupid's bow and more to a startled carp.

The lady, as was to be expected, was demonstrably *not* charmed. Far from melting into the imagined swoon of grateful admiration, she reacted with cold promptness. A shriek of such piercing intensity that it penetrated not only her would-be ravisher's ears but probably those of every creature within a half-mile radius erupted from her throat. "Unhand me this instant, you fetid, ill-favoured brute!"

Immediately recoiling with a violence that nearly overturned the chaise and certainly disturbed its springs, she then brought her reticule — a sturdy affair of reinforced leather, likely containing smelling salts, a prayer book, and perhaps a few well-chosen pebbles for ballast — down upon Harry's unwashed cheek with a resounding *THWACK!*

Verily, the impact was of such bone-crunching, flesh-rippling intensity that it momentarily silenced the environing chorus of crickets and even caused a nearby owl, which had been observing the proceedings, to lose its grip and tumble from its branch in sheer surprise.

Simultaneously, her coachman, who had hitherto been frozen in terror, seized his advantage. With a crack of his whip, he urged the horses forth.

The consequence of this sudden acceleration was that Black Harry was ejected forthwith from the vehicle with a yelp of profound indignity. He described a brief, ungraceful arc through the night air before landing with a notable thud into a patch of particularly glutinous mud.

Indeed, there our aspiring gallant was left — or rather, there he was, scrambling with much grunting and cursing to his feet — his breeches liberally plastered with the lane's choicest mire, his cheek stinging with the imprint of the reticule, and his dignity, if such a quality could ever be ascribed to him, in utter tatters.

He stood alone in the gloom, profoundly and rather comically dumbfounded. Where, *oh where*, had his carefully planned essay into the realm of refined courtship gone so catastrophically awry? He had bowed (or at least, leant in a manner he considered bow-like), he had offered a kiss (or something approximating it), he had even addressed her as "Duchess"! What more could any woman possibly desire?

***

As we bid a temporary adieu to the nocturnal exploits of our hapless casanova, our scene flits from the shadowy, mud-splattered lanes to the extensive, and impeccably manicured, parklands belonging to Lord G. Here, the next day, we espy young Mr Vincent Grant engaged — or rather *attempting* to engage — in that most noble and traditionally aristocratic of pursuits: the scientific art of marksmanship.

Behold him, pistol in hand, adopting what he clearly deemed to be a posture both martially impressive and elegantly refined. His brow was furrowed in a frown of intense concentration; his myopic gaze fixed upon a crudely fashioned wooden target nailed to a venerable oak's stout trunk some twenty paces distant — an oak, it might be added with some sympathy, that had witnessed generations of Grants come and go with varying degrees of competence and had likely endured far worse indignities.

Beside him stood a fellow whose deeply weathered visage and ramrod-erect military bearing bespoke a long acquaintance with gunpowder, lead shot, and the often-frustrating vagaries of aristocratic pupils. With a long-suffering air, the instructor demonstrated the correct grip — firm, yet not so tight as to induce tremors. He illustrated the proper stance — balanced, feet planted as if to defy a hurricane. He expounded upon the sacred trinity of marksmanship: the unwavering alignment of the eye, the bead of the sight, and the very centre of the distant target.

"Observe closely, my good fellow," declared Vincent with the sort of breezy confidence that only the truly inexperienced can muster, interrupting the instructor's patient discourse and raising the heavy pistol with a flourish. "You shall witness a demonstration of pure triumph. Precision, you see, is merely a matter of will."

Thus, as Vincent, with an intake of breath, levelled the weapon, squinting down the polished barrel with an almost Napoleonic concentration, the good instructor (his experience having too often taught him that the 'will' of his pupils often had a remarkably poor influence on the bullet's actual trajectory) executed a manoeuvre of swift retreat — diving nigh headlong behind the relative sanctuary of a nearby ornamental rhododendron bush.

Oblivious to this rather damning vote of no-confidence, Vincent took another deep, preparatory breath. He steadied his arm and, with a final, doubtless mental command to the bullet to fly true in obedience to his noble will, squeezed the trigger.

BANG!

The report, sharp and startling as a thunderclap, ripped through the parkland's otherwise tranquil afternoon air, sending a flurry of indignant pigeons skywards from the distant manor house's eaves, while causing a nervous young footman, who was at that moment polishing silver by an open window, to knock over a priceless Georgian teapot.

A taut silence descended, broken only by the distant crow's mocking caw.

Both pupil (visibly standing proud, undoubtedly awaiting the inevitable applause of his own conscience) and instructor (peering cautiously from behind his leafy barricade) craned their respective necks, their gazes fixed upon the wooden target.

Alas, no fresh perforation marred its weather-beaten surface. Indeed, the target appeared entirely unscathed.

Another moment of profound and somewhat embarrassing stillness ensued, punctuated only by the cheerful chirping of the birds in the surrounding trees, creatures who quite probably held Mr Grant junior's marksmanship in the lowest possible esteem.

But then, a small, feathered body detached itself from a branch situated somewhat higher above the intended target — and considerably to the left of it. It described a brief parabola through the air before plummeting to the soft turf with a tiny, tragic finality.

A common sparrow, dear reader — presumably minding its own avian business, engaged in the innocent pursuit of some insectile repast, or perhaps merely enjoying the afternoon sun upon its modest brown feathers — had paid the ultimate and utterly undeserved forfeit for Mr Vincent Grant's spectacularly errant display of martial prowess.

Precision, it seemed, was considerably less a matter of aristocratic will, however forcefully and dramatically asserted, and considerably more a question of basic competence — a quality that, in the case of our young marksman, was as conspicuously absent as humility in a preening peacock or hair on a boiled egg.

Chapter the Eighth — Tales of the Page and Road

August 21, 1865

Let us, by the nimble and infinitely agreeable conveyance of our narrative (a vehicle much swifter and more comfortable, one trusts, than any mail coach), trundle away with all deliberate speed from Mr Vincent Grant's sunlit follies to the drawing room of Mr and Mrs Russell, whom we recently encountered upon His — or in this instance — Her Majesty's road.

'Twas now evening, and here, ensconced upon a sofa whose plump cushions bespoke a comfortable existence, sat Mrs Russell and her daughter, Miss Jenny. Their heads — one crowned with the matronly cap of established respectability, the other with the unadorned locks of maidenly innocence — were bent close together in an attitude of intimate conspiracy, their collective gaze fixed upon a shared volume.

This literary treasure in question was *not*, we may confidently surmise from either their expressions or what we thus far know of them, a weighty tome of profound philosophical inquiry. Nor was it a labyrinthine disquisition upon intricate theological doctrine, such as might tax the intellect or fortify the soul. Rather, it belonged to that burgeoning, and some stern moralists might observe with considerable alarm, prolific class of popular novels — those delightful, cheaply printed opiates of the imagination. These were the very literary confections, consumed with such enthusiasm by a reading populace hungry for escape from the mundane realities of daily existence, that offered a potent distillation of adventure, passion, romance, and peril — and all from the safety of one's own parlour.

The title emblazoned upon this book cover in letters of a suitably dramatic font proclaimed it, with shameless boldness, to be: "*The Lady and the Highwayman.*"

As mother and daughter pursued the narrative with a dedication not unlike that of scholars studying sacred texts, their steady progress was sprinkled with perfectly synchronised sighs; exhalations that spoke eloquently of shared sensibility and vicarious excitement. From their enrapt countenances and the occasional clutching of each other's hands during moments of dramatic tension, one could scarcely doubt that the fictional exploits of the indubitably dashing and impeccably masked protagonist — who, we wager, possessed both a silver tongue and a heart of pure gold beating beneath his villainous exterior — resonated with a peculiar and rather powerful intimacy.

Indeed, given their own recent and decidedly less romanticised brush with a genuine practitioner of the very same dubious art, their hearts perhaps never beat so inappositely, so contrarily, so indecorously. With each turned page, it appeared the line was becoming, for the Russell ladies, most delightfully, and perhaps just a trifle dangerously, blurred. One might almost imagine them comparing notes, *sotto voce*, on the relative merits of their own highwayman versus the fictional hero.

***

Meanwhile, in another chamber, within another house altogether — a residence of considerably greater opulence — a similar scene of literary absorption was unfolding.

We find Lady "Plenty" lolling with magnificent abandon amidst a veritable Alp of downy pillows upon her vast, canopied bed. She, too, was utterly held captive in the thrall of the printed word, her plump fingers — still vainly adorned with rings that flashed in the candlelight — delicately turning the pages.

Her chosen volume, bound in a considerably more sumptuous leather than the Russell ladies' modest acquisition, bore the suggestive, gold-leafed title: *"The Masked Lover."*

This literary work promised thrills of a perhaps even more explicitly titillating nature than its penny-press cousins, having been designed by its anonymous author to set the feminine pulse a-flutter with hazardous excitement and send the carefully sheltered imagination a-gallop across forbidden terrains of romantic possibility.

As her ladyship's wide eyes — aided by a pair of elegant mother-of-pearl lorgnettes that perched upon her nose — devoured the impassioned prose, a distinct and rather condemning blush bespattered her ample cheeks. Her breathing grew shallow and quick. Her capacious bosom — that monument to feminine abundance which had been the despair of countless corset-makers, and recently the willing victim to Francis' mischievous hands — rose and fell with an almost rhythmic excitement as if keeping perfect time with the galloping hooves of the fictional hero's midnight steed.

Lost entirely to the narrative's intoxicating spell, she suddenly clasped the leather-bound volume to her breast. With a convulsive movement, she emitted a breathless exclamation that was half yearning sigh, half ecstatic gasp:

"Oh!" Her eyes — which lifted beyond the silk drapes to the ornate ceiling with its painted cherubs — shone with moisture. "What a *man*! What magnificent ardour! What indomitable courage courses through those noble veins!"

One might hazard a fairly-confident guess that the fictional hero currently inflaming her ladyship's well-fed imagination bore precious little resemblance to the unfortunate Master Francis Sheringham. His own courage, lest we forget his scuffle with Black Harry, had proved a rather more fragile and easily discountenanced commodity. Indeed, the literary paragon probably delivered rather than received such deadly blows; conquered rather than fled from danger; possessed the sort of masculine fortitude that would never require rescue by a hearty slap — or several so — to the face.

***

Yet *another* tableau of literary devotion presents itself to our roving eye, this time within the stern-aired dining room of Thornfield Hall. Here, amidst the lingering aroma of roasted meats and the generations of dour-faced ancestors glowering down from their portraits, sat Lord and Lady G. They were partaking of their customary post-prandial cup of tea.

For Her Ladyship, too, had sought refuge from the crushing tedium of her existence within the captivating embrace of a popular novel. Her chosen literary escape bore the deliciously promising title, "*The Handsome Stranger*." To be sure, its very name promised a world of adventure, passion, and romance far removed from the predictable arctic chill of her present surroundings and the even more predictable emotional frigidity of her marital companionship.

So utterly captivated was she by the dashing exploits and heart-melting sentiments contained within those precious pages — so thoroughly lost was she in a world where men possessed the revolutionary qualities of being noble, brave, passionate, and, above all earthly virtues, genuinely *attentive* to the needs and desires of their ladies — that the simple act of conveying a delicate porcelain teacup from its saucer to her expectant lips proved to be a navigational challenge. Her hand, guided solely by a mind distracted by the handsome stranger's thrilling escapades and romantic declarations and not by the basic laws governing the movement of objects through space, repeatedly missed its intended target. The cup would hover uncertainly in the air, a few inches shy of her mouth, before descending back to the saucer with a delicate clink.

Lord G, whose own literary pursuits extended no further than the endless columns of his prized stud book and his adored bank ledger, observed his wife's fumbling attempts at basic tea consumption with an expression of mounting irritation. His thin lips, which seldom curved into anything approaching a smile, tightened into a sneer of outright contempt — a look which evinced his opinion regarding both romantic literature and the feminine weakness for such frivolous entertainments.

That his wife yet again fumbled for the cup, causing it to rattle most indignantly on its saucer, His Lordship's patience finally snapped. "Heavens above, woman!" His voice sliced through the room's quiet solemnity. "Collect yourself! Are you utterly incapable of conveying liquid from vessel to mouth without professional assistance? Shall I summon a footman to guide your apparently helpless hand, or perhaps engage a nursemaid to oversee your beverage consumption?"

Violently startled from her fictional reverie with all the shocking abruptness of being doused with a bucket of icy Wessex water, Lady G looked up. Her gaze, still clouded with the roseate hues of imagined romance, fell with crushing finality upon her husband. A flicker of profound disappointment crossed her features. The contrast between the noble, passionate, and utterly devoted hero of her treasured book — the dashing *beau* who would doubtless have slain entire armies of dragons for her, or at the very least, remembered, without prompting, her preference for two lumps of sugar in her tea — and the unpleasant, mercenary, and emotionally barren man seated opposite her, was stark, sudden, and deeply unflattering to the latter.

Without deigning to answer him, she lowered her eyes back to the printed page; but the spell, alas, was irrevocably broken. The tea, when she finally managed to sip of it, tasted intolerably bitter, as if all the disappointment of her existence had somehow leached into it.

***

The waning-crescent moon, gazing down upon the follies and fluctuating fortunes of mortal men, now cast its palest illumination upon a lonely stretch of country road. This particular ribbon of ill-maintained thoroughfare was bordered on one side by a dark and brooding wood, and on the other by fields that lay sleeping under a blanket of dew.

Here, once more astride his unwilling accomplice of a steed, lurked Master Francis Sheringham. He wore again the dark attire of his new and decidedly illegal profession: the flowing cloak, the concealing mask, the broad-brimmed hat.

His ears, sharpened by the twin forces of necessity and the constant thrum of adrenaline that accompanies such brazen enterprises, soon detected the rhythmic beat of approaching hooves. A lone rider, it seemed.

With a subtle pressure of his knees, Francis urged his mount from the roadside shadows into the track's very centre, his gloved hand resting upon the butt of his pistol. As the unsuspecting horseman drew near through the scant-silver-washed darkness, Francis projected the customary demand of his newfound trade: "Stand and deliver!"

The solitary rider, a gentleman well-muffled against the chill and bearing a small travel lantern, pulled his horse to a halt. "I beg your pardon?" came the reply in a cultivated tone which, alas for our highwayman's already shaky composure, struck a chord of familiarity.

"Stand and deliver!" repeated Francis, lacing his voice with a sterner edge as he nudged his horse a determined step forwards, drew his pistol, and levelled its unwavering barrel at the shadowy traveller. "Your purse, sir, and any valuables you possess! And make haste!"

"Here now! What's the meaning of this unconscionable outrage?" protested the unlucky fellow, holding aloft his lantern. "This is a most unseemly and illegal imposition! Have you no respect for the queen's peace or the sacred rights of property?"

As Francis closed the remaining distance between them, intent on concluding the increasingly uncomfortable transaction with his customary efficiency, the waning moon, as if delighting in a scene of high drama, chose that very moment to conspire with the lantern. Together, like a celestial spotlight, the meagre silvery beams and the dim orange glow played upon both their faces, cruelly penetrating the carefully constructed disguise of the one while illuminating, with pitiless clarity, the astonished features of the other.

"Francis!" gasped the rider in a tone of absolute horror and disbelief.

"Father!" exclaimed the highwayman with equal shock and considerably more mortification.

The pistol, which mere moments before had been a symbol of his desperate resolve, now felt as if it had become white-hot, a burning brand of filial shame in his hand. He lowered it with a convulsive movement. Looking at his father — shivering in the damp night air, his proud shoulders hunched over a meagre lantern — Francis saw the terrifying, unvarnished face of their ruin. Poverty stripped away all titles, all pomp and show, all dignity.

And there they sat, good reader, father and son united in the most improbable of circumstances, frozen upon their respective steeds in the desolate middle of a deserted country road, staring at each other in a tableau of mutual, unutterable, and profoundly horrified amazement.

'Twas a scene so laden with tragicomic irony that it seemed to belong more properly to the exaggerated contrivances of a Drury Lane melodrama than to the sober realities of English county life.

***

An hour hence, we find our hero and his father ensconced within the study at Brookside House. The air crackled not with the scholarly quietude that had once made this room a haven of peaceful reflection, but rather with the palpable tension of unspoken accusations and bitter recriminations.

Now divested of his highwayman's gear — the cloak, mask, and hat lying in a discarded heap upon a chair — Francis paced the worn Turkish carpet. As for Sir Andrew, he slumped deep into his favourite armchair, appearing less overtly angry than devastatingly shocked. His face, already etched with the lines of worry and financial strain, was further marked by an almost spectral disillusionment that seemed to have aged him by a decade in the space of a single, terrible hour.

"To think," began Sir Andrew at last, "that a son of mine... a Sheringham... should stoop to common thievery! Waylaying honest travellers upon the king's highway! Threatening unsuspecting folk with firearms! Have you entirely taken leave of your senses, Francis? Have you no shred of decency, no particle of honour left within your soul?"

Francis halted his agitated pacing. He whirled to face his accuser. "*Honour*? And what, pray tell, of *your* honour, Father? What of your solemn promises? You sold my mother's bracelet! The one thing — the *only* thing — we possessed that was truly, inviolably hers! The keepsake I explicitly, tearfully, begged you to preserve above all else! How *could* you? Was *that* the measure of your love for her? Was *that* the extent of your respect for her precious memory? To barter away her last tangible presence in this house for... for what? A few more weeks of solvency before the wolves are at the door again?"

The accusation, so directly and so passionately delivered, struck home with the force of a perfectly aimed artillery shot. Sir Andrew shuddered violently. "It was... it was *necessary*," mumbled he, his eyes fixed upon the floor. "We needed the funds... desperately... But at least," added he, likely attempting to regain some semblance of moral high ground, "at least my actions, however painful, however regrettable, did not transgress the sacred laws of this land! I did not turn common thief! I did not become a... a highwayman!"

"And starve virtuously on the roadside, I suppose?" retorted our hero. "Is *that* the noble fate you envisioned for us? To maintain our impeccable, threadbare honour whilst our stomachs gnaw with hunger and our creditors hammer upon the door? This" — he swept a hand wide to encompass not only the room but the entirety of his desperate nocturnal activities — "this desperate path is the *only* means I could devise to acquire sufficient funds with the speed that our dire circumstances demand, Father! To stave off the grasping clutches of Grant! To reclaim what we have so carelessly, so tragically, lost!"

"And what if you are apprehended, boy?" Sir Andrew's voice rose. "Think of the inevitable consequences! The infamy! The *gallows*, Francis! The gallows await such men!"

With a dismissive wave of a hand, Francis resumed his pacing. "I shall *not* be caught. I exercise the *utmost* caution. Furthermore," continued he, his self-assurance boiling within and climbing upwards into his voice, "Fortune has provided an unexpected and rather convenient degree of cover. It seems there is another practitioner of the highwayman's art abroad in the county — a clumsy, brutish fellow by all accounts, whose methods are as crude as his intellect. His oafish activities serve only to muddy the waters and confuse the already less-than-brilliant constabulary, thereby... *diverting* suspicion away from my considerably more refined operations..."

Sir Andrew only shook his head; his face was the very picture of paternal despair.

Francis stopped his pacing once more. "Enough of this. There will be time for recriminations later, perhaps even for repentance. Tell me, Father. *Who* has the bracelet now? To whom did you sell that last piece of my mother's soul?"

The question hung in the air, heavy and accusatory, demanding an answer that Sir Andrew clearly dreaded to give.

Chapter the Ninth — An Unexpected Bargain

August 22, 1865

The ensuing day found Francis within the bustling Taunton market town's sunlit heart, specifically, within the hushed confines of the premier jewellery establishment of one Mr Phineas Stephens.

Here, amidst walls lined with polished mahogany and beneath glass counters that gleamed, lay treasures enough to tempt the most resolute of saints and, indeed, to bankrupt princes of profligate habits. Diamonds glittered with a cold fire; rubies glowed with the deep, passionate hue of pigeon's blood; pearls gleamed with a soft luminescence; and gold, in myriad forms of exquisite craftsmanship, shone with the warm, reassuring promise of enduring wealth and immutable consequence.

'Twas, as the common saying has it (and common sayings often encapsulate a world of truth), a veritable Aladdin's cave, a burglar's paradise — though Francis' purpose on this morning was not illicit acquisition, but rather, of retrieval.

Behind the main counter stood the proprietor himself. He regarded Francis with that minutely scrutinising gaze peculiar to those whose profession it is to assess, with swift and unerring accuracy, the potential worth of both the jewels laid before them and the customers who came to acquire them.

"Mr Stephens." Our hero adopted a tone of polite enquiry. "I believe my father, Sir Andrew Sheringham of Brookside House, had occasion to conduct some small business with you yesterday? He parted with an item — a lady's bracelet of diamonds and gold, most intricately engraved."

Mr Stephens blinked, his expression as unchanging as if he were accessing some internal ledger, some mental archive of every transaction transpired at his premises. "Sheringham, you say?" He tapped a thoughtful, well-manicured finger on the counter. "From the Wellington direction, is it not?"

"The very same," confirmed Francis.

"Sheringham...?" Mr Stephens' gaze drifted into the middle distance. "Engraved gold bracelet... diamonds... Ah, yes." His focus returned to Francis. "Indeed, sir, I do recall the piece. A most charming example of older craftsmanship, quite delightful in its detail. Yes." He paused. "In point of fact, I was *most* fortunate. I found a discerning buyer for it almost immediately. Resold it, as it happens, this very morning, not an hour past."

"*Resold?*" echoed our hero, accompanied by a sickening drop in his stomach. "*Already?* May I be so bold as to enquire, sir, to whom this piece was sold?"

Mr Stephens blinked again; his memory, it seemed, required another moment's consultation with its internal ledgers. "The purchaser..." murmured he, his brow furrowing slightly. "Let me see now..." He made a small show of fumbling through some papers beneath the counter, though Francis suspected the information was already perfectly clear in his mind. "Ah, yes. Here we are. It was acquired by Miss Vanessa Lockwood."

"*Lockwood?*" Francis' thoughts raced to connect the name with the local constellations of wealth and influence. "Might this be any relation, perchance, to the late Sir John Lockwood of Staplegrove? The industrialist? Proprietor of Lockwood Mills, the tannery near the river, and owner of some eight hundred acres of prime agricultural land besides?"

"Sir John's sole issue and principal inheritor, I understand," confirmed Mr Stephens with a slight inclination of his head. "His daughter, and now, by the sad event of his demise, a very considerable heiress in her own right."

For sure, as Francis absorbed this intelligence, his wits galloped with an acuity sharpened by his not-small anxiety. An heiress. A *wealthy*, independent heiress. The owner now of his mother's bracelet. "Miss Lockwood resides, I believe, at Springfield Castle?" at last replied he. "That rather imposing edifice overlooking the valley?"

***

Behold, gentle reader, the imposing edifice of Springfield Castle, rising from its extensive and meticulously sculpted parklands like some venerable, moss-encrusted giant. A truly majestic pile it was, fashioned from enduring grey stone in that glorious age when Good Queen Bess reigned supreme upon the throne of England. Its turrets and battlements, though now serving purposes more ornamental than defensive, spoke of a history far grander, and, it must be confessed, considerably more solvent than that of poor Brookside.

Down the sweeping, immaculately raked gravel pathway, which crunched beneath his horse's hooves, our hero trotted in the suit of a gentleman caller; a suit that had seen better days, much like its owner. He surveyed the imposing façade before him — the vast, rolling lands, the almost aggressive evidence of immense wealth — with an admixture of emotions: awe, certainly, at such magnificence; envy, perhaps, for a life so cushioned from the harsh winds of penury; and a significant degree of shrewd calculation, as his mind, ever active, began to assess the strategic possibilities this fortress might present.

Upon reaching the arched entrance, he was immediately noted by a footman. This liveried sentinel approached with that carefully calibrated air of polite yet firm enquiry, perfected by those whose solemn duty is to distinguish welcome guests from unwelcome petitioners.

A brief, murmured exchange ensued, during which Francis stated his name and the purpose of his visit — or, more accurately, a carefully edited and suitably vague version thereof, designed to pique curiosity rather than invite immediate dismissal.

The result of this parley was that the footman, with a nod that conveyed neither surprise nor enthusiasm, accepted the reins of Francis' somewhat jaded steed and, with a subtle gesture of a white-gloved hand, indicated that the caller should proceed towards the castle's main door.

Ushered in by a subordinate functionary, Francis found himself deposited in what was discernibly a visitors' waiting room. This chamber had manifestly been designed with the express and unambiguous purpose of impressing upon all who entered the profound antiquity and unimpeachable importance of the Lockwood lineage. Here was luxury indeed, though perhaps of a slightly oppressive kind. Austere-faced progenitors, clad in ruffs, robes, or armour, glowered down from massive, ornate gilt frames. Panoplies stood sentinel in shadowy corners, their polished surfaces gleaming dully in the filtered light as if recalling glorious battles they had, in all probability, never actually witnessed. Coats of arms, displaying a menagerie of heraldic beasts adorned the oak-panelled walls in ostentatious profusion alongside an assortment of weaponry — swords, pikes, and maces — arranged in decorative patterns, a constant reminder perhaps that the Lockwood dynasty had been rather formidable individuals to cross.

Yet, amidst this somewhat overwhelming display of genealogical bombast, Francis' eye, ever susceptible to beauty in its finer *and* feminine forms, was drawn to a rather more refined and captivating object. Perched with incongruous delicacy upon the marble mantelpiece stood a statuette: a female figure, fashioned from what appeared to be ivory or fine alabaster, in a state of classical undress.

Thus tempted, our hero — veritable libertine that he was — approached the mantelpiece. Casting a quick glance towards the heavy oak door through which he had entered to ensure that he was unobserved by any liveried guardian, he then reached out and took the figurine in his grasp. This way and that he turned it, admiring its craftsmanship — its cool contours, the pleasing curves, and graceful lines of the maidenly form.

'Twas precisely at this moment of — one might charitably call it "artistic" — contemplation that a door at the room's far end swung open with a rather ominous creak.

"*Ahem-hem!*" came an abrupt female voice.

Thusly startled from his reverie, Francis turned his eyes accordingly. My, how he practically leapt clean out of his own skin at the sight of a young lady of striking beauty framed in the doorway! So violent was his jolt that the statuette flew from his grasp, taking flight in a perilous arc through the air, destined for annihilation upon the polished floorboards. With an agility born of utter panic, and, one suspects, a fervent desire not to commence an acquaintance with a wealthy heiress by destroying her property, Francis lunged forth. He executed a clumsy dive that culminated, most miraculously, in his catching the falling figurine mere inches from catastrophe.

At this undeniably undignified spectacle (the sight of a strange fellow prostrated upon her floor, gasping for breath whilst clutching a naked nymph) Miss Vanessa Lockwood (for 'twas she stood in the doorway) raised a gloved hand to her mouth.

For a single, unguarded heartbeat, the imposing heiress vanished, replaced by a young woman utterly disarmed by absurdity. Her eyes danced with a bright, unfeigned mirth.

Though the spell of ancestral solemnity was, for that moment at least, comprehensively broken, our shame-faced hero scrambled to his feet. Having supposed that the lady might rather have shrieked in alarm and summoned the footmen to eject the apparent lunatic than laugh at his *faux pas*, he, with as much decorum as he could muster, replaced the statuette upon its marble perch.

With a bracing breath taken, he smoothed down his waistcoat, adjusted his cravat, cleared his throat, and turned to face the lady.

But alas, though now afforded a bona fide view of Miss Vanessa Lockwood — the very *belle* from Lord G's gathering — he found his tongue cleaving stubbornly to the roof of his mouth whilst his jaw plummeted like a drawbridge under assault. Indeed, it seemed his body's most essential appendages were bent entirely on sabotaging his mission this day. But what else was to be expected when, now disrobed of the uncompromising black of her mourning attire, Vanessa Lockwood possessed an even greater *je ne sais quoi* that blazed through with overawing intensity?

Here, it must be confessed, Francis' eyes did rather more than politely observe; they lingered, they appraised, they perhaps even — in the swift, silent language of masculine admiration — conducted a complete *inventory* of her charms. But let us hastily abandon such indelicate considerations...

Francis, a self-proclaimed *connoisseur* of beauty in all its manifold forms — whether sculpted in ivory, alabaster, or embodied in breathing womanhood — executed a low, sweeping bow. "Miss Lockwood," began he, his voice a trifle unsteady. "Good afternoon."

Her earlier expression of humour had now vanished. "Good afternoon, sir," replied she, her voice, in contrast to his own, clear and steady. A pause ensued, during which her gaze seemed to take his full measure. "You are...?"

"Forgive my unannounced intrusion. Francis Sheringham, entirely at your service." He offered another bow.

"Mr Sheringham...?" She inclined her head in a gesture that acknowledged his presence without necessarily welcoming it. "I trust your business is of some pressing importance?"

"Indeed, M-m-miss Lockwood. M-most assuredly." Francis gulped hard, striving to stay the ridiculous jitters that mocked his speech. Her tone, though impeccably polite, held a distinct note of briskness. She clearly suffered no fools, or fumblers of statuettes, gladly. "And permit me, first and f-f-foremost, to offer my sincerest, heartfelt" — again, he gulped — "and belated condolences upon the loss of your esteemed father, Sir John."

"Thank you. Your sympathy is noted." Her voice softened momentarily; yet it immediately resumed its former curtness. "Now, your purpose? What *exactly* do you want?"

Once again, our hero swallowed hard — quite the thunderclap in the taut silence. He shifted uneasily on the floorboards, which creaked beneath his trembling tread. What the deuce was wrong with him? His carefully rehearsed and elegantly phrased approach felt suddenly, woefully inadequate. He fiddled with his collar. "It concerns..." began he, faltering ever more grievously under so steady and intense a gaze. "... 'Tis about... a certain item of jewellery. A bracelet. I understand from Mr Stephens, the jeweller in town, that you purchased such an item from him this very morning?"

"That is correct." As she spoke, she raised a hand to adjust a stray lock of dark hair that had escaped the confines of her hairpiece; in so doing, she revealed, upon her slender wrist, the unmistakable gleam of the very object in question.

There it was! His mother's bracelet.

"W-w-well," stammered he, somewhat like a village idiot, "the fact of the matter is, Miss Lockwood... I find myself in the slightly awkward position of... wishing to... to *repurchase* it from you. If... if you would be amenable, of course."

A deep line appeared between Vanessa's arched eyebrows. "Repurchase it? But why on earth should you wish to do so?"

"It... it possesses considerable sentimental value, you see. That bracelet had belonged to my family for nigh on a century. It was my mother's. My father, facing certain... exigent *financial* pressures... Sadly, he was compelled to sell it only yesterday."

Anew, our hero gulped audibly. His breath lodged in his throat. His palms grew clammy. Would this tale of fallen fortunes and filial devotion strike a sympathetic chord in her clearly well-guarded heart?

Vanessa glanced down at the bracelet. A smile appeared to touch her lips. "I see..." She lifted her gaze at Francis; her smile vanished. "No. I think not. I find myself rather taken with it. It is quite the finest piece of its kind I have encountered in some time."

Blast and botheration! Seeing his direct, heartfelt appeal fail so comprehensively, Francis *had* to act. 'Twas time to deploy a tactic that had, on several prior occasions, proved remarkably effective on the fairer sex:

"But *surely*, Miss Lockwood," declared he, re-adopting the rich, honeyed tones he reserved for moments of attempted gallantry, "a lady of your evident taste and discernment... has no genuine need of such... such *mere* baubles." He fixed

Vanessa with what he fondly hoped was a look of disarming sincerity — a gaze designed to melt the iciest of resolves. "You already possess, if I may be so bold, the rarest and most precious ornament of all: the radiant, incomparable lustre of your own celestial beauty."

Such mellifluous flattery, however, elicited an effect quite the reverse of that which he had so confidently anticipated. Miss Vanessa Lockwood did not blush. She did not simper. She most certainly did not melt in feminine acquiescence. Instead, she folded her arms with military precision, and her expression hardened into one of unequivocal — nay, positively *arctic* — displeasure.

"Sir!" Her dark eyes flashed with a dangerous light. "Whatever notable success such glib and frankly impertinent pronouncements may have earnt you with other, perhaps more susceptible, members of my sex, I assure you they are entirely, and I mean *entirely*, wasted upon me. Kindly refrain from employing them further in my presence."

Hot, condemning blood rushed to our hero's cheeks. With a gesture of profound self-reproach, he involuntarily slapped his forehead. *A fool! A blunderer! I'm an idiot of the first order!* He had misjudged his audience with a spectacular lack of perception. This was no easily flattered matron, no impressionable, giggling miss to be swayed by saccharine compliments.

With a decisive movement, Vanessa glided forth and reached towards the ornate mantelpiece for a small silver bell, which she rang with a clarity and firmness that brooked no argument.

That his opportunity, and indeed his entire stratagem, rapidly dissolved before his very eyes, Francis made a final plea: "Please, Miss Lockwood. I implore you! Reconsider. That bracelet... it is the only tangible memory I possess of my mother! I lost her, you see... when I was but ten years old."

Surely, this revelation of past sorrow must touch some chord of human sympathy?

Vanessa's stern expression appeared to soften. A hue of something akin to compassion crossed her features. "I too lost my own mother," replied she at length, "when I was but *four* years of age. I retain scarcely any coherent memory of her dear face..."

Amid the ensuing pause, Francis, for a breathless instant, felt a tiny flicker of hope ignite within his breast. Perhaps this shared experience, this common ground of early bereavement, might unite her opinion and ultimately her decision in his favour?

"A faded memory is a cruel inheritance, Miss Lockwood," ventured he, his voice — even his soul — stripped momentarily of its bravado as his sensibilities fell in sympathy with hers.

"However, *such* is life..." resumed she, though her tone had lost a fraction of its former frost. "While you have my sympathy, this changes *nothing* whatsoever regarding the bracelet. I am sorry for your loss, but I am *not* selling it. Especially to a complete stranger whose rather... *dramatic* story — you must forgive my candour — I have absolutely no way of verifying."

"But I assure you, Miss Lockwood, upon my honour as a gentleman, every word is true! It is desperately — *vitally* — important to me!"

"Absolutely not," flatly stated she. "You presume greatly, sir, upon a very short, and I might add, rather trying, acquaintance."

At that precise moment, the door through which Francis had initially been ushered opened again, and the footman re-entered.

"Thomas." Vanessa turned away from Francis with an air of utter finality, as if he had ceased to exist. "Mr *Sheridan* is departing."

The indignity of being misnamed, on top of all his other spectacular failures, stung Francis more acutely than he would have cared to admit. "*Sheringham!*" corrected he with a flash of his former spirit, though it sounded even to himself more petulant than dignified.

"My apologies," replied Vanessa, without deigning even to glance in his direction; "Shering*ham*. Please show him out, Thomas."

"This way, sir," intoned the servant.

Francis cast one last pleading look towards the cruel heiress; but she presented him once more only with her shoulder, a study in elegant, unyielding dismissal that could have frozen hellfire itself!

Defeated, mortified, thoroughly outmanoeuvred, and, most painfully, bracelet-less, Francis allowed himself to be shepherded from the room.

Indeed, that woman — that obdurate, unfeeling, self-centred she-devil — while admittedly excessive in external beauty, possessed all the tender warmth of a tombstone! She was as heartless as the very statuette that had nearly met its demise. To be sure, our hero's wounded dignity, first lacerated by her aloof at Lord G's gathering, festered with even greater vehemence!

***

Our scene, by that magic of narrative which allows us to be in several places at once, now transports us to the Game Room at Thornfield Hall, that chamber dedicated to those pursuits deemed fitting for gentlemen of leisure. The oaken-panelled space was already thick with the aromatic, and some might say, acrid, haze of expensive Virginian tobacco smoke — blue wreaths of which curled upwards to join the shadows that clung to the high, beamed ceiling — and the low murmur of cards being shuffled and dealt. Chips clicked with the satisfying sound that speaks of fortunes, however small, in flux; brandy, amber and potent, was sipped with thoughtful deliberation; and the serious business of whist was well underway.

Gathered about the table, sat our familiar quartet of gentlemen: the ever-calculating Lord G; beside him, his somewhat inept son Vincent; opposite them sat the recently relieved (in more ways than one, perhaps, after his encounter on the highway) Mr Jonathan Russell, his usual air of mild anxiety subdued by the brandy at his elbow; completing the foursome, was the hitherto largely unseen Sir Burton, a stout gentleman of middle years whose chief distinction, for our present narrative purposes, lies in his marriage to the lady whom we have, with affectionate accuracy, dubbed "Plenty".

Yet, beneath this placid veneer of convivial gaming, a shadow of disquiet seemed to flicker across His Lordship's features. Setting down his cards with an almost ponderous slowness, he turned his gaze upon Mr Russell. "Jonathan, my dear fellow," began he, "a word, if I may, between hands. My wife happened to mention earlier, quite in passing, her firm intention of attending a ladies' gathering at your residence this very evening. A party of some description, I believe she termed it? A little soirée, perhaps?"

Mr Russell, who had been contemplating his own hand of cards with the furrowed brow of a man facing a difficult choice (or perhaps merely a poor selection), looked up, his expression one of genuine surprise. "A party? At *my* house? This evening? Surely not, my lord. There was no mention whatsoever of such an event when I departed."

The skin tightened and rippled around Lord G's cold eyes. "Curious. *Most* curious. Virginia was *quite* specific, you see. Mrs Russell *directly* invited her, she claimed."

"Impossible, my Lord! Utterly impossible!" Mr Russell shook his head. "Both my wife and my daughter left the house some considerable while before me; 'tis true. They ordered their carriage, and they departed with some air of... of purpose. But their stated destination was the home of Lady Burton — for taking tea."

At this pronouncement, all eyes about the table — those of His Lordship, keen and suspicious; those of Mr Russell, still bewildered; and even those of young Vincent, momentarily roused from his contemplation of his dwindling chip pile — swivelled towards the fourth member of their party: Sir Burton.

The baronet, thus made the focus of collective attention, blinked like an owl disturbed in daylight. "*Tea?*" echoed he, his voice rising to a note of high incredulity. "Tea, you say, Russell? At *my* house? My dear fellow, you jest surely! Or your good lady wife is practising some harmless deception upon you! For my poor Beatrice has been most grievously afflicted with a ferocious megrim throughout the entire course of this day. When I took my leave, she was confined to her bedchamber, demanding absolute quiet, darkened rooms, and smelling salts. She was, I assure you, in no fit state to entertain guests for *tea!*"

A moment of profound and rather perplexed silence descended. The rhythmic clinking of chips ceased. These three husbands, pillars of their community, were suddenly and simultaneously confronted with the unsettling — nay, the rather *alarming* — realisation that their respective spouses had, with a remarkable and somewhat suspicious uniformity, entirely fabricated their stated evening plans.

Lord G drummed his fingers on the table's surface; his eyes narrowed in a gaze of intense contemplation. "Most peculiar," muttered he, more to himself than to the others. "*Exceedingly* peculiar. One begins to wonder, gentlemen, what *precisely* these wives of ours are... plotting... when left entirely to their own devices..."

Chapter the Tenth — Masks and Mayhem

Meanwhile, good reader, upon that self-same stretch of lonely country road, now shrouded in the deeper darkness of advancing night, another plot was hatching. 'Twas a plot driven less by conspiracy and more by a shared, and profoundly misguided, romantic fantasy — a fantasy that had, it seemed, taken firm and riotous root in the fertile imaginations of our local gentlewomen.

Herein, we observe not one but *three* coaches — a most unlikely convoy in the dead of night — standing altogether stationary in the road's very middle. No accident was apparent; no fallen tree or overturned cart obstructed their passage. They were simply... waiting. And besides said carriages, illuminated by the carriage lamps' flickering light, stood four silhouetted figures: Lady G, Mrs Russell, her daughter Miss Jenny, and, bringing up the rear, the substantial and unmistakable form of Lady "Plenty" (otherwise, and more formally, known as Lady Burton).

Far from enjoying a convivial tea party or a sophisticated soirée, these *female pillars* of polite society were engaged in a most unladylike, and indeed astonishingly vigorous, altercation. Their voices, usually modulated to the cultured cooings of the salon, were now sharp, shrill, and carried with distressing clarity through the still night air.

"Out of my way, you presumptuous chit!" was snarling Her Ladyship, delivering a most unceremonious shove to young Jenny. "*I* arrived at this appointed spot first! He is *mine* to encounter! Mine alone!"

At this, Mrs Russell, her maternal instincts naturally ignited like a she-bear for her cub, sprang to her daughter's defence with a spirited shove of her own. "Take your arrogant, aristocratic hands off my child, you painted harlot!" shrieked she.

Lady G, disdaining the mere artillery of words, responded with a swift, stinging slap delivered with considerable force across her accusing adversary's equally (if truth be told) painted face. "Do not you *dare* address me in such disrespectful tones, you meddlesome old *hag*!"

As was to be expected, Mrs Russell, incensed beyond all mortal endurance by this physical assault and being newly christened "Old Hag", did allow the last vestiges of ladylike restraint to give up the ghost. With quite a guttural cry, she lunged forwards.

Behold, gentle reader, as she grasps Lady G firmly by that elaborate edifice of coiffured hair! Observe how the theatre of war degenerates from a mere verbal skirmish into a full-blown, flailing, clawing, slapping *mêlée*. Their elegant gowns, their carefully arranged speeches, their very dignity, were all quite forgotten in the passionate heat of battle as they, having taken on horizontal postures, got to rolling around one upon the other on the dusty roadway like two rabid badgers.

Lady "Plenty" tried a commendable display of peacemaking only to find herself caught in the crossfire. A stray fist from one combatant crashed into her sturdy jaw and sent her stumbling. She collided with the still-discombobulated Jenny, whereupon the pair of them tumbled ignominiously together into a nearby ditch. There they lay, a tableau of such disarray — a tangle of limbs and petticoats; their legs hoisted inelegantly aloft; their underwear displayed in a most unseemly fashion to the indifferent gaze of the stars and any nocturnal creatures that might happen to be passing.

Into this scene enters Master Francis Sheringham, once again cloaked, masked, mounted, and patrolling this familiar territory. The sting of his recent failure at Springfield — Miss Vanessa's abode — had lent a sharper, more desperate edge to his pressing need for financial success. As he rode cautiously along the verge, keeping to the hedgerow's concealing shadows, his attention was naturally arrested by a sight and sounds that defied easy explanation.

To be sure, the sheer absurdity of the situation was positively potent. A philosopher as well as a layman might have paused for some moments to contemplate the curious spectacle before him. For what cause, pray tell, had these leading county ladies been reduced to a squabbling, scratching, hair-pulling rabble?

An intervention was imperative, if only to restore a semblance of order. As was the no-less-pressing business of larceny. With a sigh that was part amusement, part exasperation, Francis dismounted. After adjusting his mask, ensuring it was firmly in place, he stepped boldly from the bushes' concealing shadows, adopting the commanding presence of the very figure that they, unbeknownst to him, so eagerly awaited: "Ladies!"

The effect was instantaneous — nay, magical.

The fighting, the lacerating, the cursing, ceased as abruptly as if a switch had been thrown. Hair, dishevelled and wild, was hastily patted down. Bodices, strained and askew, were quickly adjusted. And skirts, dusty and disordered, were straightened with frantic tugs. The four women scrambled rather gracelessly to their feet, staring at the materialised figure with that species of reverent astonishment usually reserved for apparitions, saints, and visiting royalty — or, mayhap in this instance, the heroes of popular novels.

"'Tis *he!*" gasped Mrs Russell; her voice, no longer an instrument of rage, now trembled with breathless awe as her hand flew to her bosom. "'Tis the gallant highwayman!"

Indeed, they *all* stood mouths agape for some seconds, a picture of startled femininity, gazing with rapt attention upon the object of their collective, and somewhat fevered, imaginations.

"You," breathed young Miss Jenny, her eyes, wide and luminous in the carriage lamplight, shining with a rather alarming adoration. "*You* are the very man of my dreams! Even more mysterious than in the novels!"

Not to be outdone by her own daughter: "Take me! Oh, take me now!" declared Mrs Russell, adopting a pose that would not have disgraced a tragedian on the London stage; one arm flung wide, the other pressed to her forehead as if overcome with emotion. "Take all I possess! My jewels, my purse — my very heart is yours for the taking, brave sir!"

Lady "Plenty", recovering her composure with remarkable speed, fluttered her eyelashes with a suggestiveness that was anything but subtle. "Oh, sir," sighed she, "pray, do not keep us in suspense! Show me... show me your... your formidable weapon!" She underscored this truly shocking invitation with a glance directed perhaps a little too south of our hero's belt, a gesture at which this humble chronicler can only blush and avert his gaze for shame.

As for Lady G, ever determined to seize the prize for sheer audacity, she cast Francis a look so laden with unspoken promise that it verged upon the positively indecent. "For the very first time in my dreary existence," purred she, "I find myself wishing, with every fibre of my being, that I might exchange places with your magnificent steed, and enjoy the exquisite, unimaginable delight of conveying your noble person hither and yon!"

Now, notwithstanding our hero's criminal vocation and his usual sangfroid in the face of feminine charms, a wave of acute, almost painful embarrassment did wash over him. This was not quite the gratifying fear he sought to inspire; nor was this the customary acquiescence he often met with; this — *this* — was a species of competitive adoration for which his nefarious trade had left him utterly unprepared. "Ladies, please!" stammered he. "Such... such *unbridled* enthusiasm! You... you make me blush!"

Indeed, good reader, he spoke the unvarnished truth. His cheeks, beneath the concealing anonymity of his mask, did burn most vehemently. Had it been daylight, a flush of a most un-highwayman-like shade of crimson would have betrayed him to the world. He was, perhaps for the first time in his illicit career, utterly routed — not by fear, or the threat of the law, *or pistols*, but by an excess of flattery.

***

A short while later, our hero took leave of his peculiar triumph, his saddlebag considerably heavier with jewels, trinkets, and coin — a testament perhaps more to the surprising generosity... no! the competitive spirit! ... of the ladies involved. Seeking, with a sigh of mingled relief and bewilderment, the nearby forest's shadows to audit this singular enterprise, he failed to notice a pair of avaricious and decidedly unfriendly eyes watching his every move from above.

Perched amidst the twisted branches of an ancient apple tree, like some malevolent, low-born sprite, was Black Harry; that unlovely specimen of rustic villainy. Within his brutish breast, an unholy trinity held congress: Revenge, for a prior humiliation; Envy, for the dandy's success in a trade he considered his own; and Greed, that most eloquent of persuaders, which argued for the immediate possession of the bag that swung so tantalisingly from our hero's saddle.

As Francis rode directly beneath his arboreal perch, Harry launched his descent. He fell upon his quarry with a guttural cry that grievously offended the sylvan quiet. The sudden violent impact sent both ambusher and ambushed tumbling to the earth. Startled by this commotion and the unexpected addition of a second, unwelcome rider, Francis' horse registered its profound objection by whinnying in fright and bolting into the darkness. As for the precious bag, the very cause of this commotion, it flew from Francis' grasp and landed several yards away, half-hidden in the undergrowth.

Undoubtedly more accustomed to such rough-and-tumble encounters, Harry regained his feet with remarkable celerity and lunged for the prize. But Francis, though dazed and winded, shot out a hand and secured his adversary's ankle. "Unhand that property, you snot-nosed, ill-bred rascal!"

Harry's response to this inconvenient injunction was a vicious kick from his free boot that connected with excruciating force against Francis' ribs. The grip was lost in our hero's agony, whereupon Harry, seizing his advantage, snatched up the bag.

Barely had the reprobate turned to flee with his booty when Francis, spurred by that boldness which attends a man whose entire night's plundering is about to vanish into the woods, launched himself forth. By a hair's breadth, he grasped the rough canvas bag's trailing lower edge.

And so, in the star-dappled woods, there ensued a most undignified contest of wills. One might call it a pastoral ballet of avarice and covetousness, with Harry pulling by brute force and Francis — his gentlemanly muscles straining, equally determined to retain what he considered, by a rather twisted logic, to be rightfully his — resisting.

Alas, the humble canvas, being unequal to the task of mediating between two such determined proprietors, surrendered its integrity with a rip. Utterly ignorant of this breach, Black Harry, feeling the sudden release of tension as a victory, merely resumed his flight, crashing clumsily through the undergrowth with the now-damaged sack clutched tightly. Yet as he ran with a triumphant cry, a muted but glittering trail began to mark his path through the forest: rings, brooches, necklaces of pearl and garnet, gold coins, and silver shillings — the very treasures Francis had so courteously plundered earlier that evening — winking in the stray beams of starlight that penetrated the canopy.

Oh, how capricious Fortune is, good reader! How in her inscrutable whims she does delight to play with the hopes and aspirations, the triumphs and disasters of mortal men! One moment, a man believes himself possessed of a prize; the next, it is slipping, quite literally, through his fingers, or in this case, through a hole in his bag.

And so, Francis was not long abandoned to kneeling on the damp ground, gasping for breath, his ribs aching, clutching a useless scrap of canvas. As his eyes adjusted to the gloom, he caught a faint glint near his knee. A diamond earring.

Then another glint, a little further off — a gold coin, nestled amongst the fallen leaves. "Aha!"

Thus, we leave our hero on his hands and knees in the dirt and leaf-mould, transformed by necessity from a dashing rogue into a common grubber after trifles, diligently harvesting the scattered remnants of his perilous night's work.

***

The next afternoon arrived and we now shift our gaze to nearby Wellington town, to the noisy interior of a principal public house — known as "The King's Head" (or perhaps "The Plough and Harrow", for such names are common to these havens of refreshment) — where commerce and conviviality often walk hand-in-hand, lubricated by the free and generous flow of good English ale. Here, amidst the general hubbub of ruddy-faced farmers discussing the price of corn, and merchants debating the late shipments from London, sat young Mr Vincent Grant. With a diligence that somewhat outstripped his natural aptitude, he endeavoured to project an air of shrewd negotiation. Opposite him sat a Mr Fox, a man whose well-cut coat, confident demeanour, and keen eye bespoke a thorough familiarity with transactions involving the buying and selling of equine flesh.

"Well, Mr Fox," began Vincent, swirling the amber contents of his pewter tankard with what he fondly hoped was a knowledgeable and discerning air, "my father informs me, and indeed, the county concurs, that you possess an expert eye for horseflesh? Your candid opinion, therefore, I seek on the humble offerings of the Thornfield Hall stables?"

Mr Fox took a slow, appreciative-looking sip of his own drink. His gaze rested on Vincent. "Ah, young Mr Grant," replied he, wiping a fleck of foam from his lip with a flick of his finger, "your esteemed father does me too great an honour with his kind words. And indeed, the beasts I had the distinct pleasure of inspecting at Thornfield this very morning are, without exaggeration, prime specimens of their kind. Truly exceptional. Excellent bloodlines; one can see it in the set of the head, the depth of the chest. Strong, clean limbs, well-muscled quarters, and most importantly, sir, they possess both the requisite stamina for a long day's run and that fiery spirit so ideal for the rigours of the hunt. Capital animals, young sir, capital indeed! My client, a gentleman of considerable discernment, will be most pleased, I am certain. He has, in fact, expressed a keen interest in acquiring all three of the geldings."

Mr Fox paused. After some thought had evidently crossed his brain, he leant across the table. "Perhaps another draught of this excellent ale, Mr Grant," said he, his voice dropping to a more confidential tone, "to seal our mutual understanding, eh? And then, if you are amenable, and your time permits, I shall be delighted to escort you directly to my client's current lodgings here in town to conclude the matter with the necessary paperwork and, of course, the agreeable transfer of funds."

Without even waiting for Vincent's formal assent, Mr Fox signalled to a passing, apron-clad waiter, who was navigating the crowded room with a tray laden with tankards. "Landlord! Ho there, landlord! Two more of your finest, if you please! And be quick about it, there's a good fellow!"

As for Vincent, flattered by such praise of his father's horses and buoyed by the ale already consumed, he readily agreed to this proposal. He felt himself in that moment quite the man of business, a worthy scion of the Grant lineage.

***

Later that same evening, the transaction involving the Thornfield steeds having been presumably concluded to the satisfaction of all parties, Vincent Grant rode homewards along the dark, winding country lanes. The perceived success of his mission, combined with the several draughts of ale consumed in its celebration, had left him in a state of cheerful inebriation. He whistled a jaunty, off-key tune, which no doubt served the dual purpose of expressing his good spirits and discouraging any phantoms, real or imagined, from sharing the lonely road.

His whistling, however, died an abrupt and strangled death. Out of the shadows of an overhanging oak, a figure on horseback materialised as silently and suddenly as an apparition, the cold starlight glinting on the barrel of a levelled pistol.

Vincent gave a startled yelp. He sawed ineptly at the reins, causing his mount, already unsettled by its rider's somewhat askew course, to sidle and threaten a complete dissolution of their partnership.

"Halt!" commanded our masked hero, his voice deliberately roughened, designed to inspire terror. "Stand and deliver!"

Terror did visibly take possession of Vincent. His hands flew into the air in a frantic parody of surrender, nearly unbalancing him. "Mercy!" came the piteous bleat of a lamb addressing a wolf. "Don't shoot! Pray, kind sir, don't shoot!"

Abroad to recoup the losses from his earlier misadventure with the treacherous Black Harry, Francis instantly recognised the voice. A spark of irresistible malice ignited within. Fortune, having recently played him a most scurvy trick, now offered a measure of compensation. Here was an opportunity not merely for pecuniary gain, but for a far sweeter dividend of sport at the Grant family's expense. He guided his horse gently and circled the terrified young man, much as a hawk describes its leisurely arcs above a field mouse that has lost its way.

This motion, acting upon a constitution already rendered unstable by ale, produced a most visibly distressing effect upon Vincent. Were the night not so dark, a greenish hue would have been observed spreading across his already pale features. "S-sir, I b-beg you!" stammered he. "Could you... possibly... stand still for but a moment? You induce a most dreadful, whirling dizziness! I fear I may... I may be unwell upon your very boots!"

"Faster, man!" barked Francis, further deepening his voice, thoroughly enjoying the spectacle. "Your purse, your watch, your very bootlaces if they be silver! Before my patience, which is notoriously thin, wears entirely through!"

With a swift, contemptuous movement, he reached out and plucked the fashionable riding hat from Vincent's head. "A fine piece." He examined it with mock connoisseurship. "A trifle ostentatious, perhaps, but of good quality felt."

"Yes! Yes! By all means, keep it, sir! A gift!" cried Vincent with a palpably despairing eagerness. "It would become you admirably, I am certain!"

Francis tossed it into the dust. "On second thought... it is a rather *foolish* sort of hat, is it not?"

"Entirely stupid, sir! As you so rightly observe!" Vincent nodded so vigorously he nearly fell from his horse. "A truly ridiculous confection!"

"Much like its owner, perhaps?" Francis leant forwards, shaking the pistol under Vincent's twitching nose. "*You* are rather stupid yourself, aren't *you*?"

'Tis a rare thing, Reader, to witness a man so thoroughly convinced of his own imbecility, and so eager to proclaim it: "Yes! Oh, yes!" whimpered Vincent, no doubt utterly convinced that his final moments were at hand. "Profoundly stupid, sir! A veritable dolt! An imbecile of the first order, I assure you!"

"Excellent! Honesty is a virtue, even in a dolt! Now, divest yourself of your money, and any other pretty trifles you may possess, before this pistol grows impatient and decides to speak for itself."

At this, a new terror seized the unfortunate youth. "Oh, Lord! Not the *money*! Anything but the money! My father entrusted it to *me*! He will positively... positively *flay me alive* if I return without it!"

Francis leant even closer still; the cold steel grazed Vincent's trembling chin. "You face a clear, if unpleasant, choice, my dear fellow. You may incur the considerable wrath of a terrestrial father, or you may face the immediate, and I assure you, far more permanent, consequences of *my* displeasure. Choose wisely, young sir. And choose quickly." To emphasise the point, he cocked the pistol with an audible *click*.

"Alright! Take it! Take it all!" Vincent fumbled within his coat, producing a bulging leather wallet.

Our hero snatched it. A brief but expert rifling confirmed a satisfying heft of banknotes and the pleasing clink of coins. "My sincerest thanks for your most generous contribution. Your business here is concluded. You may depart. And I wish you a most pleasant, if somewhat poorer, journey home."

Naturally requiring no further encouragement, Vincent vanished into the night with a velocity that suggested the very legions of Hell were at his heels, leaving Francis alone on the road to contemplate the satisfactory weight of his new acquisition and to reflect upon the curious truth that one man's terror is so often another man's profit.

***

The following day, as the morning sun cast its revealing light upon the county of Somerset, the repercussions of this, and indeed other recent and rather unsettling nocturnal events, manifested themselves within the newly established Wellington town office of the local constabulary. This modest outpost of modern law enforcement, intended to bring order and a more systematic approach to the keeping of the king's peace in these rural parts, boasted whitewashed walls; a sturdy oak desk, upon which lay an inkstand, a blotter, and a neat pile of official-looking documents; and, lending an undeniable air of official gravity and patriotic loyalty, a framed portrait of Queen Victoria gazed down upon the proceedings with a look of regal solemnity.

Behind the desk sat Inspector Swords, a man whose almost bulldog-like build, impressively luxuriant and impeccably waxed moustache, and whose general air of no-nonsense authority marked him clearly as a veteran of the Metropolitan Police. He had been recently, and some whispered, not entirely voluntarily, transferred from the smoky complexities of London policing to the (supposedly) quieter pastures of Somerset.

Before him, tapping his silver-headed cane with an impatient, rhythmic beat upon the scrubbed floorboards, stood Lord G, his face a picture of aristocratic displeasure. Also present, standing respectfully a pace or two behind and to the side of his superior officer, was Sergeant Morris, the inspector's diligent and long-suffering assistant.

"I tell you, Swords," declared His Lordship with a distinct lack of respect for the inspector's office, "your constables, these newfangled policemen, are proving themselves utterly, shamefully, inadequate! This... this highwayman, this masked menace has been operating with brazen impunity for weeks now! He plagues our public roads, he frightens our womenfolk — indeed, I hear tales of ladies swooning at the very mention of his name! — and he pilfers our hard-earnt property with contemptuous ease! Last night he had the unmitigated audacity to accost and rob my own son, not a mile from my own home!"

Inspector Swords twiddled his formidable moustache while regarding Lord G with a calm, steady, and entirely unimpressed-looking gaze that betrayed not even a hint of intimidation. "Rest assured, Lord Grant," stated he, "we're pursuing this matter with all available resources. I've men making inquiries; patrols 'ave been doubled. I shall 'ave this rogue apprehended and under lock and key before you can say Jack Robinson, sir. You 'ave my word."

His Lordship sniffed in a manner that eloquently conveyed his scepticism and his inherent distrust of such confident pronouncements from a mere policeman, however moustachioed. "See that you *do*, Inspector. Your predecessor in this county understood the importance of swift, decisive results when dealing with matters affecting gentlemen of property and standing. He knew how to keep the rabble in check. Fail in this, Swords, and I shall not hesitate to use what influence I possess — and I assure you, it is considerable — to see you posted back to the London rookeries whence you so recently came."

A dangerous-looking glint flashed in the inspector's eyes. "Let's be perfectly clear, *sir*! While I fully respect your 'ereditary position and your influence within this county, *I* am the duly appointed Queen's officer of the law in this district now. I'll tolerate no meddling, 'owever 'ighly placed, in the conduct of my official duties. Neither will I be swayed, intimidated, or otherwise influenced by such threats. You'll permit my men and me to conduct our investigation thoroughly and without 'indrance or unsolicited advice. Now, I must, with all due respect to your title but none to your current be'aviour, ask you to leave my office immediately, before I'm obliged to place you under arrest for attempting to intimidate a police officer in the lawful execution of 'is duty!"

Lord G's face flushed a deep, apoplectic crimson. He opened his mouth as if to unleash a torrent of aristocratic fury. Then, visibly, he thought better of it. Perhaps there was something in the inspector's gaze, something in the set of his jaw, that suggested this was not a man to be trifled with, moustachioed or not. His Lordship drove anew his silver-headed cane into the floorboards in a gesture of profound frustration, turned abruptly on his heel — his back rigid with unspoken rage — and stomped out of the office without uttering another word.

Inspector Swords watched him go with an arched expression; then, with a sigh that seemed to carry the weight of bureaucratic battles fought and won in the grimy warrens of the capital, he turned to his silent, and no doubt awestruck, assistant. "In London, Morris," began he, running a contemplative hand over his magnificent moustache, "a slow day meant only five arrests before luncheon. Pickpockets, drunks, counterfeiters, and the occasional murderer. 'ere?" He gestured around the small, quiet office. "Three months I've been stationed in this... this *rural* paradise, and not a *single* felon clapped in irons! Not one! Ti's unnatural, Morris! Positively unnatural for a policeman of my experience! We *must* apprehend this 'ighwayman. Ti's rapidly becoming a matter of professional pride! And," added he, a grim smile touching his lips, "it'll do wonders for discouraging unsolicited advice from the local nobility."

Chapter the Eleventh — An Interrupted Journey

August 25, 1865

We find ourselves once more upon the sprawling Grant estate, near that self-same patch of sun-dappled woodland where, on a previous occasion, a member of the local avian population paid the ultimate price for aristocratic incompetence. Here anew stood Vincent Grant, a duelling pistol clutched in his hand with that awkwardness which is the hallmark of the uninitiated. Beside him stood his long-suffering shooting instructor.

The familiar ritual commenced: the tutor minutely adjusted the pupil's stance (a slight shift of the left foot here, a subtle straightening of the back there); the weighty weapon was raised with a determination that did valiantly battle with a visible tremor in the wrist; and the aim was taken with a fierce concentration that might suggest the fate of nations, rather than a simple wooden target, hung in the balance. And, as was his custom, the instructor, subscribing to that sound philosophical principle which places the integrity of one's own person above the dubious spectacle of another's progress, executed a remarkably agile dive for cover behind a broad-trunked and accommodating oak.

BANG!

The shot rang out, imposing a sudden and violent caesura upon the woodland's tranquil verse, momentarily silencing the chirping of unseen birds and causing a distant rabbit to bolt for its burrow.

Abandoning all pretence of decorum, Vincent rushed eagerly towards the target. The instructor followed at a considerably less enthusiastic pace. No fresh hole, it must be reported, marred the painted circles. Yet, significantly, no innocent feathered casualty plummeted from the sky either. No unsuspecting pigeon, no unwary sparrow, met an untimely end. Progress, perhaps? At any rate, a scrutiny of the vast expanse of bark surrounding the wooden circle revealed, at last, evidence of impact — a distinct bullet mark.

Vincent spun around, his chest puffed with a newfound confidence that was entirely disproportionate to the actual achievement. "Remarkable improvement, wouldn't you agree, my good fellow?" cheered he, grinning wide. "Hitting the *very tree* itself! I am acquiring, I believe, a definite, an undeniable knack for this most manly of arts. Another few sessions, and I daresay I shall be splitting hairs at a hundred paces!"

Such is the power of self-regard that it can transform a miss of several inches into a near-bullseye. The instructor, alas, still contemplating the considerable acreage of the tree trunk versus the minuscule, and still inviolate, target pinned thereon, appeared to force a thin smile. "Indeed, sir," replied he, with an admirable — nay, a masterpiece of diplomatic insincerity. "Your trajectory is... is *undeniably* closer to the mark than on... *previous* occasions."

***

Let us now, as if by the swift rotation of some grand theatrical stage, shift our scene some hours later to a travelling coach's somewhat cramped and jolting interior.

This vehicle was proceeding at speed along a darkened, rutted country road with a haste that nigh spoke of a reckless disregard for its own axles. Within, illuminated by the carriage lamps' fleeting dance upon the plush upholstery, sat Miss Vanessa Lockwood, freed from the constraints of mourning attire, dressed as the goddess Diana; a silver arrow pinned in her upswept hair; her demeanour, as ever, was one of coolness and composure. Beside her sat Ms Brown, sporting the costume of a wood nymph: a simple green gown and a wreath of ivy in her hair.

Now, it behoves your humble author to belatedly note that in fashioning Ms Brown, Nature seemed to have had in mind a commission in Her Majesty's Grenadier Guards rather than the guardianship of a young heiress. She was, to put it plainly, a woman of formidable architecture, with shoulders that might bear a musket with greater ease than a shawl, and a voice whose timbre was more suited to barking orders across a parade ground than to the gentle murmurings of polite society.

Even as the coach sped along with alarming velocity, Ms Brown's large hands twisted a lace handkerchief into a tortured knot and fiddled with her mask. "We shall be *unforgivably* late, Miss Vanessa," fretted she in baritone tones. "Lord Grant, as you know, sets great store by punctuality. He will *not* be best pleased at all."

Vanessa, who had been gazing out at the fleeting landscape rushing past the window, offered a reply as cool and crisp as the night air itself. "His pleasure, or indeed his displeasure, Ms Brown, is, I assure you, of remarkably little consequence to me." She affixed her own mask in place. "Let him frown if he so chooses."

This philosophical exchange, however, was destined for a most violent interruption.

With a suddenness that threw both ladies sharply forwards, the coach lurched to a jarring halt. Yonder the carriage interior walls, a figure had, it transpired, leapt into the road directly before the horses, brandishing a pistol. The coachman squealed; yet Miss Vanessa, far from doing likewise, instantly craned her neck out of the window.

But alas, good reader! This was no elegant figure of romantic fantasy, no dashing rogue from the pages of a lady's novel. Nor was it our hero. No, the apparition that blocked their path was none other than Black Harry.

"Stand and deliver, ye fine ladies!" growled he. "No fuss now! 'and over yer sparklers and yer coin, and ye'll come to no 'arm!"

Far from swooning or dissolving into terrified hysterics as many a young lady of her station might have done, Vanessa, briefly lifting her mask, only regarded the ruffian with an expression of haughty indignation. "How *dare* you impede our progress, you insolent fellow? Remove yourself from our path this instant!"

Quite unaccustomed to such defiance from his victims or critiques of his chosen profession, Harry merely leered, flashing a brief, uncomely glimpse of those decaying teeth. "No time for fancy talk, missy!" retorted he. "The pretties, now! And the purse!" He wrenched open the coach door, his grimy, calloused hand reaching towards the string of pearls adorning Vanessa's neck.

But just as Harry's dirty fingers were about to close upon their prize, and just as Miss Vanessa and Ms Brown let out ear-splitting shrieks — the latter emitting a sound that might have startled a sleeping regiment — Harry's collar was seized from behind. Yanked backwards with a force that nearly dislocated his scrag, he stumbled out of the coach, his feet tangling, his pistol clattering onto the dusty road.

Soon towering over him, silhouetted against the star-studded heavens, stood a cloaked and masked figure — hoorah! Our Francis Sheringham, a veritable *deus ex machina* of the public thoroughfares, arriving as if by theatrical cue.

"Unhand the ladies, you ill-favoured, misbegotten ape!" Francis' voice carried the ring of righteous authority. "Find some other path to perdition, you monkey-faced, gutter-bred poltroon!"

Black Harry, however, possessed of a greater measure of brute stupidity than sage caution, only let out a roar of outraged villainy and clambered to his feet. With a volley of curses too profane for this genteel history exploding from his mouth, he launched himself, head down, at his rival-rescuer-turned-tormentor.

Indeed, never has the art of pugilism been reduced to its most primitive elements. Instantly, the two champions crashed to the ground, a single, grunting entity of flailing limbs. Like two noisy swine squabbling over a last carob, they rolled upon the earth, grappling in the dirt and shadows.

Meanwhile, within the carriage's now comparative safety, this sudden eruption of masculine strife produced a most singular divergence of sentiment. Ms Brown, clutching her reticule, mask, and handkerchief to her bosom as a soldier might his last canteen, peered anxiously at the struggling figures. "Miss Vanessa," her deep voice trembled slightly, "perhaps it would be prudent for James to drive on now? With all possible speed? While the ruffians are otherwise... engaged?"

Rather than concur, Vanessa only leant forwards, peering out through her mask with rapt attention. "Certainly *not*, Ms Brown! This is positively thrilling! Far better than any adventure in those dreadful novels you confiscate! I absolutely *must* see how this 'Masked Hero' acquits himself in this delightful skirmish!"

Ms Brown only stared, utterly aghast that a young lady should find such brutal reality preferable to the confiscated novels which, undoubtedly to her mind, were the cause of this deplorable enthusiasm.

The struggle outside, though spirited, was in truth a brief and decisive affair. Francis, being younger, fitter, and fuelled by a simmering anger born of Black Harry's previous treachery in the forest, quickly gained the upper hand. A few well-aimed blows to Harry's unlovely jaw, delivered with a boxer's precision, sent the ruffian reeling backwards.

Francis scrambled nimbly to his feet. Taking a moment to adjust his mask, which had become slightly askew in the tussle, he smoothed down the lapels of his coat and looked at the prostrate form of his foe. "Consider that, you ill-bred cur, as but partial repayment for your cowardly ambush in the forest!" declared he.

As Harry groaned again and made a clumsy attempt to rise, Francis — with a timing that was quite comical in its precision — delivered a well-placed kick to his posterior. "And count that, you varlet, as the accrued interest on the debt!"

This final ignominious indignity proved sufficient. With more haste than grace, Harry fled into the night's enfolding darkness, nursing, no doubt, his throbbing jaw with one hand and his wounded pride (and equally wounded backside) with the other, disappearing like a malevolent, if thoroughly chastened, goblin.

Now the undisputed master of the field, Francis turned back to the coach. He dusted off his clothes and swept off his hat in a low, gallant bow. "Good evening, ladies. Pray forgive this unfortunate intrusion and the unseemly display." A formidable matron, he now observed, incongruously dressed as a wood nymph, trembled beside a lady of slenderer proportions and masked in a character of some ancient Grecian mode. "You are, I trust, unharmed by that dreadful creature's villainy?"

"Sir," replied Vanessa, all cool civility, "we *are* indeed indebted to your bravery. You have acted with commendable despatch. How might we adequately express our thanks for your most timely and indeed most spirited intervention against that dreadful creature?"

Francis, as yet ignorant of whom he was addressing — for the young lady's upper-face lay concealed behind that ornate mask — replaced his hat. Then, to the no doubt slack-jawed astonishment of his audience, he drew his own pistol and levelled it at them. "Your gratitude, madam, is duly noted." He shifted abruptly from chivalrous rescuer to pragmatic businessman. "You may now express it by handing over your valuables."

A stunned silence followed this extraordinary pronouncement. Vanessa stared at him through the slits in her mask; her perfectly sculpted brow furrowed as if she had misheard or misunderstood. "Is this some manner of... of elaborate jest, sir?"

"*Jest*, madam?" repeated Francis.

At this, Ms Brown, more accustomed to the eccentricities of the upper classes, suddenly found what she no doubt believed to be a perfectly logical explanation for this bizarre turn of events. "Ah! Of course! How foolish of me! You too *must* be bound for Lord Grant's fancy-dress ball? A highwayman costume — how *very* original, sir! And remarkably well executed, if I may say so! Perhaps, young man, as you seem so familiar with these dark roads, you could be so kind as to direct our driver? Or perhaps you can lead the way? We are, rather regrettably, late."

Francis blinked several times beneath his mask. "Fancy-dress ball? Madam, I assure you with the utmost sincerity, I am *not* en route to whatever ball, fancy-dress or otherwise, you appear to be heading for. This," insisted he, giving the pistol a slight, impatient waggle, "is a *bona fide* hold-up. Your money and jewels, if you please. And let us not dally."

Vanessa's patience, already strained by the initial delay, finally snapped. "Oh, for Heaven's sake! A *real* hold-up? How utterly... quaint! How positively archaic!" She turned to her companion. "Did you ever hear the like, Ms Brown? Actual practising highwaymen in this day and age!" Ironic indeed for our heroine, who, residing not in this region, was yet to learn the truth on this score. "This county proves more tiresome by the minute." Without another glance at our increasingly astonished hero, she leant towards the driver's box. "Drive on, James! We have dallied here quite long enough with these... roadside theatricals!"

Before Francis could utter another word of protest, the coach lurched onwards, gathering speed and leaving him standing alone in the middle of the dusty road, his pistol still clutched uselessly in his hand.

Robbed of his robbery! The indignity was almost too much to bear.

"Damn and blast!" muttered Francis. "Confound that woman's impertinence!"

And yet, as he watched the carriage lanterns disappear into the gloom, a startling thrill eclipsed his injured pride. She had not fainted, nor fluttered her lashes, nor surrendered her purse. She had looked down the barrel of a loaded pistol and found him wanting.

His bewildered stasis was, alas, shattered by a new and far more alarming sound — the unmistakable, rhythmic trampling of multiple horses approaching at a rapid gallop.

"There he is! After him, men! Don't let him escape!"

The voice was sharp and authoritative.

There was no time for further reflection; no opportunity to ponder the philosophical implications of being outwitted by a society belle. Francis leapt onto his horse and galloped headlong into the roadside forest's welcoming darkness, with none other than Inspector Swords, Sergeant Morris, and two other constables thundering in hot pursuit.

Chapter the Twelfth — Morality and Motives

Sometime thereafter, the coach bearing the precious cargo of Miss Vanessa Lockwood and Ms Brown accomplished the final stage of its journey, proceeding at a more sedate pace up the sweeping drive to Thornfield Hall. From the grand edifice's brightly lit, mullioned windows, music — a lively quadrille, if our ears do not deceive us — laughter, and the general, cheerful hubbub of a grand social occasion spilt forth to greet the tardy.

At the imposing entrance, beneath a festoon of lanterns, stood a triumvirate of welcome: an extravagantly costumed Lord G, his Lady wife, and their hopeful heir. This latter personage, it must be recorded, presented a figure of singular absurdity, being attired as a Harlequin in a riot of clashing checks and glittering spangles — a costume which conferred upon its wearer none of the wit or agility traditionally associated with that character.

"Miss Lockwood! Welcome to Thornfield!" His Lordship advanced with an eagerness that did little, however, to disguise his irritation at her delay. "Our humble abode is honoured by your presence. We had begun to fear some mishap on the road!" And while his mouth performed the rites of effusive hospitality, his eyes were engaged in the more serious business of appraisal.

"Lord Grant." Vanessa's tone was distinctly frosty. She dispensed with the required civilities with a cool economy: a curtsy so minimal as to be a mere suggestion of the act; a polite nod for her hostess; and finally, a hand extended towards the beaming Harlequin. "Vincent."

The young fop grinned with a vacuity that was entirely his own. He seized her proffered hand and bestowed upon its gloved surface a kiss whose ardour, a shrewd observer might surmise, was probably directed less at the lady herself than at the concept of her considerable dowry.

At any rate, Lady G thus escorted Miss Lockwood through brilliantly lit corridors thronged with costumed guests. Here was a veritable riot of social absurdity: shepherdesses conversed with Roman senators, pirates flirted with milkmaids, and a portly gentleman costumed as Henry VIII debated agricultural tariffs with a Grecian nymph. Through this menagerie, the ladies proceeded to the quieter sanctuary of the upper floors, trailed by several servants laden with the sundry baggage that is ever the herald of a significant visitation.

"Here we are, my dear Miss Lockwood." Her Ladyship indicated a well-appointed chamber with a welcoming fire already crackling in the hearth. "Your sanctuary for the duration of your stay. Pray, make yourself comfortable and join the festivities when you are refreshed."

"You are most kind, Lady Virginia," replied Vanessa as the last of the servants finally withdrew. "However, the journey, and... and certain events upon the road... have left me quite fatigued. If you will excuse me, I shall retire directly for the night. And Ms Brown" — the chaperone was presently fiddling with her party mask with a look both hopeful and downcast — "I shall see you on the morrow." And without awaiting further comment or persuasion from either lady, she offered a slight inclination of her head and closed the door gently but decisively.

Alone at last, Vanessa gave up the air of weary fatigue and hastened directly to the largest of her travel trunks. Unfastening its sturdy brass latches, she threw back the heavy lid and proceeded to remove sundry items of clothing. Ballgowns, feathered headpieces, delicate slippers suitable for an heiress' extended social visit were cast negligently aside. Her mind, it was abundantly clear, was occupied with plans and purposes far removed from the polite tedium of socialising with the Somerset gentry.

She held aloft a delicate nightgown; the chosen attire for her aborted night.

Elsewhere in the grand house, Lord G and his harlequin son made their way towards the increasing noise and infectious gaiety emanating from the great hall, where the orchestra was now striking up a spirited waltz. Here was a scene of determined jollity, a swirling, dizzying kaleidoscope of vibrant colour and delightful absurdity. Lords and ladies, normally staid squires and their equally prim wives, had shed their everyday sobriety and inhibitions along with their usual attire, transforming themselves for the night into the borrowed plumage of historical figures, mythical creatures, and exotic, bejewelled potentates. Wine flowed with alarming freedom; laughter echoed off the high ceilings; couples, young and old, twirled and stomped in the energetic measures of the dance.

A fatuous grin remained fixed on Vincent's face; his earlier encounter with Miss Lockwood had indubitably filled him with optimistic notions.

"Well, Vincent, my boy," remarked His Lordship, clasping a hand upon his son's diamond-patterned shoulder. "What say you to our Miss Lockwood, eh? She has blossomed considerably since she ditched the mourning frock, has she not?"

"Indeed, Father!" Vincent twitched and giggled. "Wealthy beyond all measure, *and* beautiful besides! By Jove, she is the very paragon of her sex! The very wife for me! Our fortunes, sir, are as good as made!"

And here, we observe that alchemy of an ambitious mind, whereby a lady's virtue, wit, and character are held as mere subsidiary qualities, while the true measure of her perfection is calculated in the cold arithmetic of her dowry.

Vincent puffed out his chest; the garish costume stretched across the magnitude of his burgeoning self-importance.

***

But let us for a moment leave the world of wax candles, plotting, and polite conversation, and return to the ancient forest, where a contest of a more primitive nature continued with unabated ferocity. Here, Francis demonstrated a newly acquired knowledge of the local terrain. He wove his mount expertly through the treacherous labyrinth, ducking beneath low-hanging branches that might have unseated a less experienced rider.

From time to time, he would cast a glance over his shoulder. His pursuers, led by the indefatigable Inspector Swords, were still in view, their progress much hampered by a landscape that offered no courtesy to strangers.

Suddenly, a cry of alarm, followed by a most sickening thud, echoed through the trees. It appeared that one agent of the law, in attempting to navigate this arboreal obstacle course at speed, had parted company with his mount and made an undignified acquaintance with the forest floor.

One less to worry about, thought Francis, a fleeting, mirthless smile touching his lips beneath his mask. The odds were improving.

After some distance, arriving near the woods' shadowy edge bordering the Thornfield estate, he reined in his labouring horse. Through a gap in the dense curtain of trees, the myriad lights of the great house blazed invitingly. The faint strains of music, punctuated by bursts of distant laughter, drifted towards him on the cool night breeze — quite the taunting contrast to his own precarious situation.

He glanced back into the inky blackness he had just traversed; the remaining policemen were, judging by the receding sounds of their crashing progress, still some distance behind.

A decision — swift and decisive — was needed.

Francis dismounted and gave his faithful horse a firm slap on its sweat-slicked rump, whereupon the beast galloped away into the woods' deeper darkness, its hoofbeats hopefully serving as a misleading beacon. "Go on, my friend, lead them a merry dance."

Having thus despatched his steed, and hastened onwards himself, he soon skulked amidst some ornamental shrubbery. The sounds of pursuit, though fainter now and more sporadic, still echoed from the woods behind him. 'Twas clear that escape lay forward, into the very lion's den.

In observing the great house's architecture — seeking out Her Ladyship's bedchamber window, which was, alas, closed — he espied the stone balcony projecting from the very epicentre of jollity, the ballroom itself; a potential and somewhat perilous point of entry.

Since the balcony was presently vacant, Francis bolted across the lawns and began his ascent, finding dubious purchase on the decorative stonework and trusting his weight to the aged ivy's tenacious grip that snaked its way up the cold wall.

His efforts, however, did not go entirely unobserved. Below, emerging from the treeline, Inspector Swords spotted the dark, climbing figure silhouetted against the brightly lit windows. He instantly beckoned to the nearby Sergeant Morris and pointed upwards with a finger that trembled slightly, no doubt, from the thrill of the chase nearing its quarry. The fox, it appeared, was brazenly attempting to enter the henhouse.

Into the Great Hall's intoxicating vortex of costumed anonymity slipped Francis. His own highwayman attire — the dark cloak, the hat, the concealing mask — which moments ago had been the undeniable mark of his criminality, now served as effective camouflage. To his mingled surprise and wry amusement, he was *not* unique in his choice of disguise. No fewer than *half a dozen* other gentlemen stalked the crowded room in deliberate imitation of the very rogue the constabulary so diligently sought. What is more, these ersatz brigands, these drawing-room desperados, it seemed, held a peculiar and undeniable fascination for many of the female guests — a testament, perhaps, to the enduring, if somewhat perplexing, allure of the forbidden, even when rendered in harmless satin and buckram.

In navigating this surreal landscape of masked revellers, Francis narrowly avoided the lurching embrace of a clearly intoxicated Lady "Plenty" (attired, somewhat indelicately and with a distinct lack of verisimilitude, as a pastoral shepherdess). Though her hands, in the brief collision, made free with his person in a manner one shudders to recount, her eyes had fortunately lost their faculty for precise observation and failed to penetrate his disguise. With less perilous currents sought in this sea of cacophonous humanity, Francis slipped through the throng and found himself in the relative quiet and dimness of a long corridor.

Here, after a moment's recuperation, he proceeded with renewed caution until reaching the foot of the main, sweeping carved oak staircase. Spurred by the situation's urgency, he bounded up the wide, carpeted steps, determined to secrete himself in some vacant wing.

He had barely reached the upper landing when voices — one sharp and commanding, the other deep and indignant — echoed from below. Instantly, he pressed himself into a shadowy alcove, offering a silent prayer to that deity whose portfolio, one must assume, includes the patronage of desperate rogues. Even so, curiosity, that often perverse sovereign, impelled him to the balustrade, whence he peered down into the hall below: Inspector Swords and his motley band of officers presently emerged from the vestibule, being obstructed by a red-faced Lord G.

"Search my house, Inspector?" His Lordship's voice was tight with aristocratic indignation. "On what possible grounds? This is an outrage!"

Time being a commodity Francis could ill afford to squander, he scurried along the nearest corridor. The first door he tried was locked; so too were the second, third, and fourth. The fifth, blessedly, yielded.

He slipped inside, closing and locking it silently behind him and breathing a sigh of profound relief that instantly died in his throat, reborn as a gasp of utter astonishment.

Our readers, whose sagacity in such matters doubtless outstrips that of our hero, will not be surprised to learn he found himself in none other than Miss

Vanessa Lockwood's bedchamber. The lady herself, clad in a simple silk nightdress, stood staring at him.

Francis, who had faced pistols and dangers with a certain sangfroid, was now utterly routed. "Miss... Miss Lockwood?!"

"Well, well!" Her voice dripped like icicles into the room's sudden silence. "If it isn't our gallant, pistol-wielding highwayman — paying another unexpected call!" She crossed her arms. "And how, pray tell, do you come to know my name?"

Though try otherwise he did, Francis stumbled from one poor excuse to the next, while Vanessa, having grown speedily fatigued with his presence interrupted: "Who precisely *are* you, when you are not playing the villain on the open road or, it would seem, invading ladies' private bedchambers?"

Before Francis could even formulate a coherent, let alone convincing, reply, the distinct and ominous sound of purposeful footsteps grew louder, reaching them.

"Great heavens!" Francis shuddered, his blood running cold. "The police!"

Vanessa now regarded him with arms akimbo. "The police, you say? After *you*? My, my. You must be a very *naughty* boy indeed, Mr Highwayman. I now see you *were* in earnest when, scarcely above an hour ago, if my memory serves me correctly, you attempted, and rather ineptly I might add, to rob me of my valuables!"

Francis stepped forwards. "Miss Lockwood, you *must* help me!"

One perfectly sculpted eyebrow flew to imperious heights. A hand shot out, stopping his approach. "And why should *I* extend such unsolicited assistance to you, sir? More so, given that you alluded to the police, I can only assume you are a dangerous felon fleeing the justice you so richly deserve."

At this, our hero fell at her feet. "I am no common criminal, I assure you, madam! Upon my honour! My circumstances are... *exceedingly* complex. Hide me, I beg you, just until they pass! I shall explain everything, I promise you!"

A firm, authoritative KNOCK! KNOCK! sounded on the door.

Without taking her eyes off the man kneeling before her, Vanessa called out in a composed voice: "*Who* is it that disturbs me at this late hour?"

"Police, madam! Inspector Swords," came the gruff reply. "We are searching for a fugitive. Open the door, please!"

"Vanessa," also came Lord G's voice; "open the door."

Francis, his soul about to shrivel from sheer terror, looked up at her with such earnest entreaty that it might have melted a heart of stone.

"One moment, if you please, sir!" Vanessa turned her full attention back to our hero. "Your mask, sir." Her voice was low but firm. "Remove it. Now."

"I... I cannot!" groaned he. The very idea of revealing his identity in such circumstances — to *her* of all people! — filled him with so profound a sense of dread as to almost outweigh that of Lord G and the Law's imminent arrival.

"Then," whispered she, "I shall perforce admit his lordship and the inspector." She moved towards the door. "They seem *most* insistent."

Another, more impatient, KNOCK! KNOCK! KNOCK! rattled the door in its frame.

Torn in that agonising moment between the Scylla of the law and the Charybdis of social ruin, Francis made his choice. With fingers a-trembling, he fumbled with the strings at the back of his head and, with a heavy sigh, removed the mask: he exposed not just his face, but his desperation, his ruin, and his fractured pride. There he knelt before her, entirely defenceless.

Her hand now hovering mere inches away from the doorknob, Vanessa peered at him. Her eyes widened, first with surprise, then with a dawning, unmistakable recognition. "Oh!" uttered she with a gasp. "'Tis *you*, Mr... *Sheridan*, is it not?"

Notwithstanding his extreme peril, Francis, ever the stickler for accuracy where his lineage was concerned, could not help but correct her. "*Sheringham*, madam!" grumbled he in a fierce whisper. "Francis *Sheringham*, at your rather compromised service!"

"Open the door, my lady, if you please!" demanded Inspector Swords from the corridor.

"I am coming, Sir!" Vanessa's voice now took on a sudden, surprising urgency. She indicated a large, ornate wardrobe. "In there! Quickly, man! And pray, make no sound!"

As Francis, his heart a-hammering and his limbs a-jelly, scrambled with undignified haste into the lavender-scented sanctuary, his eyes fell upon an elegantly appointed dressing-table. There, gleaming softly in the candlelight amongst silver-backed brushes, crystal vials of perfume, and other feminine accoutrements, lay his mother's bracelet. The sight of it, so close and yet so unobtainable, shot a fresh pang of bitter longing through him.

With our hero now ensconced within the wardrobe's claustrophobic confines, Vanessa turned the key and opened the bedchamber door.

Through a sliver in the wardrobe, Francis watched: Inspector Swords stood on the threshold with Sergeant Morris and Lord G hovering behind. The inspector, whose duty it was to look for villains, was evidently and most unprofessionally distracted by the vision of dishevelled beauty before him.

"Yes, sir?" enquired Vanessa. "What *is* the meaning of this unwelcome intrusion at such an ungodly hour?"

A slight, but still perceptible blush crept up the inspector's neck; he blinked, evidently recalling his duty. "My sincere apologies for disturbing you, Miss, but we have reason to believe a fugitive — a notorious highwayman — may have sought refuge in this house. And a dubious character was seen by one of the servants venturing upstairs."

Vanessa stepped back, opening the door wider. "As you can plainly see for yourself, Inspector" — she gestured expansively around the room with a sweep of her hand — "there is no one here but me, and my virtue, which I trust, is not in question. Are you satisfied now? Or do you intend to rummage through my unmentionables as well? And you, Lord Grant, *you* ought to better command your own household!"

This masterstroke of feminine aggression had its intended effect. "Come, come! Inspector!" groaned His Lordship. "My domestic was likely mistaken!"

After glowering at Lord G, Inspector Swords peered dutifully into the room; his gaze swept over the four-poster bed, the dressing table, the chaise longue and lingered, for a fraction too long, on the wardrobe — which indeed caused our hero to gulp and nigh choke on his own tongue — before returning to Vanessa's no doubt challenging face. "My profound apologies once again for the disturbance, Miss." He bowed rather stiffly. "Please ensure your door is locked henceforth. The scoundrel remains at large in this house and could potentially attempt a forced entry."

"Rest assured, Inspector, I shall take every conceivable precaution." With that, she shut the door firmly in his face, and turned the key decisively in the lock.

After a grumbling inspector, muttering sergeant, and a lambasting lord were heard disappearing down the corridor, Francis poked his head out. "Is he... is he *truly* gone?"

Vanessa leant back against the door. "He is!"

Thus, safe to do so, our hero emerged, dusting himself off and divesting his head of a lady's bonnet. He took a step towards her, intending to offer his heartfelt thanks for her unexpected intervention. But Vanessa again halted him with an upraised hand.

"Stay *precisely* where you are, Mr Sheridan!" Her voice, though quiet, brooked no argument. "I believe you owe me an explanation. A full and frank one. And for your sake, it had better be a remarkably *convincing* one!"

***

Back in the Great Hall, a state of utter, unmitigated confusion now reigned. Inspector Swords, thwarted in his upstairs pursuit and no doubt smarting from Miss Lockwood's disdain, now faced the bewildering spectacle of multiple masked highwaymen mingling, with varying degrees of *élan*, amongst the increasingly agitated guests. 'Twas a veritable convention of faux brigands, a riot of theatrical villainy.

Sergeant Morris stared about him, well and truly at a loss. "What now, sir?"

The inspector surveyed the scene, his jaw tightening, his impressive moustache bristling with professional frustration. "There is only *one* way to be certain, Morris," declared he. "Only one way to flush our quarry. Unmask every-last one of them!"

Here, good reader, let us pause to consider that forever-in-question virtue of a chaperone and governess. For Ms Brown, having availed herself of her mistress' absence to prosecute her own, less official enjoyments, was at that moment flushed with wine and a most un-chaperone-like levity. She presently received the whispered attentions of a masked Musketeer, whose volley of sweet French sentiments betrayed a most potent effect upon her ear.

But this tender scene was rudely interrupted when her amorous companion was unceremoniously shoved aside by an officer of the law. At this indignity, a sudden change came over our chaperone. Whether it was a belated pang of conscience concerning the safety of her distant charge, or — what is perhaps more probable — a sudden terror that her own dereliction of duty might be discovered, we shall not presume to say. Whatever the cause, she at once abandoned the field of pleasure and quit the ballroom to make her way with a new, and rather unsteady, sobriety towards the upper floors.

Incidentally, in a relatively quieter corner of the hall, one of these counterfeit highwaymen was engaged in flirtatious, roguish banter with Miss Jenny Russell, assuring her he was the very *bona fide* outlaw himself.

"So" — she fluttered about him in a rather spangled fairy costume; her wings slightly askew; her eyes wide with delicious excitement; her fan working overtime — "you *truly* are the mysterious, dashing highwayman everyone speaks of?"

"Indeed, my dear enchanting sprite," lied the fellow with admirable, wine-addled composure, adopting a deeper, gravellier voice which, to an ear less enchanted, might still have held a note of familiarity. "All the *others* you see are mere *impostors*, theatrical charlatans. I alone, your humble servant, am the genuine, *dangerous* article!" He puffed out his chest, nearly dislodging a decorative pistol from his belt.

"Oh, my hero!" Jenny — bless her simple soul — excitedly clasped her hands to her bosom. "The man of my wildest dreams! So daring! So... so *unsuitable*!"

Alas, for this faux outlaw, the deception was about to be unrestrictedly shattered. At that very moment, Sergeant Morris approached. "Excuse me, sir. Police business. Would you kindly oblige me by removing your mask?"

Natch, the impostor only stared, manifestly aghast. "How *dare* you!" blustered he, his disguised voice cracking a little. "Do you know who I —" he cleared his throat with the air of a man caught between a lie and a lawsuit "— who I *represent*?"

"We are searching for a fugitive highwayman, sir," explained Morris, quite unintimidated. "A dangerous felon. We have every reason to believe he hides himself in this very ball, even as we speak."

Alas, now, for poor Jenny — for the reader shall observe how Fortune delights in compounding folly with further folly — the deception only duped her further. "'Tis he, Sergeant!" squealed she. "It *must* be! He confessed it all to me just now! Oh, Sergeant, unmask my hero! Let me gaze upon the face of true wickedness!"

To be sure, the pretender, shrinking within his borrowed highwayman's cloak in a manner not unlike a snail into its shell, protested: "Nonsense! Utter balderdash! The ravings of a hysterical girl!" His disguised voice now fully faltered, reverting to his usual rather reedy and all too familiar tenor. "I am not *the* highwayman! I am" — he ripped away his mask, revealing the rather ordinary, middle-aged, and now extremely flustered face of none other than — "Sir Burton! I... I have been present at this ball for several hours! Ask anyone! Ask the lady here herself!"

Sergeant Morris, after peering at the baronet's red, perspiring countenance, offered a respectful, though perhaps amused, touch to his helmet. "My sincere apologies for the inconvenience, sir." He moved on, his gaze already scanning for the next masked suspect.

Let us first spare a moment of Christian charity for our luckless masquerader. Even as Sir Burton exhaled a sigh so prodigiously long, so unutterably deep, and so replete with shamefaced ignominy — an expulsion of air, I must add, that so thoroughly strained the seams of his, we can only surmise, corset — his natural corpus, alas, chose that precise moment to reassert its dominion over his artificially compressed silhouette.

The spectacle was nothing short of scandalous — and decidedly hazardous to boot!

His shirt and waistcoat, those valiant but ultimately inadequate sentries against the tide of flesh, surrendered with the crack of musket fire. Buttons, expelled from their textile bondage, took wing like lead balls, each seeking its own dramatic destiny. One struck a gilt-framed mirror, shattering the glass into a thousand glittering fragments. Another sailed through a nearby French window, transforming that portal into a shower of crystalline rain. A third found its mark upon a chandelier's pendant crystal, which chimed once — a pure, sweet note of destruction — before tumbling earthwards like a fallen star. But the *pièce de résistance* of this sartorial catastrophe was one particularly ambitious button that hit a passing waiter squarely between the eyes. The poor fellow — silver tray of flutes and all — his orbs rolling backwards into their sockets, crumpled to the parquet with all the noise and commotion to be expected.

And so, we find poor dumbfounded Jenny staring at the revealed face of the rather portly and entirely un-heroic Sir Burton — a man who, with every heave of her palpably indignant bosom, looked less the dashing brigand and more an overripe turnip in a tricorn hat. Her countenance flushed an unbecoming scarlet, passing through several shades of mortification before settling upon fury. "You... you deceitful... *old scamp*!" And with that, her dreams of a dangerous liaison visibly turning to ash, she delivered a resounding slap across his now fully exposed cheek — a blow that echoed through the hall like a pistol shot — before flouncing away in a torrent of angry tears, her fairy wings drooping forlornly.

This unfortunate incident, good reader, was merely the prelude to a wider and far more entertaining breakdown of social decorum. As the police moved systematically through the hall, unmasking the revellers, the ball's whimsical fantasy did not merely dissolve; it detonated. Gentlemen caught in compromising scenarios protested this infringement of their liberties. Ladies discovering their husbands' attentions had strayed shrieked with a fury that was anything but theatrical. Accusations and counter-accusations flew like poisoned darts. A volley of glazed canapés sailed through the air like miniature, sticky cannonballs, bespattering guests and officers alike. Indeed, we observe a volatile duchess wielding her fan against the head of a portly Bacchus, whom we must presume to be her husband. Lady Burton herself, having learnt of Sir Burton's rascality, was now — notwithstanding her own hypocrisy on this score — thumping his divine skull with a vigour that promised thunderbolts of agony. Meanwhile, intoxication working its wicked wiles exacerbated several scuffles between elaborately costumed guests and the uniformed, increasingly harried constables, who found themselves grappling with everything from Roman gladiators to Egyptian priestesses. Even the orchestra escaped not the chaos: a cello was unluckily wielded as a shield, whilst a pilfered violin, brought down upon a constable's head, expired with a final, splintering shriek of strings. In short, the ballroom had become a bedlam; a theatre of absurdity where social grace had been categorically routed by the baser instincts of men and, more terrifying still, of women scorned.

Finally, Lord G, his face a shade of purple that clashed alarmingly with his costume, bellowed above the din: "STOP!!! STOP THIS INSTANT, I SAY!!!"

A semblance of quiet, punctuated by indignant gasps and muttered curses, fell grudgingly upon the mightily dishevelled hall.

"Inspector Swords!" His lordship, trembling with fury, pointed towards the main door. "Remove yourself and your uncouth men from my property this instant! Before I take such steps as will make you rue the very day you ever set foot in the county of Somerset! You shall hear from my solicitor in the morning, I assure you!"

***

Back upstairs in Miss Lockwood's room, after a somewhat slurred interruption from Ms Brown, whereupon Vanessa bade her through the wood of the door to leave her be, the young lady sat before her ornate dressing-table, observing Francis in the mirror's polished reflection.

Feeling distinctly out of place and uncomfortably aware of his dishevelled appearance and questionable status, our hero perched awkwardly on the bed's very edge.

"I confess, Mr Sheringham, your *situation* evokes a certain sympathy," conceded Vanessa at length, breaking the charged silence. "Poverty, I am given to understand, *can* indeed drive men to desperate, ill-advised acts. Nevertheless, resorting to outright lawlessness is hardly a commendable solution to one's financial embarrassments."

To be sure, this cool, almost clinical assessment stung Francis even more. "Do you truly imagine I *relish* this damnable existence, Miss Lockwood? Playing the masked bogeyman on public roads? Dodging constables and risking the gallows? 'Tis a sheer necessity, I assure you! But I swear to you, upon what remains of that honour, I have never preyed upon the needy or the defenceless. My victims, if we absolutely *must* call them that, have all been persons of considerable, often ostentatious, means."

Vanessa raised an eyebrow. "Ah, so you fancy yourself a modern-day Robin Hood, do you?"

"Not precisely. Robin Hood, as I recall, gave his spoils to the deserving poor. My own... ah... *acquisitive* activities, I confess, are directed primarily towards alleviating the pressing poverty of... well, of myself."

"What impeccable, self-serving morality!" A hint of dry amusement crept into her voice. She picked up a silver-backed brush and began drawing it slowly through her long, dark hair.

Indeed, our hero caught — or at least he believed he caught — that fleeting note of amusement. She was perhaps not so scandalised by his confession as he had feared. She appeared more to dissect his hypocrisy with scalpel-like precision. Thrilled, indeed, was he by her sharp, unforgiving wit.

Francis rose restlessly from the bed and moved closer to the dressing-table — and, more specifically, to the bracelet lying upon it. His eyes fixed upon the gleaming gold, the familiar diamonds winking in the candlelight. "So, I hear you are betrothed to Vincent?"

Vanessa's hand stilled abruptly. Her reflection in the mirror seemed to darken. "There is no earthly need, Mr Sheringham, to remind me of *that*."

"You do not seem... overjoyed... at the prospect?" observed Francis.

Vanessa made a small gesture of profound contempt with her hand.

"You are wise in your assessment," agreed our hero. "He is naught but a feather-brained, preening dandy."

"The Grants," explained she, devoid of emotion, "are distant relations on my mother's side. On his deathbed, my father appointed Lord Grant as my legal guardian. The terms of his will are quite explicit: I *must* marry by the age of one-and-twenty a man of Grant's choosing. Should I refuse, my entire inheritance — the tanneries, the land, everything — will go to my father's closest male relative, his third cousin Nicholas, a London philanderer who will most assuredly sell it all to finance his extravagant lifestyle."

Vanessa rose abruptly and paced the room, her agitation palpable, her rustling silk nightdress whispering curses around her person. "Of course, I can hardly allow my father's fortune to be lost like *that*! My twenty-first birthday is merely two months away. To save my inheritance, I *must* make this sacrifice and wed Grant's choice, Vincent."

With her back momentarily turned, Francis' hand crept stealthily towards the dressing-table, his fingers inching closer, ever closer, for the coveted bracelet, whilst simultaneously he maintained the flow of conversation. "Surely young Vincent lacks the necessary acumen and commercial shrewdness to oversee your late father's extensive industrial concerns, which I imagine are considerable? It requires a keen mind, a firm hand!"

Vanessa spun around, fixing him with a sharp, suspicious look.

Francis snatched his hand back.

"And who do you suppose *has* been overseeing them, Mr Sheringham," demanded she, visibly affronted, "during the long, weary months of my dear father's final, debilitating illness? I assure you, sir, I am perfectly capable of managing my own affairs, both personal and commercial, without the interference of fops *or* fortune-hunters!"

Francis inwardly cursed himself for his clumsiness. The opportunity, so tantalisingly close, was lost. And he had mistakenly provoked the lady.

"Running away is not a viable option either," continued Vanessa, resuming her agitated pacing. "Where would I possibly go? I have no other family to turn to, no independent means whatsoever if I defy the will."

Francis stood perfectly still. Usually so quick with a glib retort or a salacious proposal, he found a new sensation, quite unknown to him, commandeering his faculties; perhaps it was sympathy?

Whatever the case, looking at her — wealthy beyond measure yet utterly confined — the bitter irony of their shared predicament struck him. "It seems," said he, his gaze meeting hers with a tense, quiet solidarity, "that I have spent the night dodging the law only to find that you are already in a prison. We are both captives of Lord Grant's greed, Miss Lockwood. Caged birds, merely kept in different wings of the same house."

She stopped pacing, the defiance in her posture wavering as the truth of his words landed between them.

"My own humble home, Brookside, is a mere handful of miles distant," offered Francis — the words coming out before he could properly consider their implications; the spell immediately broken.

Again, Vanessa stopped pacing; she turned to our hero and pointed at the door. "Out! Leave my room. Now!"

Indeed, Francis *had* pushed his luck. He lifted his hands in a gesture of apology and surrender. "Very well, Miss Lockwood. As you wish. Pray, do not raise an alarm until I am clear of the grounds."

Vanessa simply folded her arms, visibly waiting.

Francis retrieved his hat and mask, settling them back into place. He strode not to the door, however, but to the window overlooking the gardens below. Unlatching it swiftly, he swung a leg over the sill and, intending to scale the wisteria trellis, rather fell and landed with painful accuracy in the thorny embrace of yet another large rose bush.

"Damn and blast!" yelped he, extracting himself from the thorns that snagged flesh and fabric most fiercely. "Not again!"

Chapter the Thirteenth — A Wallet and A Fight

Sometime later, with the police being beyond all doubt gone, Francis, in need of his own absent horse, had acquired another suitable mount by means less than strictly legal. He was back at his accustomed trade upon a solitary stretch of country road, seeking to soothe his bruised ego with a fresh dose of larceny. Fortune, it seemed, was inclined to oblige, for a lone horseman soon approached at a steady trot — a solitary traveller whom Providence had seemingly delivered up for this very purpose.

Our hero urged his pilfered mount from the shadows and levelled his pistol. "Stand and deliver!"

But lo! As if the stage manager of this nocturnal theatre had a particular taste for symmetrical absurdity, another shadowy figure emerged from the road's opposite side, likewise brandishing a pistol. 'Twas none other than Black Harry, seated with a singular and infuriating impudence upon Francis' own horse.

"Yer money or yer miserable life!" snarled he at the traveller.

The fellow in question, a poor wretch now caught between two armed and competing practitioners of the same nefarious art, fumbled in his waistcoat pocket and produced with nervous haste a thin wallet.

"Give it 'ere, cully!" demanded Harry, clumsily urging his stolen beast beside the palpably terrified gent. "I'll take that!"

"Certainly not, sir!" interjected Francis, impelling his own plundered animal to the poor fellow's other side. "You will deliver it to *me*, if you please!"

Indeed, the unfortunate would-be-victim, his eyes wide with starlit terror, could only stare left to right from one determined highwayman to the other, utterly baffled, we doubt not, by the procedural complexities of his own roadside robbery.

"'e's *mine*!" Harry emitted a rather porcine grunt, reaching out to pluck the still-held-aloft wallet. "I saw 'im first from be'ind yon 'edge!"

"A baseless claim, you witless, malodorous oaf!" Francis shot out a hand, grabbing Harry's wrist. "*I* had already commenced the transaction! *I* stopped him first!"

Alas, Harry proved unyielding, his skull being of that peculiar thickness that renders argument futile and violence inevitable. "Maybe so, Mr 'igh-n-

Mighty!" He yanked his wrist away with a volley of blush-inducing curses. "But I *spotted* 'im first!"

Francis could scarcely contain himself. "Out of my way, you snaggle-toothed baboon!" He gave a shove that nearly unseated his foe and sent both horses dancing nervously. "Before I lose my temper and forget I was ever taught to behave as a gentleman!"

"Er... excuse me, gentlemen," interrupted the traveller somewhat hesitantly whilst discreetly retracting the would-be-plundered wallet into his lap. "Might I impose upon you to reach a mutually agreeable decision as to which of you is to have the distinct honour of robbing me? Only, 'tis getting rather chilly out here."

Francis put a hand up to the man. "One moment, sir, if you please. A small matter of professional demarcation to resolve." With a lithe movement, he dismounted, thrust the reins of his horse into the hands of the befuddled, would-be-plundered traveller, and, circling to the other side, dragged Black Harry from the saddle. "Now, be off with you, you incompetent buffoon!" He shoved him again. "Find your own victims! And I'll take back my horse now, if you don't mind!"

Harry, as we have erenow observed, whose courage was ever more robust than his intellect, shoved back with considerable force. "You be off, you foppish dandy!"

In mere seconds, the two rivals were grappling anew furiously in the dusty road — much like they had before Miss Vanessa's coach — forgetting entirely about their intended victim. Punches, mostly ill-aimed and occasionally landing upon their own persons rather than their opponent's, were thrown; a volley of curses, both inventive and profane, were exchanged with gusto.

'Twas to be expected that the would-be-robbed traveller — no doubt being a prudent philosopher who understood that when two dogs fight for a bone, a third may carry it away — would seize the golden opportunity. Releasing the reins so recently given into his charge, he rather galloped down the road as fast as his startled mount could carry him, no doubt vowing to forever avoid a region where the highwaymen were so lamentably disorganised.

The sound of the rapid departure finally penetrated the combatants' thick fog of fury. Breathing heavily, and grunting immensely, they broke apart, their fine highwayman personas rumpled beyond sufferance.

"He's gone!" Harry tugged at his own hair, staring at the now empty road.

"And whose fault is that, you blithering, addle-pated booby?"

"*Yers*! Mr 'igh-nd-Mighty-Know-It-All! Always stickin' yer fancy nose in where it ain't wanted!"

After pausing only for breath, they immediately fell upon each other with a fresh torrent of shoves, clumsy slaps, and oaths of imminent despatch. Francis, his patience now utterly exhausted, landed a well-aimed punch that sent Harry rolling into a ditch with a splash and a yelp. As the rascal attempted to rise, dripping and spluttering, Francis delivered his now-customary kick to his rival's posterior, sending him sprawling once more — head first, too!

"The next time our paths cross, Harry," declared Francis as he remounted his own horse whilst securing the reins of the other, "consider yourself deceased!"

With that, he turned the horses and trotted away, leaving his vanquished, grovelling rival to curse his ill fortune in the ignominious theatre of the king's highway.

Chapter the Fourteenth — Desperate Times

August 26, 1865

The next day, the Thornfield Hall drawing room — a chamber dedicated not only to the stilted rituals of polite conversation but to the solemn veneration of forebears, whose stern or simpering likenesses lined the panelled walls in heavy gilt frames — proved a most indifferent stage. Here stood Mr Vincent Grant, striking a pose of what he clearly considered knowledgeable reverence before the impressive, life-sized portrait of a bewigged gentleman clad in slightly archaic military attire. His audience consisted solely of our heroine, whose expression, alas, suggested an interest level significantly below that demanded by the weighty subject matter.

"Observe, my dear," declaimed Vincent, "the esteemed William Grant, the second son of a most noble Scottish laird. A man of sound, pragmatic principles, you understand, who most prudently chose the winning side during that unfortunate and rather messy affair at Culloden Field. His loyalty did not go unrewarded by His Majesty King George. Indeed, besides considerable lands, he was offered the hand of a Somerset heiress of immense fortune, whose own lineage, mark you, bore connections to the Royal Household itself!"

Vincent paused, further puffing out his chest. "Thus, you see, my dear Vanessa, there flows within these very Grant veins a not insignificant tincture of royal blood."

At this momentous and evidently much-rehearsed revelation, Vanessa merely emitted a delicate yet unmistakable yawn.

Pretending with admirable fortitude not to have noticed this lack of appreciation for his heraldic distinction, Vincent cleared his throat and moved briskly, with a swish of his coattails, towards the next portrait. "And this formidable lady, Vanessa, with the rather severe countenance —"

"Vincent," interrupted she without any ceremony, "I am quite certain your glorious ancestors will patiently await our further inspection on some future, and perhaps less clement, occasion. The day, as you can see, is remarkably fine, and the hour advances."

A fleeting shadow of irritation crossed his features before being smoothed away by practised insipidity. "As you wish, my dearest Vanessa. Your desires are naturally my command."

As Vincent turned away from the gallery and strolled towards the room's exit, his path took him directly past a large mirror. Habit, that most powerful and often most revealing of human impulses, compelled him to pause and consult this oracle on the state of his own person. A gasp of horror escaped his lips. "Good Lord!" He leant closer to the glass. "Can it be? I appear positively spectral! The very image of Banquo's Ghost!" Utterly forgetting his companion, who observed him with an expression of mingled pity and amusement, he began frantically pinching his own cheeks. "Ah!" He stepped back to admire the effect. "That is much improved. Considerably improved. One simply cannot greet the world, can one, looking like a corpse freshly disinterred from the family vault."

Vanessa rolled her eyes with... well, *little discretion* and moved to the window. "It appears a truly lovely day," said she. "I find myself possessed of a sudden desire for a ride."

Vincent consulted his gold watch. "Alas, a most pressing prior engagement prevents me from having the distinct pleasure of escorting you on your equestrian excursion. My regular shooting practice, you see, commences in half an hour. One must keep one's eye in, you know. Though you are, of course, most welcome to attend and witness my improving marksmanship, should you so desire."

To this generous offer — an invitation which, had she known the true state of his prowess, she might have accepted purely for the sake of its comic potential — Vanessa offered no reply. She continued to gaze out of the window.

****

Elsewhere, the Brookside study presented a somewhat different aspect. Here, upon Sir Andrew's mahogany desk, lay spread not learned treatises nor estate accounts, but a pile of banknotes — the total sum for all the stolen items thus far sold. Sir Andrew and Francis bent over this accumulation, their expressions reflecting not the triumph of successful enterprise, but the grim, furrowed concentration of men engaged in a most unwelcome and disheartening calculation.

"It is insufficient, Francis!" Sir Andrew ran a hand through his thinning hair. "Woefully insufficient. By my reckoning, we remain some three thousand pounds shy of the required sum. And the deadline... curse their impatient souls... is merely seven days hence! We shall not achieve it, my boy. The vultures, as they say, will descend, and Brookside will be picked clean."

Francis slammed a fist upon the desk, scattering a few loose shillings that rolled and spun before coming to rest. His gaze drifted to the generations of leather-bound books and the faded Turkish carpets. They were going to lose it all. The masquerade was over; this was the precipice.

"There must be some way!" said our hero. "Some avenue unexplored!"

A thin, humourless smile overspread his father's visage. "Oh, undoubtedly there is. Perhaps if we contrived to kidnap Her Most Gracious Majesty the Queen herself from Buckingham Palace? The ransom, I imagine, would be quite substantial. Short of such a feat, I fear our prospects are bleak indeed."

Presently, a liveried servant (one of the few remaining, rather threadbare vestiges of former prosperity) approached Francis and handed him an envelope.

His curiosity both piqued and aggravated, Francis broke the Grant seal. Inside, he found a stiff card, elegantly engraved. 'Twas an invitation. Lord and Lady Grant requested the pleasure of Mr Francis and Sir Andrew Sheringham's company at a garden party to be held at Thornfield Hall on the following Monday; the occasion being the formal engagement of their son to Miss Vanessa Lockwood of Springfield Castle.

Francis stared at the invitation, then slowly tapped it against the palm of his hand. The hunter invited into the preserve... Intriguing.

***

Night fell once more, draping the familiar, whispering forest in its customary mantle of deep shadow and mystery. Francis rode through the rustling trees, the waxing moonlight painting fleeting silver patterns on the path before him. But tonight, curiously, he wore not the customary dark cloak and mask of the highwayman, but the respectable attire of a country gentleman. He moved with quiet deliberation, his gaze scanning the dense undergrowth on either side in search of something or someone.

Suddenly, the distinct sound of frantic crashing through the woods reached his attentive ears. A figure burst into view, running with the headlong speed of the well and truly hunted. 'Twas Black Harry. Behind him, growing louder with each passing second, came the ominous sounds of determined pursuit: Inspector Swords and his indefatigable constables were, indubitably, closing in on their hapless quarry.

Francis positioned his horse directly in Harry's path. The fleeing robber skidded to a halt, staring at Francis with wide, bewildered-looking eyes.

"Do not stand there gaping, Harry! They are nearly upon you. I shall create a diversion. Conceal yourself in those bushes. Quickly now!" He pointed with his riding crop towards a particularly dense and uninviting thicket of brambles and ferns to their right.

Though Harry was verily baffled, likely deliberating upon who it was who knew him by name, he hesitated for only a fraction of a second. Trapped between the proverbial devil of this unknown allegiance and the deep blue sea of the constabulary, he opted for the devil. He plunged headfirst into the bushes' thorny embrace just as Inspector Swords and his men thundered into the silver-speckled clearing.

Affecting a gentlemanly fright, Francis held up a hand, halting their progress.

"Your pardon, sir." Inspector Swords reined in his horse, which was champing at the bit, clearly eager to continue the chase. "We are in pursuit of a dangerous fugitive. A highwayman — the very bane of my existence!"

Francis now feigned an expression of appal. "A *highwayman*? In these very woods? So *that* was the scoundrel! Cannot a law-abiding gentleman ride through his own neighbourhood without fear of being molested or assaulted by these villains?"

The captain peered at him more closely. "Has the rascal troubled you then, sir?"

"Indeed, he did!" declared Francis. "Not five minutes ago! Attempted to rob me, the scoundrel! Thank God, your timely and most welcome arrival frightened him off before he could perpetrate his vile deed!"

"Did you happen to observe the direction of his flight?"

"Aye, that I did!" Francis pointed with his crop towards a particularly dense clump of trees to the left — the very opposite direction to Black Harry's place of trembling concealment.

"My sincere thanks, sir. Your assistance is invaluable. We shall have him this time, I promise you!" The inspector signalled to his men, and the troop spurred their horses onwards, crashing into the woods in the direction Francis had so helpfully, and so deceitfully, indicated.

The moment the sounds of pursuit had receded, Francis directed his mount towards the bushes wherein Black Harry lay hidden. As our hero approached, Harry, trusting more to the fleetness of his own legs than to the dubious mercy of a stranger, scrambled from the thicket and commenced a flight distinguished more by haste than by grace. Francis, however, being mounted, easily overtook him.

"Hold, Harry! That is quite enough running for one night. I have, at no small risk to my own person, just preserved you from the law. Is headlong flight the only gratitude you can offer your benefactor?"

Panting and staring up at Francis with a mixture of fear and confusion written in his phiz, Harry stammered, "but... but why, sir? 'oo are you, sir? 'ow do you know my name, and why would *you* 'elp *me*?"

"Why?" echoed our hero. "Let us call it an investment. Firstly, your constant, clumsy interference in my own... nocturnal enterprises... has become exceedingly tiresome. Secondly" — he leant down from his horse — "I suspect that, under the right, more sophisticated, management, you, my dear Harry, might prove surprisingly... useful.

***

And so, half an hour later, we find ourselves in Brookside's gloomy kitchen. Divested of his immediate fear of capture and restored to that state of animal contentment which follows the removal of mortal peril, Black Harry sat hunched over a table, prosecuting a vigorous and single-minded war upon a bowl of soup and a loaf of bread. A greasy rivulet of broth traced a path through the matted thicket of his beard and onto his tattered clothes, adding yet another layer to the rich patina of his neglect.

Francis stood leaning against the stone fireplace, observing this spectacle of unbridled consumption with a mixture of distaste and pragmatic calculation. "Well, Harry?" said he, as the reprobate finally wiped his greasy mouth on the back of his grubby hand — that universal napkin of the underclass — and let out a small contented burp.

"Aye, sir," mumbled Harry, his eyes still fixed on the now empty bowl as if he hoped it might magically refill itself. "I'll work for yeh. No question. Whatever yeh say, sir. Yeh saved me bacon, right enough."

And here the good reader may note the felicity of the metaphor, bacon being perhaps the only thing Harry valued more than his own worthless hide. But I digress...

Our hero took a deep, fortifying breath. "Excellent!"

"Weren't always like this, sir, yeh know," offered the wretch suddenly, possibly feeling a primitive need to justify his current degraded state, or maybe just emboldened by the unexpected kindness of a hot meal. "'ad prospects once, I did. Decent ones. Till me fool of a brother, young Johnny, got 'imself proper mixed up in some riot against 'hem new-fangled Peelers down in London. Caused a right ruckus, 'e did. Whole family 'ad to scarper, see? Lost everything. Been on the run, one way or another, pretty much ever since." He sighed, a gusty, melancholic sound, and scratched absently at his beard.

"Your past, Harry, colourful and grimy though it may be, is of minimal interest to me, provided your future conduct remains obedient. Betray my trust, or attempt any foolishness, and I shall personally deliver you, bound and gagged, to Inspector Swords. Is that understood?"

"Aye, sir! 'onest as the night is long, that's me! Cross me 'eart and 'ope to... well, you get the picture, sir!" Harry tapped his chest with what he, we doubt not, imagined was convincing sincerity.

"Very well." Francis fell silent for a moment, subjecting the urchin before him to a thorough and frankly critical scrutiny, from the matted crown of his head to the dilapidated soles of his boots. "However, Harry, if you *are* to be in my employ, certain... ah... standards *must* be observed. You cannot represent me looking like... well, like *that*." He gestured towards his guest's general state of dishevelment.

Harry shifted on the bench. "Wot d'yeh mean? What's wrong with 'ow I look?"

Francis shook his head. "Tell me, if you can recall such a distant event. When precisely did you last avail yourself of soap and water?"

Harry screwed up his face in evidently a great effort of memory. "Hmm... soap and water, yeh say... must've been... let me think now... couple o' months back, I reckon. Maybe three. Near enough. Bein' chased by the constables near Bristol, I was. Tripped over a root, I did, and fell 'eadlong into a right muddy stream. Cold as charity, it was. Does that count?

Francis chuckled despite himself. "Not precisely, Harry. No, more formal, more deliberate ablutions are required. We must rectify this... pungent... situation immediately."

Hence, some hour or so later — a duration that had no doubt seemed an eternity to both Harry and the unfortunate servant charged with his reformation — in a small bedchamber, a truly miraculous transformation had occurred. Standing somewhat sheepishly before a looking-glass was a man almost unrecognisable as the grimy fugitive from the forest. Here was a Lazarus scrubbed clean and raised from the tomb of his own filth, his tangled beard shaved off to reveal a surprisingly ordinary, if weathered, face, and dressed in a suit of decent, if worn, clothes borrowed from the wardrobe of some long-dead Sheringham ancestor.

Our hero stood near the doorway, observing the result of these sartorial and hygienic ministrations with quiet satisfaction. "Well, Harry? What is the verdict?"

Harry slowly turned from the glass, his hand rising tentatively to touch his clean-shaven chin with the airy wonder of a man discovering a new continent. "Gor blimey, sir," breathed he, all childlike awe. "Is that... truly *me*?" He looked again at the reflection and then back at Francis. "But... but where are me old clothes, sir? Me comfortable rags?"

"Your former attire, Harry, has been consigned to the flames of the kitchen furnace. Their aroma, it must be said, bore an unfortunate and quite overpowering resemblance to that of pig dung mixed with stale beer. A fresh start, my dear Harry, requires fresh garments. And if I may say so, a significantly less pungent personal atmosphere."

Chapter the Fifteenth — Desperate Measures

August 28, 1865

We return once more to that familiar patch of woodland adjacent to Thornfield Hall, the designated theatre for Vincent Grant's ongoing struggle with firearms. On this day, however, the audience for his endeavours had expanded. Joining the painfully resigned instructor were Miss Vanessa Lockwood and her chaperone, Ms Brown. The two ladies were observing the proceedings from a strategically safe distance.

Puffed up with a self-importance that still far outweighed his actual skill, Vincent took his stance, raised the pistol and sighted down the barrel towards the distant wooden target. Significantly, the instructor did *not* on this occasion execute his customary dive for cover. Instead, he merely clamped his hands firmly over his ears, bracing for the inevitable ear-splitting report.

Progress, it seemed, was being made on all fronts.

BANG!

The shot, loud and startling, echoed through the tranquil trees, causing a flock of indignant pigeons to erupt from the canopy above.

All eyes turned towards the target.

And there, clearly visible, was a fresh, undeniable bullet mark!

'Twas not, admittedly, anywhere near the coveted bullseye, residing instead closer to the wooden circle's outermost edge. Nevertheless, 'twas beyond any shadow of a doubt *on* the target. A palpable hit!

A complacent smirk spread across Vincent's face. He lowered the still-smoking pistol with a ridiculous flourish, as if he had just single-handedly defended a breach in the walls of Badajoz. The instructor allowed himself what resembled a smile of relief; progress, no matter how marginal or accidental, was still progress. And, more importantly, he had survived another lesson unscathed.

From their vantage point beneath a shady elm, Vanessa and Ms Brown exchanged quick and full-of-meaning glances. Then, in perfect, almost synchronised unison, they began to applaud — slowly, more deliberately than sincerely.

Vincent merely basked in the warm glow of his perceived triumph. The adulation, however insincere, was music to his ears.

Chapter the Fifteenth — Desperate Measures

***

Simultaneously, a scene of far greater activity was unfolding in Thornfield Hall's rear garden. Here, preparations were in full swing for the garden party, intended to formally present Miss Vanessa Lockwood to the local gentry as Vincent's intended bride.

An army of servants scurried about, erecting marquees, arranging seating, polishing silverware, and positioning floral displays under the watchful eyes of their employers. Lord and Lady G supervised these efforts, each according to their distinct temperament. His Lordship, embodying aristocratic detachment, observed the proceedings from a shaded vantage point, occasionally offering a vague gesture or a noncommittal grunt. Her Ladyship, conversely, was a whirlwind of managerial energy, bustling amongst the staff, pointing imperiously, adjusting decorations, and issuing a constant stream of sharp, often contradictory, orders.

***

Elsewhere, we find Sir Andrew upon the terrace, deriving from a modest meal of cold mutton and pickles a kind of stoic contentment that was, in its own way, a profound philosophical statement.

A short distance away, on a bandstand, unfolded a theatre of a far less tranquil and considerably more exasperating character. Here, Francis was prosecuting a most singular and arduous campaign: the instillation of gentlemanly conduct into the freshly scrubbed person of Black Harry. The lesson concerned that most complex of all sciences, more obscure than mathematics and more perilous than alchemy — the proper method of approaching the fairer sex.

"Observe, Harry." Francis demonstrated a graceful, controlled bow from the waist. "When presented to a lady of quality, one inclines the body thusly. Not too deep, mind you, lest you resemble a tradesman soliciting custom, nor too shallow, which might imply disrespect." He now mimed assisting an imaginary lady from an equally imaginary coach. "You will offer your hand, so. Firmly, yet with a gentle touch — think of holding a bird's egg, Harry; something delicate that might shatter if gripped too enthusiastically." He then extended a hand, palm upwards, taking an invisible, feminine one. "And when taking her hand in greeting, a light pressure, perhaps a brief, courteous glance towards her eyes is permitted; but no prolonged leering, and certainly, Heaven and all the saints forbid, no vulgar squeezing or pumping as though you were drawing water from a well."

Harry watched these demonstrations with a look of painful concentration, occasionally scratching his head as if trying to physically implant the information.

"Now, Harry" — Francis stepped back, preparing himself for the ordeal — "a little role-play, if you will. Let us imagine that *I* am a lady of quality —"

"But you ain't a lady?" interrupted Harry, stumbling at this first imaginative hurdle.

"As I said, Harry," replied Francis sternly, "let us *imagine*... So, I am a beautiful, refined young woman you have just encountered at, say, a garden party. How would you address me? What charming pleasantries might you offer to initiate a conversation?"

After some visibly perplexing internal struggle, Harry puffed out his chest like a bantam cock preparing for combat and thrust out a hand in a manner more suited to demanding payment than offering a greeting. "Ello there, birdie!" His voice reverted to its usual coarse tone. "Fancy a bit o' fun, eh, me lovely?" He embellished this roguery with a wink. "You and me, we could 'ave a right old time! I got a shilling or two if yer interested!"

Francis recoiled as if he had been struck by a blunt instrument. Then, he delivered a sharp, percussive critique with the flat of his hand across Harry's cheek.

"Ouch!" cried the rapscallion, flinching back in disgruntled bewilderment. "What was *that* for?!"

"That, Harry, is *precisely* what you will receive — or, more likely, far worse — should you ever *dare* address a respectable woman in such an abominable, utterly reprehensible fashion! Have you learnt absolutely nothing?"

Harry only rubbed his smarting cheek with an air of injured innocence wronged. Indeed, we may safely surmise he could scarcely conceive of a universe wherein such a direct and, to his mind, friendly overture could be met with anything other than reciprocal enthusiasm. "But... I was just bein' friendly-like, sir... Most birds appreciate a fellow that speaks plain!"

Francis pressed his fingers to his temples. "Perhaps a different pedagogical approach is required," muttered he, more to himself than to his hapless pupil. "We shall try again. Perhaps the judicious addition of a few simple French phrases might lend an air of continental sophistication to your discourse. A 'trick,' they say in certain circles, that often proves remarkably effective with the ladies, particularly those of a romantic disposition."

Alas, Harry's gaze had already drifted longingly towards Sir Andrew, still peacefully consuming his meal. From the depths of Harry's stomach, a loud, resonant rumbling emanated. "Beggin' yer pardon, sir" — he cradled his belly like a woman in travail — "but I'm fair famished, I am. All this... this bowin' and scrapin'... it's 'ard work. Makes a man's insides feel all 'ollow-like."

"You will eat, Harry, only when you can execute a simple, passable bow and offer a polite, coherent greeting without sounding like a drunken navvy attempting a clumsy seduction in a dockside tavern! Now, for pity's sake, *concentrate!*"

Let it be recorded that after a further interval of diligent — nay, heroic — instruction on the one part, and of profound incomprehension on the other, the state of our pupil's education had progressed remarkably little, if at all. Harry's stomach continued its mournful, rumbling protest, a constant and eloquent counterpoint to Francis' increasingly strained directives.

"Once more, Harry," demanded he. "From the very beginning. Remember the bow. And the smile. A *charming* smile, if you please."

Upon this command, Harry thus attempted said smile. He aimed for sweetness and light, for an expression of amiable gallantry, but succeeded only in revealing that grim, desolate landscape of sundry gaps and general decay.

Francis closed his eyes as though by shutting out the sight he might somehow erase it from memory. "Harry, I believe I have explained this *repeatedly*. When employing a smile for social purposes, it is generally advisable to keep the lips *closed*. Firmly closed! Now, if you please, *try again*. The bow. *Just* the bow."

Looking thoroughly miserable, Harry hence executed a sudden contortion of the torso which, had a physician been present, might have been diagnosed as a violent affliction of the lumbago rather than any recognised form of polite salutation.

At this, Francis threw his hands up in surrender. "Enough! I can bear no more! I believe we have both reached the absolute limit of our endurance for one evening."

He turned on his heel and strode to the house.

Harry shuffled along behind him, muttering under his breath just loud enough for the retreating Francis (and, indeed, for us, good Reader) to hear: "Wouldn't be so bleedin' difficult, this lady-charming lark, if I 'ad a proper woman to practise on, now, would it? Instead o' this moody fancy-pants governess yellin' at me all blessed evenin'..."

***

Later, in the small bedchamber now designated as Harry's own, a council of war of a most delicate and critical nature was convened. Francis, his brow furrowed with the gravity of a certain impending enterprise, stood before his accomplice. In his hand, he held a small glass bottle, its contents a clear, volatile liquid that shimmered in the dim candlelight.

"Pay close attention, Harry. Here, my friend, is the very linchpin of our endeavour this evening. The substance within is called *chloroform*. A recent and remarkably effective scientific discovery." He held the bottle aloft. "A few drops, judiciously applied to a cloth, held firmly beneath a person's nostrils for but a moment, will induce a temporary... a temporary loss of..." He paused, searching for a term that might successfully navigate the barren terrain of his companion's intellect.

Harry peered at the bottle with a mixture of suspicion and childlike curiosity. "Loss o' wot, sir? Loss o' their valuables?"

"Consciousness, Harry," clarified Francis. "They faint, you understand? Pass out. Become insensible, unhearing, unseeing, for a short, convenient period."

"Ah! Right then!" Harry nodded slowly, a glimmer of something akin to comprehension (or probably just unquestioning compliance) dawning in his eyes. "Knocks 'em right out, it does! Like a good clout with a cosh, but quieter, eh?"

"Precisely," conceded Francis, wincing at the analogy's crudity as he pressed the precious bottle into his accomplice's hand. "You will guard this as if it were the Crown Jewels themselves. And you will employ it *exactly* as I have instructed, at the precise moment this evening. Discretion, Harry, is paramount. No heroics, no improvisation."

Harry nodded again, clutching the bottle.

119

"Very well." Francis was satisfied, for the moment at least. "You understand your role? The sequence of actions I have outlined?"

"Clear as crystal, sir!" Harry adopted an air of breezy confidence that did little to reassure his mentor. "Piece o' cake, it'll be. Yeh can trust ol' Harry."

Here, the reader may perceive the desperate strategist who, lacking a trained soldier of any competence whatsoever, must needs arm a baboon and hope for the best.

Indeed, a fleeting, prophetic shudder — a vision of impending disaster — did cross Francis' mind. But time was short. Harry, for better or decidedly worse, was the sole instrument at his disposal. "Good. See that you do not fail me." With a final, curt nod, he turned and quit the room.

And now let us observe the inevitable and eternal triumph of innate stupidity over imparted wisdom. The moment the door closed — the very instant the latch clicked into place — Harry's irrepressible curiosity overcame all oaths of caution. "Chloroform, eh?" muttered he, holding the bottle to the light. "Wonder what it smells like? 'E made it sound like powerful stuff... but" — and here he caught his own newly respectable reflection in the glass, producing an effect all too reminiscent of those noble lords so often puffed up beyond reason or counsel by their own imagined superiority — "'e's a bit of a nervous Nellie, ain't 'e? Probably all exaggerated, like them windy ghost stories."

With this profound but fatally inaccurate assessment of both his master's character and the properties of modern chemistry, he uncorked the bottle and, ignoring all explicit instructions, raised the vial's open neck directly to his own unsuspecting nostrils. "Mmm... that's a bit like ripe pears, ain't it...? Or maybe..." Sniff-sniff. "... apples...? Don't know what all the fuss was..."

Alas — and not that your humble author needs to point out with any great emphasis the disastrous, inevitable, and frankly richly deserved consequence of this inadvisable sniff — his eyes, which had lit up with olfactory appreciation, suddenly glazed over. His brief expression of delight slackened into one of vacant, bovine surprise. Then, without another sound, without even a gurgle of regret or recognition that he had been a damned fool, his knees buckled beneath him. He crumpled to the floorboards in an untidy, insensible heap, the uncorked bottle rolling from his outstretched hand and spilling nearly all its precious contents onto the planks where it would do precisely no good to anyone.

Scarcely a minute later — Fortune, it seems, possessed a keen sense of comedic timing — Francis, having remembered one crucial detail concerning the timing of their enterprise, returned.

"And one more thing, Harry, regarding the signal for…" His words died in his throat. Before him lay a tableau of catastrophe: his carefully briefed accomplice, spread-eagled and comatose upon the floorboards, the uncorked bottle beside him serving as mute testimony to precisely what species of idiocy had transpired.

Indeed, our hero stared with paralysed fascination. He blinked once, twice, thrice, disbelieving the evidence of his own eyes. "Sweet merciful heavens!" groaned he to the senseless form of his protégé. "I simply *do not* believe it! Of all the idiotic, imbecilic, harebrained…!"

Chapter the Sixteenth — A knock-out Soirée

The extensive lawns behind Thornfield Hall presented a picture of elegant festivity. Lanterns cast a warm glow about, illuminating clusters of well-dressed guests mingling amidst the fragrant flowerbeds and along the neatly gravelled pathways. The balmy night air, redolent with roses and honeysuckle, carried the pleasant sounds of society at its leisure: the polite babble of conversation, decorous bursts of feminine laughter, and the delicate clinking of champagne glasses. Dominating the lawn's central expanse, three long, linen-draped tables groaned, quite literally, under the magnificent weight of a lavish buffet: lobsters reclined in aspic, game pies rose in golden-crusted glory, and jellies trembled in a rainbow of jewel-like colours.

Lord G, looking suitably proprietorial, held court near the largest of the punch bowls with his usual coterie of cronies, the portly — and still shamefaced — Sir Burton and the perpetually anxious Mr Russell. This triumvirate most likely discussed matters of local importance or perhaps merely complained about the incompetence of the local authorities.

Elsewhere, our hero found himself, as *per se*, the centre of a feminine constellation: the effusive Lady "Plenty", the ever-flustered Mrs Russell, her skittish daughter Jenny (who fluttered nearby), and, inevitably, their gracious hostess, Lady G herself, surrounded him in a tight, perfumed circle. Their combined chatter and delighted giggles formed a constant, slightly dizzying, and frankly rather overwhelming backdrop to his thoughts.

Though Francis smiled, nodded, and offered cordial responses, his attention was fixed elsewhere. Across the lawn stood Vanessa. My, how she dazzled this evening, attired in an evening gown of shimmering sapphire silk that seemed to capture and reflect the lantern light with every subtle movement. As she placed her empty plate on the buffet table and reached for a flute of champagne, the candlelight caught the intricate gold links of the bracelet encircling her slender wrist.

Just as she turned, glass in hand, Vincent materialised behind her. Vanessa visibly stiffened; then, with a gentle but firm movement, she disengaged herself from his unwelcome conversation and turned with a cool, deliberate grace — that left him looking momentarily foolish — to Ms Brown.

As she did so, her gaze, having swept the crowded lawn, collided with Francis'. For but a fraction of a second, she appeared to allow her mask of polite indifference to slip, sharing, what was undoubtedly, a silent, exhausted exasperation with him before turning fully away. Such was this miniscule intimacy, that it verily made our hero's pulse race!

The night deepened, the champagne continued to flow, and 'tis here, amidst the noisier revelries that we find Francis and Vanessa standing somewhat apart from the party, having, as if by chance — or, perhaps intention — congregated near a fragrant rose arbour. Engaged in a most agreeable and absorbing conversation, they each held a half-empty glass, their postures relaxed, suggesting a degree of comfortable familiarity that was not lost on certain other observers across the grass.

"One wonders who precisely extended *him* an invitation to this affair!" muttered Vincent somewhat sourly, standing beside the buffet table and spearing a cream-filled vol-au-vent as if *it* had personally affronted him. "He seems to have made himself rather too much at home, in my opinion. And *where* is that chaperone of hers?!"

"I believe, my dear boy," said his father, "I possess a fairly accurate and deeply regrettable suspicion on that particular score." Lord G took a large, thoughtful bite of game pâté, chewing with slow deliberation. His equally vexed gaze shifted pointedly from his soon to be daughter-in-law towards his wife, who was at that very moment engrossed in devouring a substantial slice of rich fruitcake nearby.

Francis and Vanessa, meanwhile, shared a low, conspiratorial-sounding laugh; the sound of which carried quite freely on the air.

For the first time since their disastrous introduction, the invisible walls between them had begun to fall. They were no longer merely the desperate debtor and the trapped heiress, but rather a man and a woman delighting in the rare, intoxicating relief of being a little more understood by one another.

"Tell me, Mr Sheringham, are there no ladies present this evening worthy of your... *professional* attention?" Vanessa's eyes sparkled with something like mischief. "No coaches to intercept on the driveway as they depart?"

Indeed, dear reader, we may readily wonder what transformation of sentiments might yet account for this proximity and burgeoning affinity between the heiress and the highwayman. Yet is it not the very office of Fortune — that most capricious and theatrical of all the deities who govern human affairs — to delight in bringing together those whom society, reason, and common sense would keep forever apart? Does she not take pleasure in watching the proud humbled, the certain confounded, and the incompatible made intimate? The author, a humble servant to this mischievous mistress, can only chronicle what she decrees, however improbable it may seem.

His eyes having rarely strayed from her face throughout their discourse, Francis allowed a sly grin to touch his lips. "You never know, Miss Lockwood. One must always remain vigilant. Opportunity, like beauty, can appear when least expected, and often in the most surprising of disguises."

His words, uttered with well-placed gallantry, proved startlingly prophetic.

With a velocity and violence that would have astonished even a Delphic oracle, at that very instant, a dark shape erupted with a great crashing of branches from behind a section of shrubbery. A horse and rider cleared the bushes, less in a graceful leap and more in a calamitous scramble, landing with a heavy thud upon the lawn and sending divots of turf flying in all directions.

'Twas, good reader, none other than Harry, clad in black, sporting Francis' own hat and mask, and clutching the fateful bottle of chloroform.

Spooked by the sudden blaze of lanterns and the cacophony of startled cries, the horse bolted with wild and uncontrollable energy. Harry, poor wretch, sawed frantically at the reins with all the effectiveness of a man trying to steer a hurricane, shouting curses as he strove to impose his will upon the rampaging beast.

From that precise point, events escalated with a catastrophic and frankly quite glorious speed: the panicked steed, still ignoring its rider's desperate efforts, charged squarely into the longest of the buffet tables. Let the Muse of Gastronomy weep! For with a tremendous, ear-splitting crash, the entire structure overturned. Its contents — a veritable avalanche of salmon mousse, jellied eels, shattered porcelain, slivers of crystal, and cascading rivulets of champagne — descended directly onto the unsuspecting forms of Lord G and his son. Verily, they vanished from sight beneath this glistening, sticky, and altogether unappetising inundation — much like Pompeii buried beneath Vesuvius' wrath — their muffled screams of outrage the only testament to their continued existence.

At the same time, the horse's charge, thus faced by the obstacle of aristocratic flesh and overturned furniture, abruptly halted. Obeying the inexorable laws of physics, poor Harry was launched from his saddle. Through the lantern-lit air, describing a decidedly un-heroic arc, sailed he — much like a human cannonball — emitting not a warrior's cry, but a high-pitched, rather un-highwayman yelp.

But lo! The disaster ended not there; for Fortune, it seemed, was in a particularly mischievous and destructive mood this evening.

Simultaneously, during said arc through the air, the bottle of chloroform, that linchpin of Francis' carefully arranged plan, slipped from Harry's grasp. It flew across the intervening space, striking the lovely Vanessa squarely on her elegant forehead. Her beautiful eyes rolled back in their sockets, her expression one of fleeting surprise before dissolving into utter vacancy, and she collapsed onto the soft grass, instantly, and most effectively unconscious.

Harry's airborne trajectory, meanwhile, concluded not upon the turf, as he might have hoped, but directly upon the person of Lady G, whereupon she let out a sound that could only be described as a startled squawk. The combined mass of highwayman and hostess then toppled, with very little grace, into what had been a magnificent, tiered celebration cake, boasting a sound — a deep, satisfying, and distinctly wet, cream-and-jam-spraying SPLAT! — as they became one with the confection.

And there they flailed amidst the gluey detritus (very much like two exuberant infants creating angelic patterns in freshly fallen snow, albeit with considerably less grace, and one suspects, significantly less pleasure). Indeed, they resembled nothing so much as two dishevelled Christmas puddings — all cherries, cream, pastry, candied fruit; an insult, we may easily imagine, to the pastry-cook's art — given the breath of life only to mutter ear-tingling expletives.

Oh, lest we forget the horse! Having wreaked such devastation, it planted its hooves with triumphant firmness upon the overturned tabletop, effectively pinning the food-bespattered, groaning forms of Lord G and his son beneath it.

Francis and the others — now including Ms Brown, who made her reappearance — could only stare, mouths agape, like a tableau of universal stupefaction.

As for Her Ladyship, after the initial shock of having been propelled into a mountain of desert by a masked, airborne man, she now seemed to enjoy the situation's novelty. "My goodness!" A delighted giggle escaped her as she licked a smear of buttercream from her fingers and looked up at the disoriented — unbeknownst to her who he truly was — Harry, still sprawled atop her person. "And who, pray tell, might *you* be, my handsome and most unexpected visitor?"

As we know, Harry had more pressing priorities than engaging in polite, if somewhat gooey, badinage with his current, cake-adorned cushion. A series of grunts and quite a few slips upon the treacherous sugary terrain now passed — during which Harry's mouth, as if guided by some naughty deity, made repeated and distinctly moist contact with Her Ladyship's own. Poor Lady G, if only she knew these 'moosy' lips, tasting faintly of desperation and cheap tobacco, belonged to the largely toothless oaf beneath the mask and not the dashing, romantic highwayman of her fantasies!

At any rate, Harry finally extricated himself from the not entirely displeased hostess. "Not *you* I'm after, ma'am, beggin' yer pardon," grunted he, lurching with a singular, if unsteady, purpose towards the spot where the unfortunate Vanessa lay motionless upon the dew-kissed grass.

Her Ladyship sighed with a theatrical pout of disappointment as he staggered away. "Oh, dear! Must you go quite so soon, my mysterious cavalier? The night is yet young!"

Let us not forget Francis; remembering *his* vital role in this increasingly ludicrous charade, he — after ordering Ms Brown to stand down (for she, with a martial air exuding from her every huff, puff, and glare, was poised to attack with a serving ladle) — stepped forwards to block Harry's path. "Stand back, villain!" commanded he. "Leave the lady alone, I say, or you shall answer to me!"

Harry, alas, following his somewhat muddled and now largely forgotten instructions, delivered an ill-aimed punch. It connected, after a fashion, landing more as a glancing blow to our hero's cheekbone. Francis, nonetheless, ever the consummate actor, collapsed onto the grass as if felled by a Titan's blow, clutching his face and groaning with a somewhat exaggerated agony.

"Not like *that*, you blithering fool!" Francis hissed under his breath. "And you don't *throw* the blasted bottle at her head! The instructions were *a cloth*, you imbecile!"

"Well, it worked all the same, didn't it?" Harry gestured with a thumb towards the still-unconscious Vanessa. "She's out cold, right as ninepence."

With that, ignoring Francis' next volley of whispered castigations, Harry produced a pistol, waved it about like a Fury, causing all guests to cower and duck for cover, and bent to lift Vanessa's limp form. With considerable effort, he carried her to the horse, which still stood, a conquering hero, upon the ruined landscape of the toppled buffet.

With some further struggles, our ersatz highwayman hoisted our dangling heroine onto the beast's broad back, slinging her over the saddle with all the tender care one might afford a sack of grain. Then, vaulting up behind her, he seized the reins, turned the horse sharply, and galloped away into the night with his captive prize.

By-the-by, amidst the chaos that continued to reign, that small, innocuous-looking chloroform bottle lying forgotten on the grass, glinted in the lantern light. And Sir Burton, having espied it, and seeing the several ladies in the throes of what appeared to be the vapours, his mind immediately leapt to a plausible, if fatally erroneous, conclusion.

"Smelling salts, by Jove!" cried he in a tone all too heroic. "Just the ticket for these distressed damsels!"

He snatched up the bottle with a flourish that betrayed his would-be-chivalric intervention and, no doubt seeking to restore some small lustre to his heretofore desecrated honour — for the reader will recall his earlier humiliations — presented himself before his first subject: Miss Jenny Russell, who was at that moment leaning heavily against a footman, her hand pressed to her forehead.

"Courage, Miss Jenny!" declared our new physician. "A restorative sniff is all that is required!" He uncorked the bottle and, in his soon-to-be-regretted ignorance of its true nature, waved it with brisk confidence beneath the young lady's nostrils.

To be sure, her swoon did not so much abate as it deepened, transitioning rather speedily from a picturesque languor into a most profound and unequivocal unconsciousness.

Pleased with the manifest efficacy of his remedy (for was she not now perfectly still?), Sir Burton turned his philanthropic attentions to his wife, who was fanning herself with agitated vigour. "Allow me, my dearest!" chirped he, presenting the open bottle.

Lady Burton, much like the lady before her, merely leant in for a genteel sniff. Her lamentations ceased abruptly as her eyes glazed over, and she subsided onto a nearby garden bench with a soft, contented sigh, joining Miss Jenny in the blissful republic of oblivion.

"Excellent!" cheered Sir Burton. "Most excellent!"

A third lady, Mrs Russell — mother to the aforementioned Miss Jenny, lest we forget — loudly proclaiming that such outrages would never have occurred in her grandmother's day, was next to receive Sir Burton's well-intentioned ministrations. One brief, incautious inhalation later, and the lady's declamations on the moral decay of the age were summarily cut short as she, too, crumpled silently to the ground.

Having thus *assisted* three ladies into a state of insensibility that rather resembled death than restored health, Sir Burton finally paused, a slight frown creasing his brow. "Remarkably effective potency," mused he, holding the bottle up to the light as though doubt, that small voice of reason which arrives, alas, always too late to prevent disaster, had entered his skull. "One wonders as to its composition... Smelling salts are generally not quite so... *decisive* in their action."

And here, scientific curiosity, that fatal flaw of so many great minds and the downfall of countless men, overcame all caution. "Perhaps a small sniff for oneself, merely to ascertain its particular aroma...?" enquired he of no one in particular. "Surely it will prove ineffective against a robust male constitution such as mine?"

With this supremely confident assertion of his masculine superiority — that pride which, as the ancients knew, inevitably precedes a fall — he raised the bottle to his own nose. He took an exploratory sniff, and, with an expression of brief, almost academic-looking surprise that suggested his final thought was something along the lines of "Oh, I say, this is rather —", he slumped to the ground, thereby joining his erstwhile patients in the land of nod.

Enter Mr Russell, alarmed by his companion's collapse hard upon the ladies' heels. "Good heavens, man! What *are* you playing at?" He first prodded the insensible Sir Burton with his cane, as if to ascertain whether he was truly defunct, before snatching the bottle from his grip. "What *is* this? Some psychedelic opium, perhaps? Some new and potent species of laudanum?"

He too, with the same magnificent lack of strategic foresight that had felled his predecessor, was about to conduct his own nasal investigation when a third gentleman — a young, aspiring poet, invited, I think, by Lady G — seized the bottle from him. "Fear not, gentlefolk!" He struck a pose. "I, Algernon Quill, shall ascertain the nature of this insidious peril that lays low both beauty and valour!"

So saying, he sniffed the bottle with an air of Byronic intensity and collapsed with remarkable speed, his half-formed verses dying on his lips.

"Give that to me!" now rasped a rather ridiculous-looking Lord G.

With the assistance of two footmen, he had finally shoved aside the overturned table and escaped the erstwhile feast's adhesive mess. My, what a singular figure of horror is presented: his fine evening clothes stained, smeared, and utterly mullered; dripping with assorted sauces; his hair matted with cake crumbs and glistening with aspic. He slapped away Mr Russell's hand (which was again reaching for the liquid with similar intentions), seizing the bottle for himself, which he — possessed of just enough wit to observe the pattern of unconsciousness that had followed the container's use — sagely pocketed.

To be sure, young Vincent, standing by his side, his face adorned with a fetching combination of trifle, salmon mousse, and profound humiliation, presented an equally and truly comical sight.

Judging the moment opportune, Francis now pushed himself to his feet with an air of dizziness, still rubbing his nose and cheek with feigned, lingering pain.

Visibly incandescent with a rage that far outweighed his father's weary disgust, Vincent spun around — flinging droplets of custard and cream hither and yon — and stormed over to our hero. "You!" He levelled a finger that was liberally coated in what looked suspiciously like raspberry jam. "Why did not you stop him? You just *stood* there! You let him take her!"

"*Stood there*? My dear follow, I tried!" Francis indicated his supposedly injured face with a faux wince. "He struck me down! A foul, unchivalrous blow!"

"You should have fought harder!" raged Vincent. "You should have defended Miss Lockwood! Defended her with your very life if necessary! It was your duty as a gentleman!"

Francis raised an eyebrow, his affected pain momentarily forgotten. "Risk *my* life, Vincent? Forgive me for posing the question, but why precisely should *I* undertake such a perilous and potentially fatal endeavour? She is, after all, *your* fiancée, not mine."

Yet, even as Francis delivered this line with his trademark flippancy, the words turned bitter in his mouth. Speaking the reality aloud — that she belonged to this preening fop and not to him — struck him with a knife-like sharpness.

***

Later that very night, when the owls had begun their mournful calling, we find ourselves within a less-sparsely furnished bedroom at Brookside. Here, Vanessa lay on the last of the silk-sheeted divans, still held fast in the unyielding embrace of unconsciousness. Upon her alabaster forehead, an angry bruise was already beginning to bloom — a prominent peak that might have done credit to the wildest and most rugged of the Northern Districts! Yet even with this disfiguring blemish, bathed as she was in the soft, economical glow of a single oil lamp, she resembled nothing so much as some enchanted princess of ancient fable — a Sleeping Beauty, perchance, awaiting that chivalrous kiss...

Beside her on the bed's very edge sat our hero. With a clean cloth, dipped into a basin of cool spring water, he gently dabbed at the swelling contusion. His touch, for a man whose hands were more accustomed to the rough leather of reins, the cold steel of a pistol, or indeed, the swift acquisition of another's property, was surprisingly tender. Indeed, a philosopher studying this unexpected beneficence might have been moved to speculate upon the hidden wellsprings of virtue that may lie dormant even in the most unpromising of soils.

He stared at the violent purple marring her pale skin — more a brutal reminder of the calculating world that constantly sought to conquer her. A pent-up sigh escaped him. Within his chest, a strange sensation took hold. What was this? *I care neither to charm nor to outwit her?* Nor did he truly wish to ransom her — *how could I?* Oddly, confusingly, incomparably, he wished only to keep her safe.

With this small comfort administered, Francis set the cloth aside on the bedside table and, for a long, silent moment, simply watched her. And here, good reader, we may observe the swift and terrible operations of Love, which can lay siege to a man's heart when it is least defended. His gaze traced the delicate, classic lines of her unconscious face. Her lips, those perfectly formed rosebuds, puckered even in slumber, as if awaiting — *Ahem*! The gentle sweep of her long, dark lashes as they lay like silken crescents against the pale, smooth canvas of her skin, drew from his breast an exquisite, swelling pang, in which both pain and a strange new pleasure were most curiously intermingled. Indeed, he perhaps already believed himself in love. And love, even in the breast of the best of men, always fruitful in invention, might have furnished him with a stratagem.

He shook his head, shuddering at the notion of indulging such a nascent passion upon an unconscious subject. Notwithstanding the attractions the lady was mistress of, our hero possessed resolution enough to withstand their effects on his libertine mind.

At length, with a hesitation that bespoke a deeper turmoil than mere concern for an injured captive, he reached out a hand and took hers — that very hand adorned with the familiar and now doubly significant circlet of gold and diamonds.

In their exploratory caress, his fingers inevitably brushed against the inviting metal. He paused, his breath held bound within his beating chest. For a fleeting, charged moment, his purpose, so long nurtured, so fiercely held, asserted its dominion. His fingers tightened. To unfasten the intricate clasp, to finally reclaim that which he so fervently desired, was but the work of an instant.

But then a sudden conflict claimed his breast. A veritable civil war was prosecuted on the field of his thoughts. On one side stood desire, long-standing grievances, and that cold, hard purpose which had been the compass of his actions. On the other stood a new and unnamed challenger — perhaps it was an incipient stirring of honour, or perhaps, more perplexing still, something dangerously akin to... affection?

Whatever the case, if he slipped the bracelet from her wrist, would he not be treating her in a manner similar to that with which Lord Grant and his rotten scion presently used her? An asset to be plundered for his own salvation. To steal from her now would be to forfeit the only thing he might later regret losing other than Brookside: her respect.

After quite a prodigious pause, he sighed, released her hand, and gently placed it back upon her breast, as one might return a sleeping dove to the fragile safety of its nest.

Then he rose from the bedside and left the room, closing the door softly behind him.

Chapter the Seventeenth — Escapes and Eavesdropping

August 29, 1865

Sunlight, bold and inquisitive, streamed through the bedchamber windows, illuminating a veritable galaxy of dust motes dancing in the air. Upon the bed, Vanessa was at last awake, rubbing at the rather prominent bruise upon her forehead — that "veritable peak," now stood proud and purple, a testament to Harry's unfortunate lack of precision. Her expression as she assessed her unfamiliar surroundings was naturally wary.

Francis, our orchestrator of these irregular proceedings, leant against the far wall, his arms crossed over his chest, observing her awakening with as detached an air of interest as his swellingly un-disinterested soul could muster.

"Good morning," said he; "or perhaps, good afternoon. I trust you slept... *adequately*, despite the somewhat abrupt and unconventional manner of your retiring. I *must*, of course, offer my sincerest apologies for your evident discomfort. Harry, whilst occasionally useful, is regrettably deficient in what one might term... finesse."

Vanessa remained silent, her gaze carrying a distinct challenge that belied her captive state.

"Please, Miss Vanessa!" Francis pushed himself away from the wall and took a tentative step towards her. "Do endeavour to comprehend the... the unfortunate *necessity* of this undertaking. 'Tis, I assure you, nothing personal directed against your charming self. Lord Grant holds the purse strings with a grip tighter than any miser. 'Tis *he* who will be invited to contribute to my... charitable fund; 'tis *he* who will pay the ransom, not yourself."

"*Ransom?*" Vanessa finally spoke. "This... this *kidnapping*... this ill-conceived abduction, Mr Sheringham, it is the most reckless, foolhardy gamble you could have employed. Do you truly believe his lordship will simply pay your demands and let the matter rest? He will hunt you down, sir! He will not permit such an egregious affront to his dignity to go unpunished."

Francis offered a small, contemptuous grin. "Grant and I, Miss Lockwood, have certain... outstanding accounts to settle."

"Perhaps, but no matter what grievances you may nurse against him, it grants you *no* right whatsoever to employ *me* as a pawn in your dangerous and dishonourable game of revenge!"

Francis opened his mouth to protest, to offer some justification, but Vanessa silenced him with a glance so fiery and direct that it seemed to scorch the very air between them.

"Lord Grant may indeed be a man of devious machinations," continued she, "but let us not, for one moment, indulge in the pretence that *you*, Mr Sheringham, are some stainless paragon of virtue, some knight errant wronged! Even in my short time in this district, whispers travel. I am not unaware of your... *reputation*. Not only your 'nocturnal ramblings' on the highway, but your 'night-time games' as some, perhaps too generously, phrase it, with certain... local ladies."

The hot blood of embarrassment rushed to Francis' cheeks. "That is nothing but malicious gossip!" He evaded her direct gaze. "Vile slander, Miss Lockwood, spread by... by *jealous* tongues and idle minds! You mustn't believe a single wretched word of it!" He found a sudden, intense interest in a crack in the floorboards.

"Oh, *mustn't* I?" replied she.

Francis fidgeted, running a hand nervously through his hair. His usually silky words seemed to have transformed themselves into heavy stones, lodged stubbornly at the back of his throat, refusing all egress.

Until this precise moment, his libertine exploits had been a source of private amusement — a rebellion against the suffocating expectations of his class. But here, subjected to the clearer, uncompromising light of Vanessa's scrutiny, the reality of his past crept over his soul with shame-inducing unease.

How was he to extricate himself from allegations, which he knew to be, in fact, *bona fide* facts?

As our hero reluctantly met her gaze, he noted how a flicker of something unreadable — perhaps amusement — lit up her eyes. To be sure, Francis' cheeks burnt only the more intensely; he gulped loudly, and again looked away, anywhere but at her knowing, challenging eyes. An abrupt change of subject was necessary.

"The... the bracelet," began he, gesturing towards her wrist. "I must still importune you for the possession of it."

Vanessa looked down at the item; her fingers traced its intricate links. "You had ample opportunity to simply *take* it from me last night, whilst I was… indisposed." She looked up. "*Why* did you refrain? What stayed your hand?"

Stirred by her acknowledgment, Francis replied, "perhaps, even in a man such as I, some small, stubborn fragment of… of honesty, some lingering scruple, yet remains."

A small, yet undeniably appreciative smile touched the corners of her mouth. The tension in the room seemed to ease slightly. However, the spark that made her so infuriatingly captivating quickly resurfaced. "In that case, Mr Sheringham, I fear you may, by your own commendable, if ill-timed, honesty, have forfeited your moment."

Perhaps it was his sudden, crestfallen expression — for his face fell, good reader, like a badly made *soufflé* — but she immediately appeared to soften. "Oh, do not look so utterly stricken, sir! I am merely teasing, indulging a wicked whim. Your offer… I *shall* give it my most careful and due consideration."

***

The hours had rolled by with that peculiar slowness which attends captivity, and we find Miss Vanessa Lockwood contemplating her own altered reflection in the looking-glass' dim surface. The single candle revealed the unfortunate state of her attire — the elegant evening gown, witness to such recent chaos, was now creased, stained, and bore the general appearance of having lost a prolonged battle with a haystack. As she endeavoured to restore some order to her tresses, while simultaneously marshalling her inner resources for the great enterprise ahead, the sound of a key turning in the lock broke the room's heavy silence.

Her heart gave a sudden leap. "Courage, my girl," whispered she to her dishevelled reflection, which seemed to nod back in conspiratorial agreement. "Fortune, as the ancients aver, favours the bold. It *must* be done." She turned to the door.

With a mournful groan that spoke of hinges long unacquainted with oil, the door creaked open, revealing the figure of Harry.

"Evenin', Miss." He rubbed his eyes, appearing decidedly sleepy, blinking owlishly and stifling a prodigious yawn. "Come for the tray, I 'ave."

"Indeed, Harry," replied she. "It is here."

She lifted the silver tray — one of the last Brookside still boasted — from the dressing table beside where her modest, and largely untouched, supper had rested. As Harry shuffled closer, reaching out a hand, she hoisted the tray high and brought it down upon his unsuspecting pate with considerable, well-aimed force.

The blow produced a dull CLANG! A sound not unlike a cracked church bell. Harry staggered backwards a pace or two, emitting a pig-like grunt of surprise and pain. "Wot the bleedin'...?" began he in his accustomarily coarse dialect, shaking his head vigorously.

But Vanessa, wasting no time on scruples or apologies — for what is a damsel in distress but an agent of necessity? — swung the tray anew. This time, good reader, she put the full measure of her desperation and no small amount of well-honed feminine fury behind the blow.

The second impact, it must be recorded, was far more decisive. Harry's eyes rolled upwards into his head like window blinds, displaying only the whites, and he collapsed onto the dusty floorboards.

Casting the tray aside, Vanessa knelt beside her vanquished gaoler. With trembling fingers, she searched through his pockets, quickly locating the iron key to her prison. With this liberating item in hand, she rose, cast a brief, utterly unsympathetic glance at the recumbent, snoring form on the floor, and hurried from the room, locking the door behind her to ensure her erstwhile captor would enjoy an undisturbed continuation of his slumber.

With the silence of a shadow, she proceeded along the dark corridor until she reached the head of the main staircase. Here she paused, her hand on the balustrade. At length, hearing nothing but her heartbeat rattling in her eardrums and the usual creaks and groans of an old house, she began her descent.

With each foot placed with care upon the wooden steps, which threatened to betray her at every moment, she soon arrived safely on the ground floor.

Barely had she oriented herself in the direction of the foyer and glided towards the main portal, crossing the quarter-moonbeams which streamed through the tall windows, when the sound of two voices from behind a nearby door arrested her flight.

The one belonging to Francis was engaged with another — unfamiliar to her ears — in earnest conversation.

"... a most advantageous match, Francis, my boy," was saying (our heroine now realised) Sir Andrew. "Vanessa Lockwood possesses not only considerable beauty but, more pertinently, a fortune sufficient to restore the standing of this family. Attractive, intelligent, and exceedingly rich — she represents precisely the sort of bride who could enable you to make a fresh start, free from these current... *embarrassments.*"

Vanessa's blood ran cold. *Am I mere cattle to be appraised and bartered, a walking dowry to be sold and purchased for the restoration of a fallen house?* Yet even as this wave of indignation washed over her, a second, more powerful, current took hold — for must not a heroine poised upon the very threshold of freedom allow but a little vanity to prevail? Believing herself undone to miss the possible sentiments soon to be expressed by a probable votary, she tiptoed towards said door. Here, pressing her ear close to the wood, she listened.

"No, Father," came Francis' reply, his voice lower, more hesitant. "Such a notion... such a transaction... is a matter I cannot, and *will not*, entertain."

Indeed? thought a somewhat bemused Vanessa, her interest further ensnared by the labyrinthine complexities of our hero. *And why not, pray tell, Mr Sheringham? Does the prospect of my fortune, so callously discussed, not appeal to your... refined sensibilities?*

"And why ever not, my boy?" probed Sir Andrew, a distinct note of impatience entering his voice. "Have you taken leave of your senses? Are we to languish in genteel poverty forever? From my own observations, I would venture that you already hold the young lady in rather high esteem. Dare I say, you appear quite... *smitten?*"

Smitten? echoed our heroine, shocked and yet strangely pleased to hear of such a feeling in one who, erenow, she believed so singularly skilled only in the art of flattery and dissimulation.

"*Smitten?*" reverbed Francis, his voice thick with an emotion Vanessa could not immediately decipher. There followed a distinct gurgling sound of liquid being poured. "Father, 'smitten' is a paltry foot soldier sent to do a general's work! I am... *utterly* captivated. Mad for her! Never, in all my dealings with the fairer sex, have I encountered a woman who affects me so profoundly!"

Indeed, to such a degree does the immoderate fondness for praise transport some people — even when held under the most inauspicious of circumstances — that to lose any opportunity of receiving it is a most unpardonable offence. 'Tis a species of music to which even the most rational ear is seldom deaf. A slow smile spread across Vanessa's face. Yet no sooner was she aware of this herself than she drew her lips into a tight purse.

"Well then," pressed Sir Andrew, his tone softening slightly. "If that be the case, why not pursue the matter? Declare your intentions! Lay siege to her affections!"

A heavy silence ensued, during which our eavesdropper pressed her ear tighter still to the wood. Alas, at this pause — which went on perhaps a trifle too long — she was only found all the more incensed, all the more intrigued, all the more... well, something! Still and all, she was just beginning to give over all thoughts of him and their talk and to abandon her post when:

"Because," said Francis at last, "because, Father... I find myself in awe of her. Intimidated by her, even."

"*In awe?*" answered Sir Andrew. "*Intimidated? You*, who waylaid patrons on the highway with naught but your wits and an old pistol? *You*, whose reputation among the ladies suggests an almost reckless degree of confidence?"

'Tis not to be wondered at that a man, in whom neither love nor honour had hitherto been known to place any great restraint upon his appetites, should, at so vital a juncture, find himself utterly disarmed by the mere idea of a woman's virtue. Where before he would merely have indulged his baser instincts, triumphed over her beauty, treated her in a fashion so accustomed to those women who are paid for their favours, there appeared to be something altogether different being fashioned in his breast.

"Ah, but Vanessa... she is not... *like* the local ladies," explained Francis. His voice, filled with a mixture of devotion and despair, ever so wonderfully flitted through the cracks in the old door into our snooper's ears. "She is... *magnificent.* A creature of a different, higher sphere. Wealthy, yes, but also possessed of such beauty, such strength of will, such... *intelligence*... She is perfection personified! Beside her, I feel... *inadequate. Unworthy!*"

Aye, at the culmination of such a confession — which revealed to Vanessa, with the sudden clarity of a lightning flash, the most astonishing and noble sentiments of humility in this most contradictory of men — she felt a warmth spread through her entire being.

Inadequate? Unworthy? The words echoed in her mind. Vincent Grant looked at her and saw only a glittering dowry. Lord Grant looked at her and saw a heavily fortified asset to be acquired. But Francis Sheringham — the shire's most infamous, arrogant libertine — looked at her and was terrified of her mind?

Again, Vanity, that persistent, universal, and most charming of human failings, urged her to linger, to savour yet further encomiums upon her manifest excellence. Yet Prudence, ever the sober-suited chaperone to Impulse, reminded her sharply that freedom lay but a few steps away, and lingering risked discovery.

Somewhat reluctantly, she drew back from the door.

Yes, she ought to go. Now.

As she moved towards the main entrance, her path took her past a centre table, which stood sentinel in the foyer. Here, she again paused; her trembling hand hovered inches from the front door's cold iron latch. A thought, sudden and decisive as a rapier's thrust, struck her. With swift fingers, she unfastened the bracelet — that glittering object of Francis' desire, symbol of his mother and, perhaps, in some strange, unspoken way, of the unwilling and complex connection that had formed between captor and captive.

Again, that Francis believed himself too unworthy to claim her, this found our heroine lost in a labyrinth of bewilderment. But she had not the time to ponder this now. By leaving the bracelet, she *was* returning his legacy, but more importantly, 'twas a silent validation of his worth — a testament that she saw the makings of a nobleman hiding beneath the rogue.

And so, with a gesture almost defiant, she hastened forth, placed the bracelet carefully upon the centre table's surface, whereupon she turned, flew back to the front door, unbolted it, and slipped out into the night's dark embrace.

As for our hero, perhaps a half-hour had transpired before he discovered our heroine had vanished. Francis stomped about the bedchamber; his words stumbled over one another in their haste to condemn, while Harry, the unfortunate catalyst of this domestic typhoon, sat miserably upon the floorboards precisely where the resourceful Vanessa had left him, nursing a truly prodigious lump upon his thick skull — a veritable second cranium, one might say. He attempted to shield his unfortunate person from the verbal — and, alas, decidedly physical — onslaught of his incandescently wrathful employer.

Sir Andrew stood by the doorway, observing the proceedings with a weary, almost philosophical resignation written in every facial twitch and readjustment of his limbs.

"You blithering blockhead!" roared Francis. He punctuated this eloquent address with a sharp slap on the back of Harry's already aching head. "You monumental, unmitigated cabbage! You were tasked with one *simple*, elementary duty! One solitary responsibility! To keep watch! And you, in your infinite stupidity, allowed her — a slip of a girl! — to overpower you with a common *dinner tray?!*"

"She took me by surprise, sir!" whimpered Harry. "Fair ambushed me, she did! Came at me like a... like a Harpy! Stronger than she looks, that one is!"

"*Stronger than she looks?*" Francis delivered yet another swift kick to Harry's backside. "That, you snivelling poltroon, is the most pathetic, the most utterly contemptible excuse for gross, unforgivable incompetence that I have ever had the misfortune to hear! Because of *your* idiocy, *your* damnable lack of vigilance, I now stand to lose everything! Everything, do you hear? The estate! My last desperate chance to restore our fortunes!"

As Francis drew back his foot for another blow, Sir Andrew intervened. "Francis, cease this futile and frankly unedifying assault! Berating this poor wretch achieves nothing. Instead of expending your energy on violence, you would be better served riding out immediately to search for the young lady. She cannot have travelled far on foot in the darkness. There may yet be time to retrieve her — *and our dwindling* hopes."

***

Elsewhere, before Thornfield Hall's imposing façade, a scene redolent of preparations for some minor, though we might say illicit, military campaign was unfolding. A quintet of men, whose rugged attire and hardened countenances bespoke occupations more familiar with the breaking of heads than the tilling of soil, were mounting their sturdy horses. Their leader, one Jimmy, possessed a shifty eye and that peculiar swagger which marks the hired bully conscious of his master's protection. He surveyed his small troop with an air of command.

To this formidable company, already bristling with ill-suppressed belligerence and the promise of rough handling, was presently added the ever-eager Vincent. Perched upon his own spirited steed, he ostentatiously displayed a rather large and menacing-looking horse pistol, which, our reader may easily surmise, he handled with considerable eagerness to discharge. Lord G stood observing this impromptu muster, one hand stroking his luxuriant sideburns with that air of thoughtful, weighty self-regard so common to men whose perceived importance resides more demonstrably in their inherited station and landed acreage than in any notable brilliance of their intrinsic substance.

Catching his employer's august eye, Jimmy offered a jerky, ingratiating wave — a gesture clearly intended to convey both deference and brutal competence. "Fear not, m'lord!" declared he. "We'll fetch 'im back for ye, right enough! Dead or alive, makes no odds to us, so long as the pay's good!"

A slight frown creased His Lordship's brow. This fleeting expression, we may suspect, arose not from any wellspring of tenderness towards the fugitive highwayman, nor indeed from any moral qualms regarding the proposed methods, but rather from a more practical, landowner's concern for the potential legal and social complications attendant upon an outright homicide. "Let us not, my good Jimmy, indulge in an excess of... unseemly zeal," cautioned he. "Alive, I believe, would serve our purposes quite adequately, and perhaps with less paperwork. Proceed with all due diligence, by all means, but also, if you please, with a modicum of discretion."

With a curt nod and a gruff signal to his ruffianly subordinates, Jimmy spurred his unprepossessing horse onwards. The small but determined posse clattered away, their departure raising a cloud of dust from the gravel driveway.

Chapter the Eighteenth — A Midnight Pursuit

Now, let the gentle reader picture our hapless heroine, lately escaped from durance vile, navigating the treacherous and decidedly gloomy forest. And at such an hour, mark you, when all honest, law-abiding folk are, or ought to be, safely abed; an hour when only creatures of the night — owls, foxes, and other such nocturnal wanderers — are abroad beneath the silent stars.

Having neither compass to guide her trembling steps, nor celestial guide save the indifferent, pale moon, which peeped occasionally through the dense canopy above, she ran with more haste than direction. Her breath came in ragged gasps. Her fine (though, as we have previously lamented) sadly abused evening gown snagged upon unseen brambles and thorny bushes, each rip a fresh assault upon her dwindling composure.

Alas! Fortune, that fickle jade, having but recently granted our heroine her escape, seemed now inclined to withdraw her favour. Through a dense tracery of interwoven branches and leaves, she espied a group of riders emerging from the inky gloom; figures, it must be said, whose rough aspect and general air of coarse belligerence bespoke little of benevolent intent.

'Twas, indeed, as the reader has no doubt already surmised, that very band of mercenary fellows despatched by Lord G, led by the unprepossessing Jimmy.

With the instinct of a startled hind, Vanessa sought concealment behind a nearby trunk, praying the gloom might swallow her whole. But fate, or perhaps more prosaically, the practised eye of professional villainy, decreed otherwise.

"'Allo there! Who goes a-skulking in the shadows?" The harsh voice belonged to Jimmy, who reined in his horse. His companions, following his lead, formed a menacing, inescapable semicircle around the spot where Vanessa trembled.

A leer, which would have disgraced a gargoyle, spread across Jimmy's coarse features as he discerned the slender female form attempting to efface herself against the bark. "Well now, lads! What 'ave we flushed out 'ere, eh? A pretty little wood nymph, is it? Lost 'er way from the fairy dance, 'as she?"

At this perilous juncture, when our beleaguered heroine believed, by all the established rules of romance, she was about to be delivered into the grasp of these uncouth ruffians to be despoiled of her innocence and what-not, another rider trotted into the clearing.

'Twas none other than Mr Vincent Grant, whose arrival at any other time would merely have repulsed her, but which now — such is the nature of desperation — was most welcome. "Vanessa!" With a rare display of alacrity and decisiveness, he dismounted and hurried to her. "Thank Providence you are unharmed! What dreadful misfortune brought you to this pass? Come, my dear, allow me to convey you from these dangers to the undisputed safety of your rightful, and soon to be marital, home!"

Our friend Jimmy watched this development with visible pique. "Oi, guv'nor," said he to Vincent, jerking an unwashed thumb towards the silent, trembling Vanessa. "This 'ere... this particular bit o' muslin... she's yer acquaintance, is she?"

"She is my fiancée; I'll have you know!" Vincent drew himself up as he helped Vanessa, who, despite her aversion as much to him as the surrounding brutes, accepted his aid onto the saddle.

A grimace, eloquent in its vulgarity, twisted Jimmy's face. "Ah," grumbled he, his voice loud enough for all, including the object of his commentary, to hear clearly. "Well, ain't that just the way of it! Just when me an' the boys was anticipatin' a spot o' 'armless, friendly diversion among the shrubbery! Dashed inconvenient, I calls it!"

Now, good reader, let those amongst you who deem the female sex capable only of swooning at the sight of a mouse, or dissolving into tears at the first sign of adversity, mark well what followed. For Miss Vanessa, perhaps emboldened by the proximity of even such an indifferent protection as Mr Vincent Grant, reacted with a spirit that would have done credit to Boadicea herself!

Before Vincent, still fussing with the arrangement of her torn and sullied skirts upon the saddle, could so much as fathom her intent, her hand darted out with the speed of a striking adder. With astonishing dexterity, she plucked his pistol from its holster.

Despite the weapon's cold, terror-inducing weight, she clenched her slender fingers around it with a vehemence that surprised even herself. She was done waiting for rescue, done being the passive prize in the games of arrogant and contrary men. If Francis Sheringham could fight for his own fate on the highway, she could certainly fight for hers in the woods!

With a swift movement, she cocked it — the sharp click echoing in the sudden silence — and, taking aim with a fury that lent a terrifying intensity to her beautiful eyes, fired directly at Jimmy's leering visage.

The shot went wide, mind you, whistling with a venomous hiss past the ruffian's startled ear and burying itself with a dull thud in the trunk of a nearby tree. Yet, its effect on Jimmy was as profound and instantaneous as if the ball had found its intended mark.

He recoiled rather violently. The very daylight (or rather, the moonlight, to be precise) seemed to have been scared clean out of him. "Whoa there, Missy! Steady on, now!" His voice, which but a moment before had been the very trumpet of low-life insolence, now pitched several octaves higher into a reedy squeak. "Steady on with the shootin' irons!!" He held up his hands in placation whilst visibly shaking from head to toe. "Can't yer take a bit of a jest? Just a bit o' 'armless fun! No 'arm meant, Missy, none at all, upon my 'onour!"

Having recovered from his own astonishment at this martial display from his intended, Vincent now found his voice. "Enough of your insolent 'jokes,' Jimmy! Your orders were to apprehend the kidnapper, not to bandy insults with my fiancée! Attend to your duty, man, and cease this buffoonery!"

Chastened, and doubtless reflecting deeply upon the unpredictable dangers inherent in provoking well-born young ladies who are not averse to the use of firearms, Jimmy sullenly signalled to his equally disconcerted men. With muttered curses and backwards, wary glances at Vanessa, the troop rode off, somewhat less enthusiastically than before, deeper into the woods, resuming their original quest for the fugitive highwayman.

***

Sometime later in a benighted quarter of that same sprawling woodland, our principal adventurer, Francis, donning his black mask and attire and accompanied by the hapless Harry (whose recent cranial trauma seemed not to have impaired his ability to cling precariously to a saddle), pursued his own increasingly frantic search.

"Lost! She is lost!" Despair, black and suffocating, clutched at our hero's heart. "Oh, cursed fortune! I am utterly undone! Ruined beyond redemption!" He turned a venomous glare upon his unfortunate companion, who trembled under its heat. "Remind me, Harry, when tonight's execrable folly is finally concluded, that I have sworn a most solemn and binding oath to terminate your miserable, bungling, and entirely superfluous existence!"

Harry merely flinched, his already aching head throbbing in sympathy with his employer's rage. Wisely, he offered no reply, deeming no doubt silence, in this instance, to be the better part of not being immediately throttled.

But Fortune, that most ingenious and cruel of playwrights, having concluded the first act of our hero's tragedy, was, it seemed, already prepared to raise the curtain on a second, even more exquisite, farce.

As if summoned by his very despair, a group of horsemen suddenly materialised from the dense curtain of trees ahead. 'Twas Jimmy, no less, that captain of ruffians, and his ill-favoured band. Francis reacted with an instinct so common to the hunted; he spurred his horse towards the sanctuary of the undergrowth.

Yet, it seemed even the heavens themselves conspired against him this night.

From the clearing's other side, there emerged a second party of riders: Inspector Swords, no less, his ever-present Sergeant Morris, and two uniformed policemen, their lanterns cutting sharp beams through the darkness.

Caught thus between the hammer of hired thuggery and the anvil of the law, Francis found himself, for a dreadful, heart-stopping moment, utterly paralysed. His mind, usually so quick, so resourceful, was brought to a dead halt by this disastrous convergence of his manifold enemies.

Harry, however, possessing that lower cunning which thrives in misadventure, reacted with greater presence of mind. With surprising agility for one so battered, he slid from his horse and dived headlong into a dense, thorny thicket of bushes, vanishing from sight just as the two hostile groups drew closer with a great deal of shouting and equine confusion upon Francis.

The representatives of the law, being marginally swifter on the uptake: "Halt! In the name of the Queen!" bellowed Inspector Swords. "Drop your weapon, 'ighwayman, and yield yerself to justice!"

Our hero raised his empty hands in weary surrender. "I bear no arms."

"Dismount, villain!" commanded Swords.

Francis swung himself stiffly from the saddle.

By now, Jimmy and his fellow brigands jostled for position, surrounding him. "Gotcha, yer rascal!" snarled Jimmy, reaching out to grab Francis' arm. "Yer comin' with us, make no mistake!"

Inspector Swords bristled visibly at this unseemly civilian interference. "And *who*, sirrah, might *you* be, to lay hands upon a prisoner of the Crown?"

"We're Lord Grant's men, that's *who*!" Jimmy puffed out his chest. "'is Lordship sent us specially to apprehend this villain! He's *our* catch!"

"Lord Grant, is it?" Swords sniffed with undisguised contempt. "'is Lordship, it would appear, entertains the entirely erroneous delusion that *he* administers justice in this county! That, sir, is the prerogative of the Crown, vested, I'll 'ave you know, in *us*, its duly appointed officers! Stand aside, fellow, and do not impede the course of the law!"

But Jimmy, loath to relinquish his prize and the reward attendant upon its delivery, refused to yield. He seized Francis firmly by one arm, just as the stalwart Sergeant Morris, obeying a nod from his superior, grasped the other with equal determination.

"'e's ours!" insisted Jimmy, tugging with all his might.

"He belongs to the law, you insolent varlet!" countered Morris, pulling with equal, if more disciplined, force in the opposite direction.

And thus, good reader, our unfortunate hero found himself the unwilling nexus of a profound jurisdictional dispute; he became, in essence, the very rope in a most undignified tug-of-war, stretched precariously between the competing claims of private ambition and public authority.

Can tonight, thought he, *descend any further into the ludicrous depths of farce? Surely, this is some grotesque, ill-digested nightmare from which I shall presently awake!*

His face now rippling with unrestrained rage, Inspector Swords drew himself up to his full, if unimpressive, height. "Un'and the prisoner immediately, you insubordinate scoundrels! Or, by 'eavens, I shall place every one of you under arrest for obstructing an officer in the performance of 'is duty!"

At his signal, the two uniformed policemen raised their own firearms.

This unambiguous display of official determination, backed by the undeniable persuasion of loaded muskets, proved at last decisive. After what was undoubtedly a swift mental calculation that a brawl with armed constables offered little prospect of profit and a considerable risk of personal injury, Jimmy released his grip. "Alright, alright, keep yer 'air on," muttered he. "Come on, lads, let these officious peacocks 'ave 'im. Seems they're serious about their work tonight."

With exceeding ill grace, he remounted his horse, whereupon he and his men melted back into the shadows, leaving Francis solely in the law's custody.

Freed from all obstructions, Sergeant Morris wasted no time. He ripped the mask from Francis' face, revealing his identity to the triumphant inspector, and then proceeded to bind his wrists securely, tying the rope to his own saddle pommel.

"At long last, 'highwayman'!" declared Swords. "Your nefarious career of villainy is, I'm pleased to announce, definitively concluded! You shall face justice, sir, and I confidently predict for you a lengthy, and doubtless salutary, acquaintance with the inside of 'er Majesty's gaol!"

Our hero offered no resistance, no word of protest. Events had transpired with such bewildering rapidity that his spirit was utterly subdued. He allowed himself to be led away, a captive bound for judgement, leaving the forest's shadows behind him.

Meantime, from the thorny bush's concealing depths, Harry watched his master having been unmasked, shackled, and hauled away like a common felon. A feeling entirely unfamiliar to his usually callous and self-absorbed breast washed over him with surprising force.

He clenched a fist and struck it feebly against the rough bark of a nearby tree. "Blast and damnation! 'Twas all me fault! All me stupid, careless, blundering fault!"

***

Some hours later, within Brookside's gloomy entrance hall, Sir Andrew Sheringham sat slumped in a high-backed chair. In his hand, he held the gold and diamond bracelet Vanessa had left behind, turning it repeatedly, its intricate links cool against his skin.

Having made his way back to the manor by circuitous routes, Harry now stood shifting anxiously before him, wringing his cap in his hands. "Well, sir?" ventured he, breaking the heavy silence. "What's to be done now? With the young master taken..."

Sir Andrew sighed deeply. Yet, even in distress, the habitual shrewdness, the instinct for calculation honed by years of precarious living, did not entirely desert him. He continued to fiddle with the bracelet, now tapping it thoughtfully against the palm of his hand.

"Well, sir?" repeated Harry.

Sir Andrew looked up, his eyes meeting Harry's. A faint gleam flickered in their depths. He held up the bracelet. "This, Harry," said he with a new note of resolve entering his voice, "this may yet prove... useful. Indeed," — he tapped the bracelet decisively once more — "I believe I begin to perceive a way forward... Yes, I think I know precisely what must be done..."

Chapter the Nineteenth — A Bit of French, Cookery, and Duplicity

August 30, 1865

Scarce had the first blush of dawn begun to chase the lingering shadows from the eastern sky, and whilst the dew still lay heavy upon Thornfield's lawns, when a figure, whose furtive movements bespoke urgent purpose detached itself from the rose bushes' concealing umbrage. Here, we find the much-battered Harry — dressed to the best standards some long-dead Sheringham's ancestor might bestow — now embarked upon a mission conceived in Sir Andrew's troubled mind.

With the haste of a fox pursued by hounds, he darted across the intervening gravel towards the great house's back regions, aiming for that portal through which domestics, and occasionally clandestine messengers, might gain ingress.

Upon reaching the sturdy oak door, he paused, casting anxious glances left and right to ensure that no prying eye, whether from whistling stable-boy or early-rising chambermaid, had marked his stealthy approach. Satisfied for the moment that his arrival remained unobserved, he lifted the latch with cautious fingers and slipped inside, vanishing into a dark corridor.

This passageway, reeking of yesterday's boiled cabbage and everyday beeswax, served as a conduit between the servants' domain and the mansion's less frequented nether regions. With sundry gulps and prayers to the deity who oversees the passage of infiltrators, Harry navigated its gloomy length until the murmur of activity and the aroma of freshly baked bread guided him towards his immediate destination — the kitchen.

Here, amidst the well-scoured copper pans and the vast hearth, presided a solitary figure — a female cook, whose comfortable rotundity and flour-dusted apron proclaimed her the undisputed sovereign over this culinary realm.

While engaged in the rhythmic kneading of a great mound of dough, she happened to look up; her brow furrowed in considerable surprise at the unheralded appearance of this somewhat dubious-looking fellow. "Saints preserve us!" exclaimed she, planting her doughy hands upon her ample hips. "And 'oo in the name of all that's 'oly might *you* be, barging in 'ere afore the kettle's even boiled proper?"

Still panting slightly from his exertions and the anxiety of his errand, Harry attempted to gather his wits. "Beggin' yer pardon most 'umbly, ma'am," said he, his voice a trifle hoarse as he straightened his cravat, his words a little more refined since his recent schooling, "but d-d-d-dire necessity, as they say, compels me. I... I must gain speech, and that right quickly, with Miss Vanessa Lockwood. Urgently!"

The cook surveyed him from top to toe with a sceptical eye. "Miss Vanessa, is it now?" She sniffed. "And what pressing business could the likes of *you* — a complete stranger and, if I'm not wrong, playing dress up, too — possibly 'ave with the young mistress, and 'er scarce risen from 'er bed, I daresay, after the... excitements... of last night?"

Recalling, perhaps, some additional fragment of instruction regarding the persuasive arts so recently and painfully imparted by his now captive master, Harry endeavoured to imbue his plea with suitably dramatic weight and solemnity. "Good lady, I implore you, don't deny me!" He attempted a tone of grave, almost funereal, importance. "Delay could prove fatal! 'Tis... 'tis a matter of life and death, no less!"

This declaration, however theatrically intoned, produced little discernible effect upon the cook's robust sensibilities. She merely shrugged her flour-dusted shoulders. "Life and death afore breakfast, is it now?" She wiped her hands on her apron. "Well, the quality do 'ave their peculiar notions, and no mistake. Very well, fellow. Since you put it so... Wait 'ere. And dare not pilfer the silver! Or I'll hunt yer down till kingdom come!"

A few minutes later, the cook returned, followed by a figure whose appearance radiated an aura of formidable propriety. 'Twas Ms Brown, enveloped in a voluminous dressing-gown of indeterminate pattern.

Having expected someone else entirely, Harry stared in open-mouthed disappointment at the woman, whose hair, he now noticed, was constrained by a mighty array of rollers that resembled more instruments of nocturnal torture than implements of beautification. "You ain't Miss Vanessa!" stated he with that unfortunate bluntness which often characterised his discourse. "'oo are you and yer spangles?!"

Thus addressed, Ms Brown regarded him down the formidable slope of her nose. "And *who*," replied she, addressing the cook rather than the uncouth intruder, "is this... *stupid fellow*, clearly dressed in borrowed finery?"

"As I said, says 'e's got urgent business with Miss Vanessa," re-explained the cook with a slight, apologetic shrug. "Life and death, 'e reckons."

"I'm... I'm Mr Francis Sheringham's assistant!" stated Harry, hoping the name might carry some weight, or at least inspire a degree of fearful respect.

And indeed, the effect was remarkably instantaneous. Upon the mention of that name, Ms Brown's demeanour underwent a subtle but significant shift. Intrigue, it seemed, that powerful solvent of social stiffness, overcame her hauteur. With a dismissive gesture, she escorted — nay, full-throttled *shoved* — the cook out of her own scullery domain.

After closing the door, Ms Brown turned her full attention to Harry. "So, Mr Sheringham sent you? What message do you bring? What does he require of Miss Lockwood?"

Mindful of Sir Andrew's explicit, and indeed reinforced, instructions, Harry stood his ground. "My orders, beggin' yer pardon, are to deliver the message only to Miss Vanessa 'erself. Directly. I must beg ye, take me to 'er presence without delay."

Ms Brown drew herself up, her dressing-gown rustling with authority. "My lady requires her rest. She endured... a most trying ordeal last night. Whatever your business, however urgent, you may confide it to me."

Seeing his direct approach thwarted, Harry found himself at an impasse. Then, inspiration, or perhaps desperation, struck. *Now* was the time, perhaps, to deploy those newly acquired, if poorly understood, weapons of social intercourse so recently installed in him. He summoned to his battered countenance what he fervently hoped was an expression of irresistible charm (remembering, crucially, and with a supreme effort of will, to keep his lips firmly sealed over his unfortunate dental imperfections). He modulated his voice: "M'dear lady," affecting a treacly and utterly unconvincing quality, "forgive me... me bold presumption... but might I be permitted to observe... that yer eyes... they're the most beautiful, twinklin' orbs in the entirety of 'er Majesty's glorious Kingdom!"

Thus astonishingly addressed, Ms Brown only stared at him, clearly baffled at this unexpected, unmerited, and frankly ludicrous encomium. Even her rollers seemed to quiver with astonishment.

Undeterred by his audience's silence, which Harry mistook for rapt adoration, he pressed on. "Aye, in London town, I've 'eard tell, there be lasses aplenty, fresh and fragrant as the roses in springtime, 'tis true! But none, m'lady, not one amongst 'em, could 'old a candle to yer own radiant, shinin' presence! Yer... yer a veritable princess amongst 'em womanfolk, a queen amongst 'em duchesses!"

A flicker of something — probably disbelief warring fiercely with a budding, deeply buried vanity — crossed Ms Brown's face. She seemed, against all reason, to be really *considering* the possibility that this questionable messenger might, in his own rough way, actually perceive these hidden, hitherto unacknowledged glories.

Sensing the potential for persuasion, Harry deployed his ultimate weapon: the French phrase taught him by Francis for exactly such an improbable eventuality. He cleared his throat with a rasping cough and declared with an accent that would have made a Parisian butcher wince in agony: "*Je vous aime, mon petit oiseau!*" (Which, for those amongst my gentle readers whose education in the Gallic tongue may be somewhat lacking, translates, rather charmingly as: "I love you, my little bird.")

Our more attentive audiences might very well recall that certain masked ball, wherein a certain Musketeer — whose identity is inconsequential to this narrative — had whispered certain French phrases into this lady's ears, provoking a certain flutter in her breast and indeed nearly breached the chaperonely citadel.

The effect, despite the execrable — nay, *criminal* — pronunciation, was astounding. The sheer audacity of it, combined perhaps with the exoticism of the foreign tongue, seemed to rout Ms Brown's remaining scepticism. An almost girlish blush rose on her mature cheeks. "Very well," conceded she. "Follow me. And try to behave yourself."

And so, within the relative sanctuary of her bedchamber, Vanessa, clad in a fine nightdress, sat propped against her pillows, still bearing the languid air of one recently roused from slumber. Before her knelt Harry, his earlier clumsy gallantry now supplanted by an attitude of base supplication. Near the door, Ms Brown stood, observing the scene with an expression of keen, and not entirely disinterested, observation.

"Please, Miss Vanessa, I is a-beggin' ya," began Harry, his plea a torrent of unlettered oratory. "You must 'elp 'im! Inspector Swords 'as 'im fast! They mean to clap 'im in a gaol, or worse! Yer 'is only 'ope, Miss! The only one as can save 'im from the gallows!"

Vanessa pulled her wrap more closely about her shoulders. She shrugged, a gesture conveying more weariness than indifference. "And why, pray tell, should his fate concern *me*? Has the man not proven himself my tormentor? Did he not attempt to rob me on the Queen's highway? Did he not invade my privacy with his unwelcome attentions? Did he not abduct my person and hold me against my will in that dreadful, dilapidated house?"

At this, Ms Brown appeared to permit herself a knowing smile. "And yet, my dear," interjected she, "despite these undeniable and quite numerous grievances... you harbour certain... tender feelings for the rogue, do you not?"

Vanessa turned her affronted gaze upon her chaperone. "It is a phenomenon I confess I have never fully comprehended, nor indeed entirely approved of. This peculiar, almost perverse, fascination that women — even sensible women — seem to possess for adventurers, for scoundrels, for men who live quite deliberately outside the respectable bounds of conventional society!"

Ms Brown cast a sly sideways glance towards the still hopefully kneeling Harry and allowed her smile to widen into something approaching a conspiratorial grin. "Ah, but such men, Miss, often possess a certain... charm, a dangerous allure; would you not agree? Especially if they have a command, however imperfect, of the French language."

"*French*?" Vanessa looked questioningly at her companion. "What *are* you talking about?" Here, she perhaps not only noted the peculiar look in her chaperone's eyes but also the direction in which they were most steadfastly fixed. "What in heavens does that have to do with my current plight?"

"Follow your heart, my child," said Ms Brown, all sentimental encouragement and perhaps an escaping blush or two. "*Suis ton cœur!* In matters such as these, the heart often perceives truths hidden from the rational mind."

This appeal, simple though it was, one might argue, is entirely inapposite to established truth! For did not King Solomon himself — or was it some other equally wise Bible person? — admonish us most sternly against the deceitful inclinations of that very organ? Even going so far, if memory serves, as to call it treacherous and desperately wicked! — Aha! 'Twas the prophet Jeremiah who elucidated on this subject. But enough of such sober moralising for now, lest we spoil the moment's tender sentiment.

Such words seemed to strike a deeply resonant chord within Vanessa's breast. She needed, if I may be so bold, little further persuasion, for, if the unvarnished truth be told, her anger at Francis was already considerably diluted. Nevertheless, the strict demands of propriety, the absolute necessity of maintaining a maidenly reluctance, required a brief, a final, a largely performative struggle.

"But I must consider..." began she, ticking off the points on her fingers, "... my dignity *must* be upheld... my virtue protected... my social standing preserved..."

A few moments of contemplative silence hung in the air, during which this brief combat between prudence and inclination was waged. The internal debate, however, was evidently short, and its outcome never truly in doubt.

"Ms Brown," declared she suddenly, casting aside all pretence of deliberation, "fetch me my riding dress and coat. At once!"

***

We now return to that chamber dedicated to the noble pursuit of public order and the stern discouragement of vice; a rather plain, somewhat gloomy space, furnished chiefly with a sturdy desk of much-scarred oak, several uncomfortable-looking chairs designed more for penance than for repose, and that faint aroma of damp wool, stale ink, spilt porter, and stubbornly thwarted justice.

Behind this very desk, enthroned like a minor deity in his own small temple of bureaucracy, sat Inspector Swords. His countenance, usually composed in lines of unbending authority, was at this moment a study in almost comical bewilderment. For seated opposite him, radiating an aura of distressed, yet captivating elegance, was none other than Miss Vanessa Lockwood herself.

"If I apprehend your meaning correctly, Madam," began the inspector, "you assert that the fellow we arrested last night in the woods... the masked individual identified as one Francis Sheringham... is *not*, in fact, the highwayman who's been plaguing our district?"

"Indeed, Inspector, that is precisely my assertion," replied she, eyes wide with simulated sincerity. "Oh, believe me, sir, I too have suffered at the hands of that dreadful predator of the highways! A most terrifying encounter!" She paused and pressed her delicate fingers to her temple.

The inspector waited, his official attention manifestly captured more by this affecting vision of beleaguered beauty than by any thoughts on the administration of justice.

"The fiend who accosted *me*," continued she, "bore no resemblance to Mr Sheringham. He was... let me see... considerably taller, *yes*, and rather stout about the middle. His hair, what little I could see of it beneath his villainous hat, was quite grey, and he spoke... most distinctly with that lilting accent one so often associates with Cornwall."

Inspector Swords stroked his moustache in a gesture indicating profound perplexity. "Extraordinary," muttered he. "*Most* extraordinary, indeed. The description you provide differs significantly from other accounts we've received regarding these recent outrages. It implies... good heavens! — it implies we may be contending with *multiple* villains on our roads!"

"It would seem possible, Inspector," gravely agreed she. "The times are indeed perilous. But of one thing I can assure you, with the utmost certainty: Mr Francis Sheringham, whatever his other faults may be" — and here she allowed a fleeting expression of private grievance to cross her enchanting features — "is assuredly *not* one of them. He is no more a highwayman than... than you are, Inspector! On that, sir, you may rely implicitly upon my word as a lady."

Now, 'tis a truth universally acknowledged (or at least, frequently observed by narrators of a philosophical bent) that a declaration made by a young lady of beauty, breeding, and evident high-social standing often carries considerably more weight with gentlemen of a certain susceptible disposition than might the sworn, corroborated testimony of a dozen less-prepossessing witnesses.

Despite his uniform, his office, and his long experience with the duplicity of mankind (and womankind), Inspector Swords was not, alas, immune to these influences. "Forgive my insistence, Madam," said he, leaning closer in his creaking chair, "but one point remains unclear. If Mr Sheringham is merely an innocent citizen, then what was 'e doing in the dead o' night wearing a mask? Such attire, you must admit, invites suspicion."

Here, Vanessa hesitated. Lowering her gaze for a second or two and allowing a delicate blush (or a masterful imitation thereof) to colour her cheeks, she appeared, to the inspector's manifestly sympathetic eye, to be grappling with the awkward necessity of confessing some feminine indiscretion.

"Ah" — she twisted a ribbon on her gown — "that, Inspector... that, I fear, requires a somewhat... a rather delicate explanation."

Undoubtedly scenting not conspiracy or villainy, the inspector leant closer still. "Pray continue, Madam. You may speak freely."

With an air of the most charming guilt adopted: "Well," faux confided she, "I am aware, Inspector, that such activities may not be deemed entirely... appropriate... for a lady in *my* somewhat conspicuous position, particularly given my recent and very public... *engagement* to Mr Vincent Grant. But..." She paused, meeting his gaze with orbs that pleaded for understanding, "... Mr Sheringham and I... we find ourselves, from time to time, occasionally drawn to... well, sir, to certain... *nocturnal diversions.*"

The inspector blinked. "Nocturnal diversions?"

"Games, Inspector," elaborated Vanessa, ensuring that the blush upon her cheeks deepened to a hue of the most becoming sort. "Innocent games, you understand, played out under the friendly, concealing cloak of darkness. Disguises... masks... charades, if you will... they add a certain... a certain *frisson*... a little spice, shall we say, to our otherwise unremarkable encounters."

As the scandalous fabrication left her lips, a very real, unbidden flush heated her cheeks. She was, after all, risking her entire reputation to save a rascal, yet the most terrifying part was not the lie itself, but the sudden, heart-racing realisation of how much she wished it were true.

And the implication, though artfully vague, was devastatingly potent.

Inspector Swords, a man perhaps more thoroughly versed in the blunt, unvarnished realities of crime and punishment than in the subtle, sophisticated nuances of aristocratic amusements, betrayed in his weather-beaten cheeks an uncomfortable warmth. No doubt, the thought of this refined young lady engaging in secret, masked assignations in the woods, however innocent she might claim them to be, was most likely enough to induce an almost paralysing sense of social awkwardness.

"Ah! I... I perceive... Yes, quite... Quite so..." stammered he, his composure deserting him entirely. He cleared his throat vigorously, a loud, rasping sound in the sudden silence. "Say no more, Madam! I comprehend perfectly! A private matter, entirely! Of no concern whatsoever to the constabulary!"

Vanessa bestowed upon him a smile of dazzling gratitude; a smile capable of melting sterner hearts than Inspector Swords possessed. "Thank you for your understanding, Inspector." She rose with a most graceful yet abashed air. "You have been most kind. And... I trust this conversation, particularly the latter part, may remain entirely confidential?"

"Absolutely, Madam! Implicitly!" He rose as well. "My word upon it as an officer and a gentleman! Discretion, Madam, is the soul of our profession... or ought to be." He bowed her out of his office with a deference bordering on reverence.

The moment the door shut behind her, the inspector's expression underwent a dramatic transformation. The flush of what was patent embarrassment faded, replaced by the pallor of frustration. He stared at the closed door, then brought a fist down upon his desk with a resounding *THWACK*!

"Curse this affair!" exclaimed he. "Just when I was certain, positive, I'd finally collared that infernal, elusive highwayman! Fooled again! Led up the garden path! Confound it all! Confound all women and their bewitching ways!"

And so, good reader, we leave poor Inspector Swords to contemplating the chameleon-like nature of criminals; the bewildering complexities introduced into the straightforward business of law enforcement by the gentler, yet infinitely more perplexing, sex; and the general unsatisfactoriness of a provincial policeman's lot in a world where masks may signify not villainy, but merely the aristocracy's eccentricity.

Chapter the Twentieth — Pretensions, Playmates, Prisons, Plans

August 31, 1865

Within that chamber at Brookside, designated as the study, sat Sir Andrew Sheringham. His posture bespoke a certain weary resignation to the slings and arrows of outrageous fortune, yet his fingers, drumming restlessly upon the desk's surface, betrayed an underlying agitation. Before him stood Francis, lately liberated, yet exhibiting none of the joyful relief or exuberant gratitude one might reasonably expect from such a fortunate deliverance.

"It avails us nothing, Francis, not a whit," flatly stated Sir Andrew. "Freedom is but a mockery when accompanied by utter destitution. The deadline approaches, and we lack the means to satisfy Grant. The estate is as good as lost."

Roused from his morose carpet-gazing contemplation, Francis commenced pacing the room. "Lost!" echoed he as the situation's bitterness stung his tongue. "To think it should come to *this*! That Brookside — the legacy of generations — should be forfeited! If only that cursed ransom had been secured! If only... if only Vanessa had not proven so confoundedly resourceful..."

While he spoke so vehemently of the lost ransom, an ache of another kind lodged in his chest. He was free, yes. But the thought of never seeing that challenging, brilliant spark in her eyes again felt, in that moment, a far heavier sentence than the gallows themselves.

"You should rather direct your gratitude, ungrateful boy, towards Providence and the timely intervention of Miss Lockwood for your present liberty. Engaging in common highway robbery, Francis, however pressing you may have deemed the need, was an act of the most reckless foolishness!"

"*Foolishness*? It was madness!" Francis struck his forehead with the loathing palm of his hand. "To have risked so much, to have imperilled my very life and liberty, and worse, far worse, to have caused *her*, Miss Lockwood, such profound distress, such terror... I shall never, never forgive myself for this catastrophic folly!"

"Regret, my son, however sincere, will not, alas, replenish our empty coffers nor satisfy the ravenous appetite of our creditors. We must face the reality of our situation. The pittance remaining from your mother's legacy may suffice to establish us elsewhere, albeit in considerably reduced circumstances. A new life perhaps free from the burdens of this place..."

Francis stopped his agitated pacing. "No! There must be some other recourse! Some avenue yet unexplored! Perhaps... perhaps if I were to approach Lord Grant myself? Appeal to his sense of decency, if such a quality exists within his grasping soul? Beg for an extension, plead for mercy, for more time to..."

The mere utterance of the word "beg" visibly ignited a spark of fierce indignation in Sir Andrew's aged breast. He bolted upright in his chair, his weary frame suddenly infused with a forgotten energy. "*Beg*?" His voice rang out. "*Beg* Grant? *Never*! Have you forgotten who you are? Have you forgotten the blood that flows in your veins? A Sheringham may face ruin; he may face poverty; he may face exile to the furthest, most inhospitable corners of the earth; but he shall *never*, do you hear me, *never* stoop to beg for crumbs from the table of a vulgar money-lender like Grant! Our honour, Francis, our dignity at least, remains to us, inviolate and untarnished!"

***

Some several hours later, Francis exited his home's shadowy doorway, beset by fortune's frowns. In his hand, he held a folded letter, sealed with an air of urgent secrecy. With a furtive gesture, he beckoned to the faithful Harry, who lounged nearby upon a stone bench, awaiting his master's orders with his customary air of indolent readiness.

Leaning close, so that his words might not be carried upon the breeze to any unwanted ear, Francis whispered instructions into his servant's ear, accompanying his low-voiced words with the delivery of the aforementioned missive. Harry listened and nodded his understanding with a gravity that bespoke the seriousness of the charge. Then, pocketing the letter, he hurried away down the gravelled drive with a sudden burst of speed, vanishing from sight.

***

Meanwhile, on a different stage, other dramas, albeit of a less financially pressing nature, were unfolding. On the verdant stretch of greensward bordering the extensive Grant estate, Vincent was engaged afresh in the practice of pistol shooting. Under the watchful eye of his hired instructor, he stood, legs planted firmly apart and pistol raised.

A little distance away, seated upon the grass like Dresden shepherdesses in some charming pastoral idyll (though conspicuously lacking in sheep), Miss Vanessa and Ms Brown were engaged in that desultory chatter peculiar to ladies at leisure.

Vincent took a deep breath. He sighted along the pistol barrel. The instructor, venturing a momentary emergence from behind a stout oak, nodded — a gesture perhaps more hopeful than confident.

A sharp, sudden CRACK! echoed through the quiet afternoon air.

Downrange, on the target's stark white face, a black hole appeared — astonishingly, miraculously, *precisely* in the painted circle's very centre! A perfect bullseye!

A look of stupefied surprise, swiftly followed by beaming triumph, spread across Vincent's face. He lowered the pistol and shook a fist in boyish exultation. The instructor permitted himself a satisfied, if somewhat tight, grin.

From their comfortable vantage point on the grass, Vanessa and Ms Brown exchanged glances of wide-eyed astonishment. That Vincent, whose previous attempts at manly pursuits had generally resulted in near-misses or minor calamities, should achieve such spectacular success was indeed a matter of disbelief.

***

Not long thereafter, a scene of an altogether different species was to be observed. Upon a secluded oaken bench, strategically positioned amidst a profusion of fragrant blooming roses, sat our erstwhile emissary, Harry. He was engaged not, as one might expect, in the immediate delivery of his master's urgent message, but rather in the far more agreeable pursuit of amorous dalliance. His companion, we may easily deduce, was none other than the recently conquered Ms Brown, her face wreathed in smiles that did battle with a becoming coyness.

Emboldened by his previous success, Harry leant close, whispering some new and audacious compliment or outrageous jest into her ear — a remark, whatever its precise content, which elicited from the lady a delighted giggle, a hand to her mouth, and some shocking colour to her cheeks.

"La, Mr Harry!" exclaimed she at length, tapping his arm playfully with her French-made fan (an instrument she now wielded with considerable flirtatious skill). "You possess a tongue dipped in the purest honey!"

A little more than encouraged by this reception, Harry, casting aside all troublesome thoughts of social disparity, class distinctions, or the proper boundaries between master and servant (or, in this case, servant and lady's companion), leant closer still. And then, good reader — with Ms Brown, far from pulling away in maidenly alarm, rather puckering her lips into what was undoubtedly the very invitation her nigh toothless lover prayed for — the two transacted a kiss. Oh, how this chronicler does wince at such an image! A kiss, it must be said, delivered with all the unfeigned enthusiasm of youthful lovebirds billing and cooing upon a sun-dappled springtime bough.

After a moment, Harry at last recalled the purpose of his visit. "Alas, duty calls, me charming nightingale!" He rose from the bench. "But anticipate me swift return. *Je vous vois bientôt, ma jolie.*" (which translates, with Harry's unique phonetic interpretation, to something approximating: "I see you soon, my pretty one.")

"*Oui!*" sighed Ms Brown, fluttering her eyelashes with a skill that quite belied her years of *supposed* innocence. "I shall count the very hours until that *moment heureux.*"

"A moment of 'orror?" replied our limited-in-the-French-tongue ambassador, his brow furrowed in confused concern.

"A *happy moment,* my irksomely charming fellow," clarified the chaperone with a chuckle.

"Ah..." Harry scratched his head. At any rate, as he turned to leave, he slapped his pocket. "Saints above! Near forgot the very reason for me intrusion upon yer delightful company!" He produced the folded letter entrusted to him by Francis. "A message, m'dear, for yer mistress. From Mr Sheringham 'imself. 'e awaits 'er reply with the utmost impatience, or so 'e charged me to convey."

He handed the letter to his new co-conspirator, offered a roguish wink that promised further delights, and sauntered away down the garden path, whistling a cheerful, if slightly off-key, tune, evidently well pleased with the unexpected progress of his own affairs, regardless, for the moment, of his master's.

***

Concurrently, within Thornfield Hall's formal dining room, a scene of quiet domesticity prevailed. Vanessa, Lady G, and Vincent were partaking of a light luncheon, the conversation perfunctory, the atmosphere almost peaceful.

Without warning, the dining-room door burst open with such explosive force that it slammed against the panelled wall. And into the room stormed the master of the house, Lord G himself, a human tempest of unchecked fury. His face was suffused with a colour that did great violence to the pastoral scenes upon the wallpaper; his chest heaved as if he had run a great distance.

"This," bellowed he, his voice hoarse, almost strangled with the intensity of his emotion, "this is an INFAMY! An OUTRAGE! A scandal beyond all bearing!"

Startled from their meal, the room's occupants could only stare at him, their forks suspended mid-air, and their expressions a mixture of shock and alarm.

Accustomed through the long and weary experience of her husband's volcanic temper, Her Ladyship was the first to reply. "Good heavens, my lord! My dear husband! Whatever is amiss?"

His Lordship ignored his wife. His accusing finger shot out, pointing directly at Vanessa. "It is SHE! This... this *viper* we have nurtured in our unsuspecting bosom! She has brought shame, invariable shame, upon *our* name! She has disgraced *our* ancient and honourable family!"

Vanessa turned pale; her hand flew to her mouth.

As for Vincent, he merely looked from his incandescent father to his stricken fiancée, his expression one of utter confusion. "*Vanessa?*" said he. "*Disgraced?*" He again looked at Lord G. "Father, I fail to comprehend... How? In what manner?"

In the corridor, meanwhile, just outside the dining room, Ms Brown had, with the quick, resourceful thinking born of long and often perilous service in a tumultuous aristocratic household, concealed herself behind a conveniently placed potted fern, peering out cautiously between its verdant fronds.

Just then, the dining-room door flew open again, with even greater violence than before. Lord G emerged, dragging Vanessa roughly by the arm. Behind them hurried the visibly alarmed and increasingly bewildered Vincent and Lady G.

"Father," Vincent attempted a placating tone. "Might I suggest that you are perhaps... over-reacting slightly? There may be some misunderstanding..."

"Silence, Vincent! Do not presume to interfere in matters beyond your grasp or comprehension!" His vice-like grip unrelenting, he propelled Vanessa down the hallway, up the stairs and along the corridor towards her bedchamber.

Upon reaching the door, he thrust it open and shoved her more than a little forcefully inside. "You will remain here, Madam! Locked within this room! Until the very day of your wedding! Perhaps a period of solitary confinement will teach you the propriety, the decorum, the basic sense of shame you so clearly, so disgracefully, lack!"

Before Vanessa could even probe what had occurred, His Lordship slammed the bedchamber door shut — the sound of which echoed through the corridor like a sharp thundercrack.

The definitive click of the key turning in the heavy lock followed immediately; a sound of grim finality.

And there she stood at the room's centre. Despite all the profit in the Lockwood tanneries, all her vast acres of prime agricultural land, she could be caged as easily as a stray dog. 'Twas as if she were not a person at all, but merely a vault waiting to be plundered.

Meanwhile, Lord G then turned to face his trembling wife and his blanching son, who stood gaping at this display of absolute, tyrannical authority. "Well?" demanded he, glaring at them as if they too were somehow complicit in Vanessa's transgressions. "What are *you* staring at, you *witless* fools? Have you nothing better to do than stand there like a pair of gormless, moonstruck statues?"

And with that, without even deigning to explain the facts behind his fury, he turned on his heel and stormed off down the corridor, leaving wife and son, and the ever-vigilant, and again hidden, wide-eyed Ms Brown — for she had transferred her base of observation from the fern to a more strategically advantageous potted palm — in a state of stunned, apprehensive silence.

Chapter the Twenty-first — Intercepted Intentions

Scarcely had Lord G's despotic departure ceased to echo along the corridor and the indignant footsteps of the retreating Grant family faded into silence than the decorative fronds of the potted palm rustled. From this leafy concealment emerged Ms Brown. Casting cautious glances along the now-empty passageway, she tiptoed with commendable stealth towards the very door behind which her young mistress had been immured.

Upon reaching this oaken barrier, this frontier between captivity and the uncertain liberties of Thornfield Hall, she executed a pre-arranged signal set aside for such times — three soft taps upon the wood.

Receiving no immediate response, yet trusting in the understanding between herself and the captive lady, she knelt and slid the letter heretofore entrusted to her by Harry beneath the narrow gap at the door's bottom.

This delicate operation completed, she rose and retreated a pace.

Within the confines of her chamber, now transformed from elegant boudoir to a veritable prison cell, Miss Vanessa retrieved the missive that had appeared upon the floorboards. Recognising not the hand, nor finding either crest or initials on the seal, yet perhaps sensing the source of the communication through that almost telepathic intuition common to ladies deeply engaged in affairs of the heart, she broke the seal with fingers that betrayed her agitation.

> *My dearest lady, permit me, your loyal Francis,*
> *before all else, to express the profoundest*
> *gratitude that fills my heart for your recent*
> *intervention on my behalf. To extricate me from*
> *the unwelcome attentions of the law, you have,*
> *I fear, placed your own esteemed reputation at*
> *considerable hazard, a sacrifice for which I can*
> *offer only inadequate thanks. I pray most*
> *earnestly that this noble act brings no*
> *untoward consequences upon your head.*

While holding the single sheet, she paced the room's length, her eyes devouring the words penned by the very man whose actions, unbeknownst to her, had precipitated her current predicament. And as she paced and read, even the voice of Francis Sheringham seemed to reverb in the troubled air around her:

> *Having presumed thus far upon your generosity, I find myself compelled by dire necessity to crave yet one final boon. It is my intention, however fraught with difficulty, to present myself at Thornfield Hall and there attempt, by reasoned argument, to persuade Lord Grant to afford some small extension to the deadline concerning my unfortunate debt.*
>
> *Might I dare to hope, Madam, that you would lend the weight of your influence, however subtly applied, to support this desperate plea? Should you condescend to perform this further act of grace, I swear you shall possess the undying gratitude of my enduring days.*
>
> *I remain, Madam, now and forever, your most humble, most devoted, and most obedient servant,*
>
> *F.S.*
>
> *P.S. Allow me also, if I may be so bold, to reiterate my sincerest, most abject apologies for any distress, anxiety, or physical harm occasioned by my regrettable, and frankly inexcusable, actions during these past tumultuous, and for you, I fear, most trying, days.*

Having concluded her reading, Vanessa sank onto the edge of her four-poster bed. With the letter clutched almost convulsively in her hand, she raised it, pressing the paper against her heart as if seeking to absorb some essence of the writer himself. A sigh escaped her lips.

Gone was the theatrical highwayman; gone was the arrogant rogue who had fumbled a classical statuette in her waiting room. Here, inked onto the page, was a man stripped entirely of his armour, beseeching her help as much as her pardon.

Her eyes (those twin stars lately employed to such effect upon Inspector Swords) now filled with tears of pity, of approbation, and, perhaps, good reader, of a more tender, more dangerously captivating, emotion still — fondness.

"Oh, Francis," whispered she to the unheeding room, "would that I could aid you! But alas, my own influence, and now my own freedom, extends no further than these four imprisoning walls!"

She pressed her fingertips to her lips, the memory of his arrogant, infuriating, intoxicating presence filling the lonely room. He had ruined her peace and endangered her life, and yet, knowing he was out there fighting for his survival made her present confinement feel a thousand times more unbearable.

Yet, even as despair threatened, the inherent resilience of her spirit — that spark of defiance that had served her so well in recent adversities — asserted itself once more. If direct intervention was impossible, perhaps indirect communication might still serve. Rising with renewed determination, she crossed to her elegant dressing-table, upon which lay the instruments of correspondence.

Seizing a pen and a fresh sheet of paper, she wrote swiftly, her thoughts flowing onto the page with urgent clarity.

With every stroke of the nib, 'twas as if the heavy chains of her father's will and Lord Grant's control were loosening with one breath and tightening with the next. She was no longer just a passive prize to be won — "I refuse to be so!" By actively plotting with Francis, she was, despite every uncertainty, choosing her own dangerous, thrilling allegiance.

When her message was complete, she folded it and secured it within a blob of molten wax. Then, hastening to the door, she raised a hand and struck the solid wood three times, mirroring precisely the signal she had received but moments earlier, trusting, with a prayer in her heart, that her faithful confederate remained within earshot.

A few agonising seconds elapsed.

Then, confirming her fervent hope, came the soft, answering TAP! upon the door's other side. Without hesitation, Vanessa knelt and slid the sealed missive beneath the barrier, entrusting its fate to Providence, to fortune, and to her chaperone's unwavering loyalty.

Chapter the Twenty-first — Intercepted Intentions

As for Ms Brown, having stooped quickly and retrieved the envelope the very moment its edge appeared, she straightened up with an in-breath of intention. But lo! What cruel, what malicious trickery! For scarcely had she turned, her heart still fluttering with a mixture of triumph and trepidation, than she found herself standing almost nose to nose with the imposing figure of Lord G himself.

He had evidently *not* departed the corridor as presumed but had lingered, concealed perhaps in some shadowed alcove, his black suspicions aroused and his cunning mind anticipating just such a surreptitious exchange.

Ms Brown let out a small cry of surprise and terror. Before she could even think to conceal the incriminating letter, His Lordship's hand shot out and grasped her wrist. With his other hand, he snatched the letter from her unresisting fingers.

A smile utterly devoid of all humanity and tinctured with a chilling malice spread hideously across his features. "So!" hissed he. "My vigilance is rewarded, it seems! I have been observing your furtive comings and goings, you treacherous, meddling weasel! Playing the secret messenger, are we? Facilitating clandestine communications beneath my very roof?"

Poor Ms Brown, caught thus red-handed and terrified! Words, excuses, pleas for mercy — all failed her. Resistance, she knew, was utterly futile and indeed dangerously counterproductive against such implacable authority.

Lord G tightened his brutal grip upon her wrist, causing her to wince in pain, and dragged her unceremoniously along the corridor like a sack of unwanted goods.

"Well," declared he, "if confinement is suitable for the mistress, it is doubly so for the interloping servant! You shall join her in captivity!"

And thus, the unfortunate, the hitherto remarkably resourceful Ms Brown was hauled away, her valiant attempt at loyal service resulting only in her own imprisonment.

***

The following morning found Francis in a state of extreme agitation. Within the Brookside study's familiar confines, he paced relentlessly back and forth. Every creak of the floorboards, every distant sound, seemed to heighten his suspense.

At length, the door opened, admitting Harry.

Francis spun around. "Well? Did you see her? Did you receive any word? Any reply?"

Harry shook his head. "Nothin', Guv'nor. Not a sausage. Went back this mornin', lurked about the kitchens like you suggested. But no sign o' Ms Brown, nor any message either. Vanished, she 'as, like smoke."

A deep, agonising groan burst from our hero's soul. He sank into the nearest chair. "Damn my impetuous folly! I have ruined everything! Sending that letter... placing Vanessa in further jeopardy... compromising her loyal servant! What madness possessed me?" He buried his face in his hands. "Oh, merciful heavens," muttered he into the shadowy obscurity of his palms, "what am I to do now? What possible course remains?"

***

Later that same day, Francis found himself once more within the decidedly hostile territory of Thornfield Hall. He had been summoned, or more accurately, compelled by the stark and utter lack of any viable alternatives, to face his ruthless creditor in his den.

He stood, a solitary, almost tragic figure, in Lord G's book-lined study.

Across the gleaming mahogany desk — a veritable battlefield of financial negotiations — sat His Lordship with an expression of unyielding indifference, while Vincent lounged in a nearby armchair, affecting an attitude of bored, almost insolent, superiority.

Both men regarded Francis with undisguised contempt.

"A regrettable situation, Sheringham," observed Lord G at length. "Most regrettable indeed. To find oneself deficient by the not inconsiderable sum of three thousand pounds... a pity."

Though his gorge rose at the man's insufferable condescension, Francis forced himself by a supreme act of will to maintain some semblance of outward composure. "My lord," began he, low but steady, "I implore you. Grant me but a little more time. Two weeks, perhaps? A mere fortnight? I assure you, my lord, upon my honour as a gentleman, the full amount, every-last shilling, shall be forthcoming!"

A thin, unpleasant character spread across His Lordship's mouth. He seemed positively to savour the spectacle of his proud neighbour: a Sheringham of

Brookside, reduced to such humiliating, desperate straits. "Your assurances, Sheringham, carry little weight, I fear. Time, like credit, has its limits. The deadline, as you are well aware, expires tomorrow evening."

Vincent, meanwhile, produced his lace-trimmed handkerchief and fanned himself with an air of exquisite tedium.

Desperation lent Francis a sudden, unexpected courage. "My lord, surely you would not — you *could* not — inflict such irretrievable ruin upon a fellow nobleman? Upon a neighbour whose family has resided, with honour and distinction, in these Somerset lands for generations, even longer, if I may be so bold, than your own esteemed lineage? Is there no consideration to be given for ancient ties, for common standing, for the simple bonds of neighbourly regard?"

To beg a man like Grant was to swallow glass, yet Francis forced every syllable past his lips. If Brookside fell, he would be a penniless exile — and an exile could never hope to offer a safe harbour to any woman, let alone a trapped heiress. In that moment, he realised he was no longer fighting solely for his father's house; he was fighting for the right to stand beside Vanessa — as improbable, impossible, as inconceivable as this sounded.

At this plea, Vincent emitted a sharp, derisive sound — a sneer thinly disguised as a delicate cough into his perfumed handkerchief. Lord G steepled his fingers, tapping them lightly against his chin.

The room's silence grew taut and heavy, thereby heightening Francis' already acute anxiety.

Then, at last, His Lordship spoke. "Very well, Sheringham, against my better judgment perhaps, and certainly against the advice of my more prudent advisors, I shall offer you one final — and I do mean *final* — opportunity. A last chance, as it were, to redeem your fortunes."

Vincent raised a questioning eyebrow, his expression clearly disapproving of this unexpected, and in his view, entirely unwarranted, show of leniency.

Hope, fragile yet undeniable, ignited in Francis' breast. "My lord! You are... you are too generous! Thank you! Whatever you ask —"

"Generosity, Sheringham, plays no part in this transaction," interrupted Grant. "Let us rather call it... sport. A little diversion to enliven a dull evening. Your fate, Sheringham — the fate of Brookside, indeed — shall be determined *tomorrow* night. By the turn of a card."

That spark within Francis' breast was brutally extinguished, replaced by a sickening dread. "Cards, my lord? But... but surely you are aware of my sentiments regarding gambling? It is a vice I abhor! Furthermore, I possess little skill indeed, scarcely any knowledge of the games involved!"

Grant's expression hardened; any pretence of affability vanished. "Your feelings on the matter, or your lack of skill, are entirely irrelevant, Sheringham. The terms are simple. Present yourself here tomorrow evening, precisely at nine o'clock, prepared either to discharge your debt in full — five thousand pounds — or to risk its recovery at the gaming table. Should you fail to appear, or refuse the challenge, you will vacate the Brookside premises by noon the following day. The choice is yours."

The chilling finality in his tone and the intransigent resolve in his eyes left no room for further argument, no possibility of appeal.

Defeated, crushed, Francis could only offer a stiff bow. Without another word, he turned, his shoulders slumped, his spirit broken, and quit the room.

When the door had closed, Vincent turned to his sire. "Why, Father? Why offer him even *that* chance? Has the insolent, penniless fellow not caused us sufficient trouble and annoyance already? Why not simply foreclose and be done with it? Seize the estate and send him packing?"

Lord G leant back in his chair. "Calm yourself, Vincent. There is no cause for alarm. Our debtor may accept the challenge out of desperation, but he possesses neither the funds nor, more importantly, the skill or the nerve to prevail. He is *not*," concluded he with absolute certainty written in every feature, "going to win."

Like a slow sunrise, understanding dawned on Vincent's face. He too now smiled, mirroring his father's smug, anticipatory satisfaction. "Of course." He chuckled. "Of course he isn't! How could he possibly? The man is a veritable innocent at the tables!"

Act the Third

Chapter the Twenty-second — The Eleventh Hour

Let the reader now picture Sir Andrew Sheringham, seated within the Brookside dining room's somewhat faded grandeur. The inclement weather, which had drawn a weeping curtain of monotonous drizzle across the Somerset landscape since dawn, precluded any form of outdoor activity. Thus, he sought a temporary distraction in the civilised ritual of afternoon tea. The porcelain clinked gently against the saucer whilst he contemplated, with a heavy heart, the imminent and seemingly unavoidable dissolution of his ancestral estate.

Into this haven of glum gentlemanly resignation, chaos, in its most abrupt and startling form, erupted.

Without so much as a preliminary knock, the door burst open. Sir Andrew jolted in his chair, sloshing a considerable quantity of hot tea onto the damask tablecloth. "Good Lord!" He clutched his chest. "Must you enter like a cannonball shot from a culverin? You have startled the very life out of me!"

Framed in the doorway stood our hero, presenting a figure both dramatic and alarming. Rainwater streamed from the brim of his hat and the shoulders of his heavy cloak, puddling upon the floorboards. Despite his sodden condition and his recent humiliating interview, his heart pounded with confident intensity.

"Father!" He strode into the room, boots a-squelching. "There's no time for pleasantries or apologies!" He stopped directly in front of the dining table. "You *must* instruct me — immediately, sir, without delay!"

Sir Andrew blinked, plainly bewildered. "Instruct you? In what, pray tell? In the art of polite conversation? In the proper manner of entering a room without causing apoplexy in its occupants?"

"In every artifice and subtlety of the gaming table! Every trick, every rule, every nuance of hazard, whist, piquet, poker — all of it! We have precisely four-and-twenty hours, sir, to transform me from a novice into a veritable card master!"

Indeed, Sir Andrew stared at his son as if questioning his sanity. The teacup trembled in his hand. "Cards?" echoed he, the single word manifestly encompassing a world of confusion and dawning apprehension. "Four-and-twenty hours? What in God's name are you talking about?"

***

And so, good reader, began a night dedicated not to restorative slumber, but to the desperate acquisition of perilous and potentially soul-destroying knowledge. Within the Brookside study, illuminated by several oil lamps, lay scattered those instruments of prospective ruin: packs of playing cards. Here, we are invited to observe an arduous nocturnal tutelage.

The master of this singular academy, Sir Andrew, first demonstrated the intricate art of dealing, his surprisingly nimble fingers manipulating the pasteboards with a practised ease. His pupil watched with a frown of such painful concentration as he followed the order of a shuffle. His lips moved silently as he attempted to commit the complex sequence to memory.

When our hero himself attempted the manoeuvre, his movements proved clumsy, his coordination unequal to the task; the cards, as if possessed of a republican desire to flee all authority, burst from his grasp and scattered across the floor like a flock of startled birds.

"Blast this infernal affair!" Francis tugged at his hair roots, nigh ready to flood the table with frustrated tears.

Sir Andrew sighed — a sound of weary resignation — retrieved the errant pasteboards and, without a word of reproach, which is perhaps the most cutting reproach of all, demonstrated the correct method once again.

Anon, the lesson progressed to the most important part of any card game — appraising what one is dealt. A tense silence filled the room, broken only by the soft flick of the cards. Here, Francis, despite his best efforts to appear indifferent, betrayed the wretched quality of his hand with a countenance of such comical disappointment — and several, albeit stifled sighs and groans — that Sir Andrew was obliged to tap the table sharply; a silent, yet eloquent, reprimand against that most fatal of all amateur errors: *honesty of expression.*

As the hours wore on, and the oil burnt lower, a single triumph — a winning sequence laid down by Francis — was met only by a curt nod from his tutor, who well understood the dangers of premature self-satisfaction.

Later still, marked by the inexorable drip of rain outside and empty teacups accumulating nearby, both men showed undeniable signs of profound fatigue — eyes red-rimmed, shoulders slumped. Yet the lesson continued, relentlessly, pitilessly on.

Throughout this ordeal, Sir Andrew provided a running commentary, imparting not just the mechanical rules, but the deeper, cynical philosophy of the unforgiving gaming table: "Observe closely, my boy," said he. "The first principle, which is to all other principles as the foundation is to the house, is the absolute mastery of one's own countenance. Beginners, Francis, invariably betray themselves. A telltale flush at an unexpectedly good hand, a tightening of the lips at a poor one — these are the open windows through which any man of sense may look directly into a fool's soul. It is fatal, my boy, utterly fatal."

"You must," continued his father, "cultivate an air of absolute, impenetrable impassivity. Keep calm, maintain an even demeanour, regardless of the pasteboards you hold. Let your opponent conjecture; let him guess; but never afford him the satisfaction, the certainty of reading your thoughts in your face. Remember, my boy, and remember it well: at the gaming table, the face is often a more potent weapon than the cards themselves..."

Francis nodded. A cold shudder seized his heart. Was he *ever* going to master this? How could he possibly mask his soul when he seethed with the thought of Vanessa? His ancestral home hung on the turn of a card, but the image of her locked in a bedroom by the very man he was about to face across the baize utterly consumed his mind.

***

As for our hero's rival in love and fortune, Vincent Grant had, under the broad and unforgiving light of the following day, engaged in his own, rather different, preparations.

We find him once more on that familiar, though somewhat damp, field of his former ineptitude, pistol in hand, facing the target. Whether it was that some latent genius, hitherto dormant, had suddenly awakened within his breast, or whether (as is perhaps more probable) mere Chance — in one of her capricious and contrary moods — had decided to make him her sport, we shall not presume to say. Encouraged, no doubt, by his previous miraculous success — as even the least promising of pupils sometimes do — he raised the weapon, aimed, and fired again.

And again he fired.

And then, yet again.

Lo! What *was* this? A veritable miracle that must set at defiance all known laws of probability?! For each shot struck true. Bullet after bullet found its mark, clustering about the bull's-eye.

Even Vincent himself, beholding this inexplicable apotheosis of his own martial prowess, could scarcely believe his eyes.

As the last shot hit the very dead centre, he lowered the pistol; his face broke into a grin of pure ecstasy. Overcome by this transport of joy, he turned to his stoic tutor and, in a spontaneous eruption of feeling that would have scandalised the morals of society, threw his arms around the bewildered man. He hugged him tightly, even going so far as to plant enthusiastic kisses upon both his weathered cheeks — much as a triumphant Roman general, in the very heat of his glory, might embrace a favoured centurion who had just secured the decisive victory.

The instructor, a man accustomed to the more reserved, more typically English expressions of satisfaction from his clientele — a curt nod, perhaps, or a muttered "Well done, old fellow" — endured this unexpected embrace with a mixture of profound surprise and professional tolerance. He reflected, no doubt, upon the unpredictable and often alarming enthusiasms of the aristocracy, particularly when they believe they have, at long last, stumbled upon a hidden talent.

Chapter the Twenty-third — The Highest-Stakes Gamble

And so, good reader, we transport ourselves once more to that chamber within Thornfield Hall's imposing walls. Here, under the flickering illumination of sundry oil lamps, the stage was being meticulously set — not for any innocent evening amusement, nor for the convivial fellowship of gentlemen at leisure, but for a far more sinister purpose: for cold-blooded plunder.

Lord G and his son moved with enterprising intent, arranging chairs around the gaming table. Yet, let the discerning eye note with particular care the placement of one *curious* oil lamp, positioned on a corner console. Its polished brass base gleaming with a baleful lustre, the lamp was situated not for the provision of light, as one might suppose, but for an insidious intent, as shall be revealed in due course.

Satisfied with the nefarious arrangements, His Lordship nodded. "Admit our guests, Vincent. Let us not keep them waiting."

With an air of smug anticipation, Vincent opened the door to two gentlemen: Sir Burton and Mr Russell.

They entered with a slightly obsequious air, common to those admitted to the inner councils of a powerful, if unscrupulous, associate. Vincent directed them to their seats, ensuring that the chair positioned most advantageously relative to the aforementioned lamp remained vacant — reserved for the evening's intended victim.

"Welcome, gentlemen." Lord G assumed the role of genial host. "Pray, be seated."

Settling himself, Mr Russell glanced towards the empty chair. "Are you certain of his arrival, my lord? Might prudence, or perhaps poverty, keep him away?"

His Lordship chuckled. "He will come, Russell, make no mistake. Desperation grants few choices. It is, after all, his final chance... though chance, I assure you, shall play very little part in tonight's proceedings. We stand ready," his voice dropped to a conspiratorial whisper, "to *break* the son, just as circumstances, aided by our own small efforts, conspired to break the father before him."

A round of low, sarcastic laughter greeted the callous remark.

Sir Burton leant across the baize. "Purely as a matter of academic interest, Grant," said he, "what odds would you lay against a complete novice prevailing in such company and under... shall we say... such *conditions*?"

Grant considered this notion for a moment, stroking his chin with an air so accustomary to men of deep thought. "Against seasoned, experienced players such as ourselves? A thousand to one, perhaps?"

At this mockery, Vincent smirked. "And should the dealer, Father, employ certain... *advantageous* techniques in the distribution of the pastecards?"

"Ah!" Lord G's smirk widened into a wolfish grin. "With a touch of digital dexterity from my astute son here? Let us say, a million to one?"

Mr Russell cast a significant glance towards the gleaming brass lamp on the console behind the vacant chair and just to its right. "And factoring in... your *strategically* placed and most helpfully angled illumination?"

His Lordship threw back his head and laughed. "With the lamp, gentlemen? Why, the odds become impossible to one! Utterly, delightfully, gloriously impossible!"

Catching his infectious enthusiasm, his companions joined in his mirth. Their collective amusement was, beyond all dispute, fuelled by the certainty of their impending, ill-got gains.

While this council of predators finalised their plans, their designated prey proceeded along the corridor leading towards the Game Room. Francis walked with a haste born not of eagerness but of grim necessity.

Hurrying behind him, her expression etched with genuine concern, was Lady G. She caught up to him just as he reached the door. "Mr Sheringham" — she laid a hand on his arm — "pray, be cautious. My husband... his companions... they are not always... scrupulous... in their play. He may seek to cheat you."

Though indeed troubled by her words, which compounded his fast-dwindling confidence, Francis offered a faint smile. "My dear Lady Grant, your concern does you credit. But alas, whether by fair means or foul, I fear my chances remain equally negligible."

Turning from her, he paused, his hand resting on the doorknob, and steeled himself for the ordeal ahead.

"Nevertheless," whispered she, leaning closer, her hand now gripping tightly his arm, "watch him. Watch everything. Carefully!"

With a nod of acknowledgement, Francis turned the knob, pushed open the door, and stepped into the unknown.

The game — poker, this novel pastime of the era imported from America, wherein the capricious whims of Lady Luck and the stern calculations of human skill so uneasily and often ruinously mingled — was underway. The air, already heavy with anticipation, hung thick and acrid with the smoke of expensive cigars and the sweetish aroma of fine French brandy. Chips — those innocent-seeming discs of ivory and bone, yet representing sums far beyond mere pocket money — lay in a growing pile at the table's centre.

Having settled into their roles, Sir Burton and Mr Russell diffused an air of relaxed, almost somnolent concentration, sipping their drinks. Lord G presided with unassailable authority. Only Francis — notwithstanding Vincent's repeated insistence as host that he partake of the glass — abstained from drink.

Now, Reader, steel your nerves and at last observe the premeditated villainy's vile commencement! As Vincent — in the role of a non-playing dealer — dealt the cards, his movements appeared almost too casual; the very model of fairness. Yet, mark you well how he positioned the deck when dealing it to the unsuspecting (though duly warned) Francis, allowing the highly polished brass surface of that strategically placed lamp to act as a most effective "shiner". This devilish device, angled with wicked precision, reflected the face of each card dealt to Francis, directly into His Lordship's unobstructed line of sight. And note further, when Lord G's turn to receive cards came. Vincent's nimble fingers, with an imperceptible subtlety, drew cards not from the top of the deck, as honesty and fair play would dictate, but slipped them deftly from the very bottom — a classic manoeuvre of the common cardsharp, ensuring that his father received a consistently, and most unfairly, favourable hand.

The inevitable, and for Francis, devastating conclusion of this first contest arrived with dismaying swiftness. Aided by his son's manipulations and the intelligence gleaned from the lamp's reflection, His Lordship swept the considerable pot of chips towards himself. He collected his winnings, a sum representing a significant loss for his opponent.

Francis stared at the depleted space before him; his face, read by his auditors, was one of dismay. And by Jove, did his eyes glisten with unshed tears of despair as his heart sank with every passing moment.

"Bad luck, Sheringham, devilish bad luck," remarked Lord G. "A costly round, that one. Five hundred pounds, I believe? A great pity, a very great pity indeed."

Ignoring the feigned, and frankly insulting commiseration, Francis looked appealingly towards the other players. "Gentlemen, surely we might play another hand? Grant me but a chance, a single chance, to recoup my grievous losses!"

Sir Burton and Mr Russell exchanged uneasy glances. They had, it may be surmised, already secured their predetermined share of the initial plunder, and now seemed distinctly reluctant to risk further entanglement, especially if their patron's victim proved entirely penniless. They shook their heads.

"No, no," said Mr Russell, making what appeared to be a show of consulting his pocket watch. "The hour grows late. And our own fortunes have suffered sufficiently for one evening, eh, Burton? We had best take our leave."

"Aye!"

Both men made to rise from their chairs.

"Stay, gentlemen, I pray you, be seated for a moment longer," intervened His Lordship, placing a restraining hand on Sir Burton's arm. He turned to Francis. "Allow me but a moment to persuade our good friends. Perhaps another round, a final round, might indeed be arranged for your benefit."

Francis nodded mutely, his heart leaping with desperate hope.

Lord G drew Sir Burton and Mr Russell to a shadowed corner of the room, ostensibly to plead Francis' case with them in private.

Left momentarily alone at the table, save for Vincent's sneering presence, Francis, though try he did otherwise, succumbed utterly to his distress. Before he even knew what he was doing, he repeatedly struck his forehead with the heel of his palm. 'Twas indeed a gesture of agonised self-recrimination, an attempt, though with little success, to regain his shattered composure, to marshal his scattered thoughts against the overwhelming tide of impending ruin.

Vincent watched this display of human anguish with a detached, ironic, almost clinical grin. For sure, that grin savoured his rival's exquisite torment.

In the room's corner, the conversation took a different turn. "You *truly* wish to continue this charade, Grant?" murmured Sir Burton. "The fellow seems utterly broken."

"Precisely!" Lord G's eyes glittered with devilish light. "Broken, but not yet utterly humiliated. I want to strip him bare, Burton! To take every-last shilling he possesses, every scrap of his damnable Sheringham dignity! I want to see him crawl, to beg for mercy!"

Mr Russell shifted with a look of mild discomfort. "Very well, Grant. We shall accommodate you. Provided, of course, that our own initial investments, plus a reasonable profit for our time, are guaranteed by morning."

"But of course, my dear Russell, but of course." Grant gestured towards our despairing hero. "Your loyalty, your discretion, shall be most generously rewarded. Consider it done."

Their scruples (if any they possessed) thus assuaged by the promise of profit, they returned to the table satisfied.

"Good news, Sheringham," announced His Lordship, resuming his seat. "My friends, in their boundless generosity, have agreed to one final round. But mark you well, Sheringham, this shall be the absolute, the unequivocal, last."

A sigh of relief escaped Francis' lips. He straightened his shoulders and steadied himself with a deep breath. This was his last — his only chance to salvage his situation. And he was going to do his all to achieve this.

"The stakes, however, remain as before," continued Grant. "An initial bet of two hundred pounds to open the play."

With varying degrees of enthusiasm, the players placed their money in the table's centre. Vincent picked up the deck, his fingers caressing the cards anew. He dealt to Sir Burton, then to Mr Russell, his movements swift and sure.

As the cards were about to come to him, Francis, pondering more assiduously Lady G's cryptic warning and his own father's sage, if cynical, counsel, observed more acutely not the descending cards, but his principal opponent.

There, in Lord G's face, our hero noticed it, unmistakably — his adversary's eyes were fixed, not on the dealer, not on the cards being dealt, nor on the players, but with an intense focus upon something behind Francis.

What has so captured his attention?

Vincent dealt the first card to Francis. Grant's gaze, however, repeatedly flitted to whatever it was behind where our hero sat. 'Twas now — whilst His

Lordship exchanged some meaningful looks with his son — that Francis shot a casual glance of his own over his shoulder. Indeed, the realisation struck him with sudden, sickening force! The lamp! Undoubtedly used as a mirror! A common, despicable cheat's device!

The wily old goat!

Vincent dealt the second card.

In that very instant, before thought could fully form, Francis acted. Feigning a sudden spasm of nerves, he flung out an arm as if overcome by a debilitating fit. His hand connected squarely with the offending oil lamp's base.

With a resounding crash, the item tumbled from the table, hitting the floor and shattering its glass chimney, extinguishing the flame and spilling its oil upon the carpet.

"A thousand pardons, my lord!" whimpered Francis with expertly affected distress. "How abominably clumsy of me! I... I find myself *quite* overcome... quite *unstrung*... with unbearable nervousness..."

A stunned silence descended upon the room, broken only by the spilt oil's faint hiss. Vincent scrambled to retrieve the fallen lamp, but a single look confirmed the obvious: its reflective surface was now oil-stained; its function as an instrument of deceit irrevocably compromised.

"No matter, no matter at all," remarked Francis, continuing in his pretended innocence. "We have sufficient light from the other lamps, I believe."

Sir Burton and Mr Russell exchanged visibly worried glances. Lord G, however, recovered quickly. He shot his increasingly nervous accomplices a subtle wink, a silent signal, no doubt, to remain calm, to trust in his resourcefulness. Clearly, he possessed a Plan B — his son's proven skill at dealing from the bottom of the deck remained a most potent weapon in their arsenal.

Finally regaining an air of composure, Vincent dealt our hero the remainder of his cards. Francis picked them up; this time, a genuine, albeit small, smile touched his lips. He had finally levelled the playing field somewhat. Vincent, meanwhile, proceeded to deal his father's hand, employing the bottom-dealing technique with clearly renewed focus.

As the players examined their hands, the silence in the room grew thicker with unspoken tension.

And so, the betting commenced.

Sir Burton pushed a small stack of chips forward with a shadow of reluctance. "With a heavy heart, I shall raise by three hundred."

"The fool that I am," added Mr Russell; "I shall match your three hundred."

Now it was Francis' turn. Notwithstanding the suffocating lump in his throat, nor the sweat which trickled down the back of his neck, he paused and glanced at his cards. Then, reorganising his countenance into one of impassiveness, he steadily met His Lordship's gaze. "I call the three hundred too, and raise it by all the cash I have left — one thousand pounds."

The pot in the table's centre grew considerably, a mountain of potential ruin or salvation.

Anon, a subtle frown claimed Lord G's forehead. He surveyed his own hand. It was strong, undoubtedly aided by Vincent's manipulation, yet perhaps not the invincible hand he might have expected. In his usual fashion, he stroked his sideburns, a tableau of calculating design. Naturally, he needed to crush Francis *now* to extinguish this nascent spark of resistance.

He signalled to Vincent, who pulled another box of chips from under the table and handed it to him. Lord G scooped a handful of discs and placed them on the baize. "I match you, Sheringham," announced he, "and I shall raise by... two thousand pounds!"

A collective gasp went around the table.

His Lordship looked at each player's face. "I can assure you, gentlemen, there are equivalent funds in my bank account."

The bet was enormous — audacious! — clearly designed to intimidate Francis and force him out of the game.

To be sure, he froze. The total pot now stood at six thousand pounds, more than enough to save his estate. Temptation tingled inside him. Yet, the sum demanded just to stay in the game — two thousand pounds — represented more than what he had left in the world, including the very clothes on his back and his loyal horse. To call the bet was to risk irretrievable ruin; to fold was to accept ignominious defeat and the loss of Brookside.

"Does any gentleman wish to exchange cards?" enquired Vincent, breaking the tension.

And now began a silent battle of nerves, a psychological warfare waged with subtle glances, feigned expressions, and trembling hands across the green baize battlefield. Sir Burton now frowned, his face a caricature of indecision; he discarded four cards, his dissatisfaction evident as he received replacements. Mr Russell exchanged three, shaking his head slightly, a clear indication that fortune had not favoured him with a significant improvement.

All eyes, heavy with expectation, turned to Francis.

Our hero hesitated; he gazed into the room's distance, then recalled his father's words:

"Try not to show your emotions. Beginners always tend to do that…"

Thus, maintaining a neutral expression, Francis spoke calmly: "Two cards, if you please, Mr Grant."

This request, so modest, so unassuming, yet entirely unexpected for a supposedly desperate man, provoked a visible flicker of surprise, perhaps even confusion, on the usually impassive faces of both Lord G and his son.

Vincent dealt the two cards.

Francis picked them up and looked at them, his face still that mask which he fervently prayed would secure him from looming disaster; and then, to the astonishment of all present, he allowed a broad grin to spread across his features.

In lieu of this confident transformation, His Lordship signalled curtly that he would stand pat, keeping his original, and presumably powerful, hand.

"The last bet stands at two thousand pounds to you, Sir Burton," announced Vincent. "Your wager, sir?"

Sir Burton sighed — and somewhat dramatically so — and tossed his cards facedown onto the table. "Too rich for my blood. I fold."

Mr Russell quickly followed suit, unwilling to risk further capital against his powerful patron, especially given the increasingly uncertain circumstances.

The contest was now solely between Lord G and our hero.

Francis, surprisingly far from being intimidated by this isolation, leant back in his chair. He projected an air of supreme, unshakeable confidence, like one who possessed a divinely ordained hand. "Well, my Lord," declared he, imbuing his voice with a newfound, almost insolent, boldness, "I shall certainly 'see' your formidable wager of two thousand pounds. And I shall raise by another thousand."

Silence. A profound silence.

"You match and raise me with what, Sheringham?" exclaimed His Lordship at last. "You have no money left."

Francis fixed him with a steady stare. He pulled a crumpled five-pound note from his pocket and tossed it onto the mountainous pile. "Along with this, I shall wager myself. If I lose, I shall become your servant until the end of my life, my lord."

Several gulps echoed through the space. To be sure, betting one's freedom was considered either an act of ultimate, almost insane, desperation, or of supreme, unassailable, god-like confidence. Even Lord G stared at Francis with a look of utter incredulity, after which he then glanced uncertainly towards Vincent, who could only offer a blank, wholly bewildered look in return.

And so, Grant looked back at his own cards — strong, yes, very strong undoubtedly from the expression one might have seen in his eyes. But were they, he indubitably thought, strong enough against the manifest certainty radiating from his opponent? He scratched his chin, then his ear. Doubt, an unfamiliar sensation, clearly began to cloud his accustomarily arrogant features.

Sensing his advantage, Francis tapped his fingers rhythmically upon the tabletop; a repetitive, almost maddening sound that seemed to amplify the room's tension.

His Lordship clearly hesitated. Undoubtedly, he pondered whether Francis' hand was truly sufficient. Were we to step momentarily into his mind, we would observe: *could Francis — the novice, this callow youth — against all odds, against all reason, possibly hold the winning combination?*

At any rate, the pressure mounted minute by excruciating minute. Beads of sweat, like tiny diamonds, appeared on His Lordship's august brow. With the back of his hand, he wiped them away. Giving up now would mean humiliation; yet accepting the bet and losing an additional thousand pounds would be even more devastating.

The silence stretched, thick and suffocating. Every eye in the room, including those of the now thoroughly unnerved Vincent, was fixed upon him, awaiting his decision.

Finally, with a low growl of frustration, Lord G slapped his cards facedown. "I fold!"

Sir Burton, Mr Russell, and Vincent stared uniformly baffled. Lord Grant, the invincible, the unyielding Lord Grant, folding? 'Twas almost inconceivable.

But for our hero, the terrible tension within him snapped. He slumped back in his chair, taking several deep, shuddering breaths. Relief, more potent and more overwhelming than ever before in his life, washed over him in a dizzying wave. "Thank God," whispered he to himself.

Then, before the others could fully process the situation, before any questions could be asked or accusations levelled, Francis pushed back his chair and stood up. With a sweep of his hand, he gestured towards the almost obscene pile now accumulated in the table's centre. "It is all yours, my lord. It's way over five thousand pounds. The largest, the most magnificent sum of money my unworthy eyes have ever beheld! But I do not care. Keep it, my lord — it settles all accounts, all debts, all obligations between us, now and forever!"

And with that, before any challenge could be issued or any astonished query voiced, Francis strode rapidly from the room.

For a rather long moment, the four remaining men — two defeated villains and two dumbfounded accomplices — sat frozen, attempting to comprehend the whirlwind conclusion to the evening's planned fleecing.

Then, Sir Burton and Mr Russell, their expressions hardening into a tableau of cold fury, slowly rose to their feet.

"A most... unexpected outcome, Grant," said the former. "We trust our earlier private arrangement still stands? You will ensure our not inconsiderable funds are returned to us, with the agreed-upon interest, by morning?"

They did not wait for an answer, but, with a contemptuous glare at their erstwhile patron, turned and departed, their profound displeasure manifest in the sudden chill that filled the room.

The moment the door closed behind them, Vincent snatched up the cards Francis had left abandoned on the table.

Indeed, as he stared at them, his eyes widened, then nearly popped from their sockets. "Father! He... he *bluffed*! The infernal, audacious scoundrel bluffed! Look! Look at this paltry hand! A pair of threes! A miserable, a contemptible, a positively lousy pair of threes!"

Chapter the Twenty-fourth — A Lady and A Vase

Flushed with the improbable triumph so audaciously snatched from the very jaws of impending ruin, Francis paused not for a single moment to savour his victory nor to contemplate the stunned faces he had left behind. His immediate concern was for another — for Miss Vanessa Lockwood.

Correctly assuming from our heroine's long-silence she had been confined to this house, he navigated the upstairs corridors, heading instinctively towards the wing where he recalled she had been accommodated.

As he hurried along — his boots echoing on the polished floorboards, his mind preoccupied with finding her, ensuring her safety, and even conveying the news of his unexpected deliverance — a particular door was wrenched open from within.

A hand shot out, grasping his arm. And before he could fully register what was happening, he was pulled unceremoniously off the corridor.

The door clicked shut behind him. He turned, startled and confused, to find that his captor, the author of this surprising abduction, was none other than Lady G, her eyes wide with a mixture of anxious enquiry and excitement.

In a state of *déshabillé* — a silk wrap loosely tied, her hair slightly disarrayed — she demanded breathlessly, still holding his arm: "Well? Tell me! What happened? Did he...?"

Still slightly disoriented by this abrupt change of location and company, our hero managed a weary but triumphant smile. "He did not. Against all odds, my lady, I... I won."

Elation, relief, covetous satisfaction exploded over Her Ladyship's features. "Oh, thank heavens! Oh Francis, my dearest Francis, I am so utterly, utterly happy for you!"

And then, good reader, casting aside all decorum, all pretence of mere friendly concern, she threw her arms around his neck, pulling his surprised face down towards hers.

Again, before Francis could react, her lips found his in a kiss that spoke not of congratulation, nor of simple relief at his good fortune, but of a rekindled, fiery passion and a deep, pent-up longing.

"Oh, Francis," murmured she against his mouth, clinging to him tightly, "how I have missed this! Missed *you*! We've been apart for far too long! Let us not waste another precious moment... let us make up for all the lost, stolen time, here, now, this very instant!"

Her embrace tightened; her intentions were, even to the most innocent observer, entirely, and thrillingly unmistakable.

Indeed, this author laments such unpardonable behaviour!

But Francis, his mind still fixed on the image of the imprisoned Vanessa, and perhaps, if truth be told, grown profoundly weary of the clandestine complexities and the inherent dangers of this illicit affair, resisted her advances.

Gently, yet firmly, he disengaged himself from her embrace.

The lady stared at him, her lips still puckered into a kissing bow, her eyes still shining with desire. Then, as his reluctance registered, her expression shifted with alarming rapidity. "Francis? What is *this*? What is wrong with you?"

He avoided her gaze and straightened his coat, trying to regain some semblance of composure in so emotionally charged an atmosphere. "Forgive me, my lady, but my thoughts, my concerns are... are elsewhere at this present moment. I must know... where is Miss Lockwood? Is she safe?"

The mention of Vanessa's name acted upon Her Ladyship like a spark to dry tinder. Her eyes narrowed into dangerous slits. Her posture stiffened. The warmth vanished from her face, replaced by a cold, almost venomous glare. "*Vanessa*?" repeated she. "Always Vanessa! It is ever Vanessa *this*, and Vanessa *that*! What, pray tell, is the precise nature of this sudden concern for my son's intended bride? What, I demand to know, transpires between you and Miss Lockwood?"

Our hero shrugged, attempting an air of nonchalance, though perhaps somewhat unconvincingly so. "Nothing untoward, my lady, I do assure you. Nothing improper. It is merely a simple, natural concern. After that dreadful, terrifying business in the woods... the kidnapping... the ransom... I merely wish to know that she is well, that she has suffered no lasting ill effects."

Lady G offered a brittle smile. "Miss Lockwood is... indisposed. Greatly overwrought by recent events. She has expressed a firm desire to see absolutely no one. She requires complete, undisturbed seclusion to recover her composure."

The implication was clear: Vanessa was unavailable, most particularly and most emphatically, to him.

A weighty gust sank Francis' frame. Unconvinced by this smooth, dismissive explanation, he saw little point in arguing the matter further; not in this place, not at this time. He turned to the door, his hand reaching for the brass knob —

"Wait!" Her Ladyship called after him; her tone shifted again. "Do not go yet, Francis! Not like this! Meet me later? In the garden? By the old fountain? Midnight? Please, Francis, say you will!"

He paused, his back still turned to her, his hand still resting on the doorknob. "No, my lady," answered he. "That chapter of our lives is concluded. This... this *entanglement*... has brought nothing but suffering, anxiety, and endless complications to us both. It must end, my lady. It truly must."

He opened the door.

"Just this once, Francis!" Her voice rose, tinged with a note of hysteria. "One last time! For the memory of what we once shared! Please, Francis! I beg you; I implore you!"

But Francis stepped out into the corridor without looking back, closing the door and leaving Lady G, a solitary figure amidst the silken drapes and gilded furniture, with her thwarted desires, her wounded pride, and her burgeoning, bitter jealousy for company.

***

The solemn hour approached midnight — that hour so oft, and with such predictable regularity, consigned by poets, playwrights, and indeed, by participants themselves, to shadowy trysts, clandestine meetings, and assignations of a decidedly amorous nature.

Within Thornfield's deeply darkened, moon-dappled gardens, concealed partially by the fragrant embrace of sundry rose bushes — bushes situated, it should be noted, with strategic precision directly beneath a specific, dimly illuminated upper-story window — a scene of lustful caress was currently unfolding. Her Ladyship, mistress of this domain, was locked in congress with a young man. His features being entirely obscured by the night's gloom and the angle of their enclasp, rendered him effectively anonymous to any casual, or indeed, inquisitive, observer.

And, Her Ladyship, for reasons best known to her own complex and devious heart, seemed utterly determined to ensure that any potential listener — particularly one who might be situated in the very room directly above this carefully staged tableau — could scarce have failed to hear. Her sighs were almost operatic in their intensity; her murmurs, laden with a voluptuous passion, were deliberately audible; her entire performance, in short, was pitched for maximum effect:

"Oh, *Francis*! Oh, yes, my darling! Just like that! Oh, Francis, my love, I adore, I simply *adore*, everything you do to me! You are simply... wonderful! Magnificent! My hero!"

Meantime, confined within her bedchamber, Miss Vanessa paced like a caged, and increasingly furious, tigress. The sounds drifting up from below grated on her already overstrained nerves, offending her jealous sensibilities to an almost unbearable degree. To hear the very woman whose husband held her captive, subjecting her to such indignity, enjoying an ardent tryst with the very man Vanessa herself now held such frustratingly burgeoning feelings for... 'twas an insult too profound, a calculated cruelty too exquisitely painful to bear in silence.

Her eyes, flashing with a dangerous light, fell upon an elegant crystal vase, filled with wilting flowers, standing upon a nearby sideboard; a poignant, and rather too obvious, symbol of her own fading state. Fury — cold, sharp, and invigorating — surged through her veins.

She snatched up the vase and strode to the window.

Heedless of the noise she might make, heedless of the potential repercussions, she flung it open with a force that rattled its frame. Taking but a moment's aim at the shadowy source of offensive, love-lorn sounds emanating from the darkness below, she hurled the delicate missile with all her considerable might.

A mere second later, good reader, the eminently satisfying sound of shattering crystal echoed sharply through the night.

This was immediately, and most gratifyingly followed by a piercing SHRIEK from Lady G, a sound that abruptly and most effectively cut short her heated and entirely dramatic performance.

Chapter the Twenty-fifth — Romance or Reckoning?

The brief respite of four-and-twenty hours afforded by Francis' improbable victory at the card table seemed mocked by the heavens themselves. A fierce wind whipped across Brookside's grounds, tearing the early yellowing leaves from the ancient oaks and sending them skittering across the gravel drive. Above, a lowering sky, bruised with shades of grey and slate, threatened imminent rain.

Into this blustery scene rode Harry, his horse looking as weary as its rider.

Francis, who had been pacing the yard in anxious anticipation, rushed forth the moment Harry dismounted. "*Well*? Did you find anything? Any word? Any news at all?"

Harry met his master's desperate gaze and slowly shook his head.

There was nothing to report.

No sighting.

No message.

No intelligence gleaned from the servants' network at Thornfield or beyond.

Vanessa remained unseen, unheard, effectively vanished.

Francis' shoulders slumped; the brief flicker of hope extinguished once more.

Later that afternoon, as the rain made good upon its earlier promise and began to lash with a mournful, drumming persistence against the dining-room windows, father and son once again sat down to the civilised ritual of tea. The contrast between the two men, however, could not, by any stretch of the imagination, have been more pronounced.

Relieved of the soul-destroying weight of imminent ruin, Sir Andrew seemed positively rejuvenated. A long-absent spark had returned to his weary eyes. The etched lines of worry on his noble face had softened. He sipped his beverage with the air of a man granted an unexpected reprieve from the gallows. He was, to put it in common parlance, on cloud nine, floating upon a sea of blissful relief.

Francis, conversely, presented a picture of the most impenetrable gloom. He sat slumped in his chair; his gaze fixed upon the murky depths of his teacup as if he, unbeknownst to himself, sought answers in the swirling leaves. His demeanour was less that of a man who had just saved his ancestral home and more akin to that of a chief mourner at a particularly sorrowful funeral.

"Come now, Francis," gently chided his father. "This is hardly the time for pulling such a long face! Brookside is safe! We are solvent! The wolf is no longer at our door! You should be rejoicing, my boy, celebrating, not moping about like a lovesick, melancholy ghost haunting his own victory feast!"

Francis offered no reply; his attention remained fixed on the porcelain oracle before him. Sir Andrew sighed, his cheerfulness dimmed by his son's persistent dolour. "Ah," said he in a tone that hinted at understanding. "Yes, I comprehend. Of course. It is not the fate of the estate that troubles your heart now, is it? It is the fate of Miss Lockwood."

Still staring into his cup, Francis finally spoke. "The wedding, Father. It is scheduled for tomorrow. And I have heard nothing. Not a word, not a sign, for three long days. Perhaps... perhaps after everything that has transpired, she truly wishes never to set eyes upon me again."

Sir Andrew pushed his own cup aside. "Francis, cease this unmanly despondency and consider the evidence! First, she deliberately and with clear intent left behind the bracelet — a token for you to find! Then, at enormous risk to her own standing and reputation, she intervened to secure your release from Inspector Swords! Do these actions speak of indifference? Do they evince a desire never to see you again? Or do they not rather demonstrate the profound depth of her regard for you?"

Francis merely shrugged. The grim reality of the present circumstances far overshadowed the hopeful memories of the past. Despite her previous acts of benevolence, this was, in his troubled mind, no guarantee that she harboured any feelings for him deeper than mere charitable regard, or perhaps, a sense of pity.

"It is as plain as the nose on your face, Son! As plain as the rain on that windowpane!" Sir Andrew's voice rose with conviction. "Grant! It must be Grant's doing! He knows or strongly suspects a connection between the two of you. Her disappearance, this sudden silence — it serves his wicked purpose perfectly! He intends to keep her isolated, to feed her falsehoods, to ensure the wedding proceeds without any interference and to keep her away from *you* until she is bound to his insipid son!"

Francis remained impassive, his gaze still lost in his cup's swirling tea leaves — a man drowning in his own sea of doubts.

At this, Sir Andrew threw up his hands in a mode of paternal exasperation. His patience, so recently restored, finally and quite spectacularly snapped. "For the love of God, Francis, cease this miserable inaction! Will you simply sit here and allow Grant to win? Allow the woman you clearly care for to be forced into a marriage she cannot desire? Do something, man! ACT!"

At last, Francis raised his head, lifting his eyes from the teacup to meet his father's. "*Act*?" Such a word felt only fruitless. "And what precisely am I supposed to *do*, Father?"

Sir Andrew's orbs blazed with a fierce — nay, almost feral — ancestral pride. "*Do*?" His voice, no longer chiding, but ringing with a sudden clarion fire, reverbed in the room. "You do what Sheringhams have *always* done! You follow the grand, the noble, the time-honoured family tradition! When a Sheringham truly wants a woman, Francis, he does not wait for permission, nor does he dither and despair at obstacles! He does not consult the tea leaves, my boy! He goes forth, and, by God, he *gets* her!"

***

Night had drawn its black and solemn curtain across the sky. The rain, which had hitherto been but a mournful accompaniment to the day's anxieties, grew at last into a storm of magnificent, and indeed terrifying, proportions. It broke with the fullest fury over Somerset.

In his bedchamber, Francis lay awake, his eyes wide in the darkness.

Sleep, that sweet balm to the troubled mind, offered no escape from the turmoil in his mind. He twisted and turned beneath the covers, haunted by his father's words, torn between the chilling fear of failure, the dread of the potentially disastrous consequences of any rash action, and the yet more unbearable, more soul-crushing, thought of Vanessa being irrevocably lost to him on the morrow.

To be sure, the wild, elemental storm that thundered without, good reader, did but serve as a pale mirror to the far greater tempest that raged, with equal fury, within.

***

Miles away, yet sharing the same stormy night, and, alas, a similar, if not greater, depth of despair, Miss Vanessa Lockwood stood by the tall window of her own bedchamber.

Clad only in her nightdress, she watched the relentless raindrops chase each other down the dark glass pane, blurring the already chaotic view of the turbulent world outside. She felt in that moment completely alone; abandoned by fortune, forsaken by hope, trapped by cruel circumstances and the inescapable, villainous machinations of the odious Lord G.

Suddenly, a blinding flash of lightning illuminated the room. With a stark, pitiless, and momentary glare, there was revealed in the reflection the glistening path of tears that coursed down her pale cheeks.

The wedding was the next day.

Hope, that last refuge of the anguished, seemed as distant and unattainable as the stars now obscured by the impenetrable blanket of storm clouds.

This was indeed the blackest moment for our hero and heroine both.

Chapter the Twenty-sixth — Confrontations and Revelations

The day dawned sullen and grey. Though the previous night's torrential rain had, for the moment, ceased its furious assault, the sky remained choked with clouds. The very air itself felt damp, oppressive, and charged with an unspoken tension, as if the world held its breath in anticipation of the day's dramatic events.

Against this bleak backdrop, decisive action was finally underway. Francis' heart thrumming with the grim determination forged during a sleepless, tormented night, he emerged from the house, followed closely by Harry.

Without a word exchanged, they mounted their waiting horses. Then, turning their steeds in the muddy, rutted road's direction, they spurred them into a gallop, riding away from Brookside and towards an uncertain confrontation.

As our hero and Harry sped along, the rain began anew, initially as a fine drizzle that quickly intensified, slicking the surfaces of the country road and rendering the going treacherous.

Presently, the sound of wheels and the rhythmic splashing beat of hoofbeats reached their attentive ears.

Upon rounding a sharp bend, they saw their quarry: a single coach, surprisingly ornate for such uncelebratory weather, its panels decorated with festive white ribbons, now drooping, limp and pathetic. Its great wheels churned through the thick mud and splattered noisily into the puddles.

Following closely behind the coach, serving as a solitary and rather miserable-looking escort, rode a liveried servant, his fine uniform already soaked, his posture slumped in weary resignation.

This, good reader, was undoubtedly the conveyance bearing the unfortunate bride to her much-dreaded nuptials.

Indeed, within said coach's swaying confines sat Vanessa, attired in a magnificent wedding dress. Its white silks and lace, a cruel contrast to the utter misery etched upon her features, she clutched between her trembling fists. Beside her sat, as always, Ms Brown, dressed in her finest frock, her face reflecting a similar gloom, her loyalty compelling her presence but her disapproval palpable.

Timing their approach perfectly, Francis and Harry emerged from a side track, converging rapidly on the wedding coach.

As they drew alongside, Harry launched himself with a wild cry from his saddle onto the unsuspecting servant escorting the conveyance.

Both men, in a tangle of limbs, curses, and fine livery, tumbled from the horse's back onto the road's bespattering surface, where they immediately grappled with furious intensity.

As for our hero, his focus was entirely on the carriage and its precious occupant.

Spurring his horse alongside the vehicle, he leant close, shouting to make himself heard above the rumble of the wheels, the creaking of the coach, and the drumming of the rain.

"VANESSA!" bellowed he. "VANESSA!"

Startled from her melancholic reverie by the unmistakable sound of Francis' voice, Vanessa, and indeed Ms Brown, turned with astonishment to the window. Through the rain-streaked glass, they saw him — Francis Sheringham, their unlikely saviour perhaps, riding hell-for-leather beside them.

A spark ignited in Vanessa's eyes, chasing away the dejection therein. Without hesitation, she wrestled with the window latch, pulled it down and stuck her head out into the driving rain, heedless of her elaborate coiffure or the fine fabric of her dress.

She, too, had to shout to be heard. "FRANCIS! What is the meaning of this?"

Seeing her face and hearing her voice, our hero succumbed to a surge of wild, triumphant elation. She had responded! She had not shut him out!

"Don't do it, Vanessa!" yelled he back, urging his horse to keep pace with the lurching coach. "Don't go to the church! For God's sake, for your own sake, for *my* sake, *don't* marry Vincent!"

Her voice came back to him — sharp, challenging, laced, perhaps, with the understandable bitterness of a perceived and very public betrayal. "And why shouldn't I? Give me one compelling reason to abandon this course, Francis Sheringham, and bring yet more ruin and scandal upon my name!"

He met her gaze, hoping his own expression — now stripped bare of artifice, of all pride — might reveal the raw and utterly compelling sincerity which consumed his universe entire. "Because I love you, Vanessa! Marry *me*! I swear to you, I shall take care of you — by some miracle, I have saved Brookside!"

She stared down at him, her heart manifestly tearing against conflicting sentiments — no doubt her duty, her father's will, and the sheer, absurd spectacle of the county's most notorious rake striving to thwart her resolution. "You know I have no choice! The inheritance — if I do not wed Vincent, I am left with nothing."

"Hang the inheritance!" Francis reached out, his gloved hand grasping futilely at the air. "The money, your inheritance, means nothing to me! It is *you* I want! Only you!"

Her expression suddenly hardened. "*Love*?! Is *that* what you call your... your *nocturnal* activities... with Lady Grant, of all people, directly beneath my window only the other night? Was that *love* you were demonstrating so very, very audibly for the entire world to hear?"

Francis stared at her, bewildered. He had to duck to avoid being taken out by a low-hanging bough. "*Lady Grant*?" replied he, catching up. "What on earth are you talking about? I haven't sought Lady Grant's company — not in *that* way — for some weeks now! It is finished between us!"

The rain, as if to punctuate this dramatic exchange, intensified, plastering their hair to their faces and soaking them both to the skin.

Overwhelmed perhaps by the force of his denial, or needing a moment to process this new piece of information, Vanessa pulled her head back inside the coach.

"Vanessa, wait!" Francis watched the window slide upwards. "Don't torture me like this! Give me an answer! Tell me there's a chance, a glimmer of hope!"

Her voice came, muffled now but still audible through the closing gap. "If I defy Lord Grant and refuse Vincent, I stand to lose everything — my home, my security, my inheritance! I cannot, I *will not*, sacrifice all that for a man known throughout the length and breadth of this county as a notorious and unrepentant philanderer!"

And with that, the window slammed shut, leaving Francis riding alongside the coach in the pouring rain, his plea met with a challenge — not a refusal but a challenge, nonetheless.

Through the rain's weeping curtain, their destination at length became visible — the ancient, stone-built Church of the Holy Cross, its square tower standing sentinel, as it had for centuries, on a slight rise of land.

Gathered under a makeshift canopy, erected at the church entrance to provide some meagre shelter from the relentless elements, stood the waiting wedding party. There was Vincent, resplendent and smug in a fine wedding suit; there was Lord G, radiating an aura of impatient, almost tyrannical, authority; there was Lady G, sporting an elaborate, and frankly quite hideous, hat; and there was a huddle of damp, shivering, and deeply uncomfortable guests, all peering down the road with expressions of mounting impatience.

Their collective gaze shifted to astonishment, then to utter, scandalised shock, as the spectacle, in all its chaotic glory, unfolded before them: the bride's coach approaching, not in a dignified procession, but pursued — harassed even — by a lone, soaking wet, and clearly very agitated, horseman. The sight of Francis Sheringham — a man they all knew — riding alongside Vanessa's carriage, clearly engaged in some highly improper dialogue, sent ripples of delicious murmuring through the assembled guests.

The coach driver, having no doubt given up on outpacing his pursuer, brought the speeding carriage to a jarring halt before the churchyard, sending gravel-shrapnel over sundry guests.

Before anyone could react, before any coherent thought could be formed, the coach door flew open. Clutching the skirts of her magnificent but now damp wedding dress, Vanessa descended — a vision of defiant, rain-drenched beauty.

In the same instant, Francis vaulted from the saddle.

Ignoring the onlookers' stunned silence, ignoring the slosh pooling around his boots, he strode directly to Vanessa.

And there, good reader, in front of her furious fiancé, her apoplectic guardian, his scheming, hat-wearing wife, and dozens of assembled, open-mouthed guests, Francis Sheringham — the rake, the gambler, the prodigal son of Brookside — dropped to his knees in the wet, sludge-like earth, seizing her hand in both of his.

"Vanessa," implored he, drunk with emotion. "Please. Say you will marry me. I love you more than life itself, more than Brookside, more than anything in this world. I cannot, I *will not*, conceive of a life without you."

Vanessa looked down at him — at this proud, reckless man, kneeling in the dirt before her, soaked to the skin, pleading for her hand before the very altar where she was meant to marry another.

At this sight — the ultimate public confirmation of her son's rejection and Francis' betrayal — Lady G emitted a strangled, almost bird-like gasp and promptly fainted dead away into the surprised, and somewhat inadequate, arms of a startled nearby guest.

As for Lord G and his son, this entire scene proved to be the final, intolerable provocation. Their long-cherished plans lay in utter public ruin; their family name unforgivably humiliated.

"This is an outrage!" thundered His Lordship, his face purpling with a vehemence so intense it seemed he might spontaneously combust. "An absolute disgrace!"

Vincent, shaking with impotent rage, strode forth, tearing his murderous gaze from Vanessa to fix it upon Francis. "You dare? You dare insult *me*, *my* fiancée, *my* family, before our assembled guests? This affront demands satisfaction! I demand satisfaction!"

With a violent flourish, he ripped off one of his leather gloves and struck Francis sharply across the face with it.

Still flushed with the victory of love, our hero reacted without a moment's hesitation. "Very well, Vincent. If satisfaction is what you require, then, by God, you shall have it."

"Francis, no!" Vanessa clutched his arm.

"Do not concern yourself, my love." He eased her hand away. "He handles a pistol like a drunken sow handles a musket. He's hopeless."

"No, Francis, you are wrong!" Vanessa tugged his arm only the more urgently. "I saw him practising! With his instructor. He has become surprisingly, frighteningly proficient! He is very, *very* good!"

A flicker of doubt, of genuine worry, now crossed Francis' mind. 'Twas, however, too late to retract. The challenge had been given and accepted in public. Honour, that cruel and inexorable taskmaster, demanded that it be seen through.

"On my family's land," dictated Vincent, his own confidence visibly bolstered by Vanessa's unwitting and most helpful testimony. "In half an hour. I shall provide the pistols myself, to save you the inconvenience."

Francis' jaw tightened. "Fine!"

"Men!" exclaimed Vanessa in exasperation. "Utterly, utterly stupid!"

Without another word, Vincent stalked away. After watching him go, Francis turned back to Vanessa, projecting a mixture of love and apology.

Lord G, meanwhile, a man attempting to salvage some shred of dignity from the wreckage of his ambitions, moved towards his guests, attempting, with a series of frantic gestures and muttered explanations, some semblance of damage control; though what possible explanation could suffice for such a societal and entertaining disaster remained entirely unclear. Lady G, abandoned by her husband, began to stir, groaning softly as she slowly regained consciousness.

Vanessa's eyes darted around the churchyard. She spotted several horses belonging to the guests tethered under a nearby shed. Hitching up the skirt of her now entirely ruined gown, heedless of the mud and puddles, she made a sudden dash towards them.

Ms Brown, recovering at last from the shock, attempted to follow. "Miss Vanessa! Where are you going?" puffed she, stopping after only a few steps, breathless.

Vanessa did not reply; her objective, whatever it was, was clearly fixed.

***

Elsewhere, back on the muddy road where the initial confrontation occurred, Harry had finally gained the upper hand in his protracted wrestling match with the escort rider. A well-aimed blow sent his opponent sprawling, knocked momentarily senseless in a puddle.

Harry rose panting, begrimed but triumphant.

***

Half an hour later, the chosen duelling ground — a secluded meadow on the Grant estate — presented a scene of the grimmest, and indeed most absurd, formality. The rain had eased to a mere listless drizzle; yet the sky remained dark and brooding, lending a funereal gravity to the occasion.

Our two combatants, Francis and Vincent, stood facing each other. Having removed their coats, they were now clad only in their fine, and soon to be much-abused shirtsleeves. As for their expressions, they offered a stark and telling contrast: Vincent appeared cool, confident, almost eager for the fray — a portrait of aristocratic arrogance. Francis looked tense and sober, his earlier bravado having been entirely replaced by a more realistic appraisal of the mortal danger he now faced — an appraisal fuelled, in no small part, by Vanessa's warning.

Nearby, huddled together like a flock of unhappy sheep, stood the small group of essential participants and most unwilling spectators: Lord G, his face all grim, almost pleasurable displeasure; Lady G, pale, distraught, and on the verge of yet another collapse; Ms Brown, wringing her hands; and the two reluctant witnesses, Sir Burton and Mr Russell, who were doubtless, at this moment, regretting their unprofitable association with the Grant family more than they had ever regretted anything in their lives.

Presiding over the dreadful affair was the referee — none other than Vincent's own shooting instructor. He held open a polished wooden case containing two identical, long-barrelled duelling pistols, gleaming darkly, along with the necessary powder and ball.

Vincent selected one pistol. He expertly checked its weight, tested the hammer's action, and squeezed the trigger mechanism.

Francis, somewhat disheartened at Vanessa's absence, as he had hoped a single glimpse of her face at this moment would be the very elixir he needed, took the remaining weapon. He mimicked Vincent's actions, though it must be confessed, he did so with a degree of less familiarity.

Under the referee's supervision, they loaded the pistols, each man preparing the instrument of his opponent's potential destruction.

The spectators watched in tense silence, their breaths held captive in their chests. Unable to bear the suspense a moment longer, Her Ladyship clung hysterically to her husband's arm, burying her face against his shoulder to block out the dreadful sight. His Lordship, however, roughly — almost contemptuously — shook her off.

"Control yourself, woman! Let the boy prove himself. This duel will demonstrate to all that my son possesses the courage of a true gentleman — the mettle of a real man!"

Lady G merely sighed, a wretched sound halfway between a sob and a gasp, and subsided into trembling silence.

Vincent and Francis now took their positions, standing back-to-back, the muzzles of their pistols held upright before their faces as the sober tradition of the duel dictated.

The referee delivered the final instructions. "The agreed distance is twelve paces each way, gentlemen." He then retreated to a safe distance. "I shall commence the count. Walk on my signal. Start... now! One... two... three... four..."

As the referee's solemn count echoed across the meadow, the two duellists marched steadily away from each other, each measured step marking a fatal increase in the distance that separated them.

"... five... six... seven... eight..."

Francis concentrated fiercely, trying with all his might to calm the frantic, wild pounding in his chest.

"... nine... ten..."

A cruel smirk touched Vincent's lips. Well before the full count, he turned, drunk, no doubt, with the evil notion to catch his opponent unprepared — a tactic considered by some to be clever, and by others to be the very height of dishonourable villainy.

"... eleven..."

At that moment, Vincent acted.

However, in pivoting on his heel, his foot landed squarely upon a wet stone concealed in the grass. With much indignity and with a desperate, comical flail of his arms, he slipped. His finger tightened on the trigger, and his gun went off, the bullet bolting towards the sky.

Upon hearing the unexpected shot ring out behind him, Francis flinched, squeezing his eyes shut, bracing himself for the ball's searing impact.

But lo! Instead of excruciating pain, the very next sensation he experienced was something soft, yet distinctly solid, landing atop his head.

A collective gasp rose from the onlookers. Everyone stared momentarily speechless.

The referee, acutely aware that the strict rules of the duel had been violated, hesitated, clearly intimidated by his employer's formidable presence and unwilling to declare the obvious foul against his own pupil.

Clearly aghast, Vincent stared at his now-useless pistol and then towards Francis.

By now, our hero had opened his eyes. He reached up a tentative hand and removed the object that had so unexpectedly fallen upon him — an innocent sparrow, the unlucky victim of Vincent's errant shot. With a mixture of relief and disgust, he tossed the creature aside and turned to face his opponent.

The sight of Francis, entirely unharmed and now standing opposite him with a fully loaded and steadily aimed pistol, had an immediate and most dramatic effect on the unlucky Vincent's mien.

Our hero raised his arm, levelling the weapon, taking careful aim at the now understandably terrified Vincent.

At this sight, Lady G, true to form, promptly fainted again, collapsing in a silent heap upon the damp grass. Lord G, also seeing his son's life hanging by the slenderest of threads, decided, we must assume, that immediate intervention was necessary — protocol, and indeed honour, be damned.

"Sheringham!" called out he. "Francis! Perhaps... perhaps we can discuss this? Reach some sort of... compromise?"

Francis lowered not the pistol. His gaze remained fixed on Vincent. "No compromise, my lord," stated he. "He demanded satisfaction. He shall now receive it."

At that, he adjusted his aim, his finger tightening on the trigger, but then he paused; a gasp, half-way between mirth and mockery, escaped his lips. All eyes, save for those of the unconscious Lady G followed Francis' gaze. A dark patch was spreading rapidly, and most shamefully, on the front of Vincent's cream-coloured trousers.

The fop had, to put it plainly, quite literally, wet himself in terror.

Lord G undoubtedly thought to seize this momentary distraction. "Be reasonable, Francis! Name your price! Money? Land? Whatever you desire! Just... just spare the boy!"

Francis paused, though the pistol remained steadily aimed. "My price, my lord, is Vanessa."

"Done!" instantly agreed Lord G. "She is yours! Take her!"

Our hero held his position, the pistol unwavering. Vincent continued to shake and looked now as if he were about to burst into tears.

"That is not all." Francis pressed his advantage. "I require a document. To be drawn up this very day. Signed, sealed, and witnessed. By which you formally and irrevocably relinquish all rights and responsibilities as her guardian and approve my good self as your choice of Vanessa's spouse according to her father's will. Effective immediately."

His Lordship's face flushed with impotent anger. Losing control of Vanessa's considerable fortune was perhaps the bitterest, most unpalatable pill he could be forced to swallow... save, perhaps, for the loss of his heir. He hesitated, visibly warring with avarice and paternal fear.

"My lord," prompted Francis, "we have *witnesses*." He gestured with the pistol towards Sir Burton and Mr Russell.

"Alright! Very well! Damn you, Sheringham! You shall have it! You shall have it!"

Francis pressed still relentlessly in his victory: "Your word is given? Before these gentlemen?"

"Yes, yes! My word is given! Now, for God's sake, put that thing down!"

At long last, Francis lowered the weapon.

A collective, almost audible, sigh of relief went through the group of onlookers (excluding, of course, the still-unconscious Lady G).

The sudden release of tension, however, proved to be too much for the deeply humiliated Vincent. His legs gave way beneath him. He collapsed onto the wet ground, buried his face in his hands, and began to sob — not like a man, mind you, but hysterically, like a small, fractious child.

Francis looked down at the pathetic figure of his rival, then at the heavy pistol still clutched in his hand. He tossed the weapon aside. "Probably for the best," muttered he quietly to himself. "Never was the finest shot, anyway."

Just as the immediate, life-or-death tension dissipated, a new sound intruded upon the scene: the rhythmic thudding of multiple hoofbeats approaching at a rapid pace across the damp meadow.

All heads (except Vincent's, still buried in his own shameful hands, and Her Ladyship's, still lost to the dark oblivion of her swoon) turned as one towards the source. Through the mist and drizzle, four figures on horseback could be discerned.

As they drew nearer, their identities became startlingly, and for some, most alarmingly, clear. Leading the group, riding with an almost martial grace, was Miss Vanessa. Beside her, his back ramrod straight, rode the stern, uniformed figure of Inspector Swords. Flanking them were the familiar forms of Sergeant Morris and the mud-spattered but resolute figure of Harry.

Chapter the Last — Love and Inheritance

The unexpected arrival of Miss Lockwood and her surprising escort cast a sudden chill over the already damp and emotionally overwrought proceedings. These would-be-duelling-death-stoppers reined in their horses and surveyed the chaotic scene — the discarded pistol gleaming darkly on the grass, the weeping figure of Vincent, the general air of ignominious disarray — with expressions that ranged from Vanessa's anxious, almost breathless, relief to the grim, unequivocal disapproval of Inspector Swords.

Lord G, that architect of calamities, merely stared at this unexpected cavalry; his face, already a study in thwarted rage, contorted further. His meticulous plans had been dashed; his precious son publicly humiliated; his iron-fisted control over Vanessa and her fortune wrested away; and now *this* — the arrival of the very woman at the heart of the mayhem, accompanied by the one figure of military authority in the county whom he despised and certainly had cause to fear.

'Twas, in short, the final, the most infuriating, the most intolerable straw.

"Sweet heavens, what *now*?" He threw his hands up to the unforgiving sky. "Cannot a gentleman conclude a matter of honour — or even abject surrender — in some semblance of peace?"

Ignoring entirely His Lordship's histrionic outburst, all four newcomers dismounted briskly.

Vanessa, heedless of the state of her dress, rushed immediately to Francis, her eyes searching his face. "Francis! Oh, thank God, you are unharmed."

Still riding the high tide of adrenaline, he replied, "and why should I not be, my dear?" though his heart softened as he took in the welcome, and most lovely, sight of her.

Simultaneously, Harry made a beeline for Ms Brown.

Having overcome her initial shock at this sudden and very public reunion, she met him halfway; the two, casting aside all thought of propriety, embraced with a warmth that verily betrayed their earlier dalliances.

Their tender moment, however, was sharply interrupted by the stern voice of authority. Inspector Swords had drawn his service pistol with the clear intention of restoring order. Beside him, Sergeant Morris produced a pair of heavy iron handcuffs.

"Lord Grant! Sheringham! Gentlemen!" Inspector Swords' voice cut through the air. "Need I remind you that the ancient and barbaric practice of duelling is strictly and with severe penalty forbidden under the Queen's Law?" He then turned his stern gaze upon Vanessa. "Miss Lockwood, as perhaps the most impartial observer here whose senses remain at present intact, pray tell me: who initiated this illegal, and potentially fatal, affair?"

Without hesitation, she pointed a trembling but resolute finger at Vincent, who was wiping tears from his pale face, looking utterly bewildered by this new, and for him, most unwelcome, turn of events. "He did, Inspector," clearly stated she. "Mr Grant issued the challenge. Mr Sheringham was merely forced to protect my honour."

Inspector Swords nodded. "Morris, arrest that fellow."

As the officer hastened forth, Lord G interposed himself, planting his feet firmly in the sergeant's path. To have his son, his heir, arrested on his own land, after the catalogue of humiliations already suffered, was an indignity too great to be borne. "Hold there, officer! You are trespassing! This is *private* property! You have *no* jurisdiction here, I say!"

Inspector Swords now stepped forth. "I care not whose land it is! We represent the law; and the law, I assure you, applies universally. 'Tis high time that some semblance of order was brought to this damned, lawless corner of Somerset! Now, stand aside!"

With a surprising display of force, Sergeant Morris shoved the sputtering lord out of his path, whereupon he advanced on Vincent, who, too dazed, demoralised, and defeated to offer even the slightest resistance, allowed the cold, hard metal to be snapped decisively onto his wrists.

"You *cannot* do this!" protested Lord G. "You cannot arrest *my* son!"

Sergeant Morris ignored him entirely as he led the bound and now whimpering Vincent to the waiting horses.

Seeing his authority so utterly, so publicly, disregarded, His Lordship most unwisely changed his tactics. He strode towards the inspector, adopting a conspiratorial, friendly air. "My dear Swords, surely this is all just a simple misunderstanding amongst gentlemen? I am quite certain... quite certain, my dear fellow... that we can find a way to... to *fix* this little inconvenience."

Inspector Swords fixed Lord G with a stare of such glacial contempt that a lesser man might have frozen on the spot. "*Fix it*, my lord?" His voice was dangerously stern. "Are you by any chance suggesting...?"

"Every man has his price, Inspector," pressed on Lord G, fatally misjudging his man. "Discretion, my dear Inspector, can always be bought. Name yours. What is it that you require? A promotion? A sinecure? A simple bag of gold?"

Swords' eyes only cooled the more. "So! It comes to bribery now, does it? Attempting to corrupt an officer of the Crown in the lawful execution of his sworn duty! Lord Grant, you are under arrest as well!" He turned sharply to his subordinate. "Sergeant Morris! Secure this man!"

Utterly dumbfounded, His Lordship stared. "Hey! Wait just a moment! I merely suggested... You misunderstand my intent entirely..."

But his protests were as futile as a whisper in a hurricane.

The sergeant efficiently relieved him of his freedom, handcuffing him securely. With merciless indifference, Morris then tied the ropes attached to both father and son's handcuffs to his own saddle pommel.

Inspector Swords and the sergeant remounted their horses, preparing to lead their two most distinguished, and now thoroughly humiliated, prisoners away.

At this catastrophic sight — her husband and her son, both bound, being led away like common criminals — Lady G, who had just begun to stir and groan upon the damp ground, emitted a despairing moan and promptly, and perhaps for the best, succumbed to unconsciousness once more.

Sir Burton and Mr Russell, looking manifestly uncomfortable and doubtless wishing themselves anywhere else on God's green earth, exchanged weary glances and moved reluctantly, as gentlemen must, to attend to the fallen and now entirely abandoned lady.

Amidst the departing commotion, Francis and Vanessa found themselves drawn together.

"My dear Vanessa," said our hero, a triumphant smile escaping from his heart and onto his lips as he watched the rigid back of Inspector Swords ride off, "you appear to wield a most remarkable and highly effective influence over our stern Inspector."

Vanessa mirrored his smile. "Perhaps, my dear Francis, he merely appreciates decisive action wherever he may find it."

Francis turned her gently, with a new and tender possessiveness, to face him. "And you, Vanessa? Have you at last reached a decision...?" He gulped. "About me?"

She tilted her head; her expression became serious again, though without its earlier bitterness. "I confess, Francis, your reputation... your past... your notorious and very public promiscuity still cause me some concern."

"Vanessa, I swear to you" — he met her gaze without recoiling — "on my honour, on my very soul, I was not with Lady Grant that night. It must have been some cruel, devious, and utterly despicable trick of hers, designed specifically to poison your mind against me."

Her brow arched. Her eyes flashed with peculiar intensity. "So, if I *were* to accept you... no more chasing every pretty skirt that happens to flutter past?"

He shook his head. "No more! That life, that foolish, empty life, holds no appeal for me now. I have learnt my lesson, Vanessa. Painfully, perhaps, but most thoroughly."

She appeared to search his gaze and then, seemingly satisfied by the sincerity found therein — she would have needed to have been blind not to — nodded slowly. 'Twas a gesture of complete capitulation to her own heart. "Alright, Francis. I believe you."

Spurred by her declaration, he lifted her chin and kissed her with an abiding tenderness that spoke of his elation and that his words as well as his heart were now fully acknowledged and gratefully accepted.

When their lips finally parted, Vanessa sighed. "Then yes, Francis Sheringham," her voice rang with a happy finality, "I *will* marry you. And I will gladly, most gladly, exchange my entire inheritance, if need be, for more of your kisses!"

Francis, now unshackled from all misery, allowed himself to laugh. "That you raise the subject of inheritances," said he, "you need exchange nothing, my love. For while Lord Grant was... shall we say... *distracted*... by the pressing matter of my pistol earlier, I took the liberty of securing his verbal agreement before two witnesses to relinquish his guardianship and all claims upon your considerable fortune and approve me as your husband. He will provide written confirmation anon, too. Your inheritance is entirely yours, Vanessa. Safe and sound at your own disposal."

Her eyes widened in astonishment, then shone with a bright, almost dazzling, admiration. "Oh, Francis! You truly are... wonderful!"

And with that, good reader, she pulled him close for another kiss, sealing, at long last, their tumultuous and now triumphant future together.

Their tender, and indeed, long-awaited moment of private communion was, however, interrupted by the polite clearing of a throat nearby.

Having assisted Ms Brown onto his horse, Harry now sat proudly behind her, beaming with a satisfaction that rivalled even that of his master. "Begging your pardon, Sir and Miss Lockwood. Just wanted to inform you... Ms Brown 'ere has done me the 'onour of agreeing to become my wife."

"Harry! That is splendid news indeed!" exclaimed Francis — though he was entirely at a loss to account for how his assistant, during such disarray, had found the leisure to prosecute and conclude a romantic campaign of his own. "My heartiest congratulations to you both!"

Harry winked broadly. "Aye, sir. And thanks to you, in a manner of speaking. You proved to be a great... teacher... in matters of persistence, sir."

A quality which, as our hero had demonstrated, is as useful in the storming of a lady's heart as it is in the pursuit of any other valuable property. Francis accepted the compliment with an air of mock humility.

"Question is, sir," continued Harry, "will you still 'ave need of my services, now that... well, now that things are, as one might say, so 'appily settled?"

"Of course, Harry! Don't be a fool! Brookside would *never* be the same without you."

"Thank you, sir!" Harry beamed and, forgetting in his transport of joy that golden rule of social aesthetics so recently imparted, allowed his lips to part and afford his auditors a most unsettling view of that ruinous dental landscape which lay within. "We'll see you back at the 'ouse later, then."

Ms Brown patted Vanessa's arm. "I'm sure I leave you in very good hands, Miss!"

And here, the reader may observe the singular spectacle of a chaperone, whose sacred duty it was to guard her charge's virtue, now abandoning her post with the greatest possible alacrity to pursue her own, more tender, affairs. She settled back with a contented sigh against Harry's chest.

With a final nod, accompanied by Ms Brown's cry of "*Allons-y, ma victoire! Vive l'amour!*" (Let's go, my victory! Long live love!) Harry spurred his horse, and they galloped away, two honest hearts heading at long last towards their own happy future. Though let us not get too carried away by this romantic spectacle. For as Harry had but a moment before declared his intention to be "back at the 'ouse later," we must piously conclude that this 'happy future' was either to be an affair of a few brief hours, or, what is more probable, was to be conveniently postponed until after the evening's chores were satisfactorily concluded.

Our hero and heroine watched them go, waving, before Francis gave a low whistle, summoning his own horse.

As they prepared to mount, they glimpsed the aborted wedding party's aftermath: the still-unconscious Lady G being awkwardly but carefully carried away from the scene by the long-suffering Sir Burton and Mr Russell, doubtless eager to discharge their duty and escape Thornfield's orbit forever.

With Vanessa soon riding side-saddle before Francis, they made their way back to Brookside. The heavy clouds at last began to break, and shafts of sunlight pierced through, illuminating the valley. The storm, it seemed, both literal and figurative, had passed.

***

That evening, the Brookside dining room glowed with a warmth it had not known for many years. Our hero, our heroine, and Sir Andrew sat together at the polished table. To be sure, our lovers beamed with unconcealed happiness, their hands often finding each other's beneath the table in that silent, tactile language peculiar to their state. As Sir Andrew watched them, his own eyes glistened with unshed tears of profound joy and relief.

As for Harry and his new bride-to-be, they had, it seems, retired to celebrate their not yet formalised union elsewhere — a matter upon which, for the sake of decorum, we shall not presume to speculate.

At any rate, Sir Andrew had need to wield the napkin rather as a handkerchief. "Oh, Francis," said he, dabbing his eyes. "You cannot know how happy you have made this old man. If only your dear mother could be here to witness this day." He paused, collecting himself. "I am truly proud of you, my son. You rescued our home, our heritage, from the brink. You won the heart of this remarkable young woman. And," added he with a chuckle, "you even managed to see that scoundrel Grant inconvenienced by the law!"

Sir Andrew picked up his wineglass, his hand trembling slightly with emotion. He lifted it high. "To Francis and Vanessa. May your lives together be filled with enduring happiness, prosperity, and love."

Indeed, this *was* a most wonderful day; though Francis acknowledged, "he'll likely be out by tomorrow, Father. Men like Grant always have connections. But perhaps even *he* has learnt a lesson." He picked up his own glass. "But I shall drink to *Love*... and to... *Money*. Two great forces that make the world revolve!"

In her turn, Vanessa lifted her glass. "And I," announced she, a mischievous smile gracing her lips, "shall drink to... Lord Grant!"

Both Francis and Sir Andrew stared at her. "*Lord Grant?*" echoed they.

"Of course; had it not been for his villainy, his greed, and his truly dreadful matchmaking skills, Francis and I might never have found each other!"

"Ah," replied our hero. "Very true... very true."

As twilight deepened, casting long shadows across Brookside's lawns, Harry and Ms Brown — aha! Here they are! — sat close together on a simple stone bench. Their arms locked together in romantic repose, they watched the sky blaze with the spectacular colours of a splendid sunset, contemplating their own bright future. And perhaps amidst such pure ruminations, they might have bestowed the odd kiss or two on each other's cheeks.

At any rate, through the mullioned window of the nearby drawing room, visible within the frame like a perfectly composed painting, a final, intimate scene unfolded. Lit by the lamps' warm glow within, two figures stood in silhouette. Francis caressingly took Vanessa's hand and, with a tenderness that spoke of all that had passed between them, fastened his mother's bracelet around her wrist.

'Twas indeed a perfect, glistening circle, as it were, signifying that which was lost, at last restored; a future purchased; and a most satisfactory conclusion, dear reader, to our little history of Love and Money.

THE END

Pray, if this author's work has earnt your good opinion, a kind word on GoodReads (preferably Amazon) would be a most welcome reward to call upon further prospective readers. Should this author's work, however, have failed to please, pray, let your judgement be rendered with mercy!

About The Authors

Justan Autor

Justan came late to the wicked joy of novels, having first tried his hand at most of the civilised arts: he painted pictures, trimmed hedgerows into obedience, stitched respectable garments, and wooed a pianoforte into confessing melodies. Only thereafter did he discover that narrative mischief suited him best.

A devotee of the 18th and 19th-century masters, he writes in a classical key with a modern tempo — history that crackles, characters with inconvenient desires, and a burlesque glint when daggers flash. His first novel, "**VANITY**" (2023) of the "**Vain & Valour**" series, ushers readers into 1790s Switzerland: mountains, intrigue, and a hero who frequently collides with his own better judgement.

If you fancy, for example, Dumas for the dash, Fielding for the grin, Austen for the bite, and Dickens for the sweep — served with present-day verve — do make his acquaintance.

Visit Justan's **website** at:
www.justanautor.com

Visit Justan's **Facebook page** at:
www.facebook.com/JustanAutor

Katerina Dunne

Katerina Dunne is the penname of Katerina Vavoulidou. Originally from Athens, Greece, Katerina lived in Ireland for 25 years and has now settled in sunny Cyprus. She has a degree in English Language and Literature from the University of Athens, an MA in Film Studies (during which the screenplay of Love & Money was written as an exercise) from University College Dublin and an MPhil in Medieval History from Trinity College Dublin. While she used to write short stories for family and friends in her teenage years, she only took up writing seriously in 2016-17, when she started work on her first novel.

Katerina's day job is in financial services, but in her free time she enjoys reading historical fiction and watching historically themed movies and TV series. She is passionate about medieval history, and her main area of interest is 13th to 15th century Hungary. She has published two historical fiction novels, ***Lord of the Eyrie*** (2022) and ***Return to the Eyrie*** (2024). Although the main characters of her stories are fictional, Katerina uses real events and personalities as part of her narrative in order to bring to life the fascinating history of the medieval Kingdom of Hungary, a location and period not so well-known to English-speaking readers.

Visit Katerina's **Facebook page** at:
https://www.facebook.com/profile.php?id=100076818802721

Staten House

www.ingramcontent.com/pod-product-compliance
Lightning Source LLC
Chambersburg PA
CBHW060314310726
48976CB00007B/2324